Derek Beaven lives in Maidenhead, Berkshire. His first novel, *Newton's Niece* (1994), was shortlisted for the Writers' Guild Best Novel Prize and won a Commonwealth Prize. *Acts of Mutiny* (1998) was shortlisted for the *Guardian* Fiction Prize. His third novel, *If the Invader Comes* (2001), was longlisted for the Man Booker Prize.

Visit www.AuthorTracker.co.uk for exclusive information on your favourite HarperCollins authors

From the reviews of *His Coldest Winter*:

'A stylish drama of espionage, teenage romance, and hard choices . . . The atmosphere of the time, with its ton-up boys, Brylcreem, paraffin heaters in freezing bedrooms and enormous red and green flasks in chemists' windows is often almost painfully sharp' *Sunday Times*

'With wonderful imaginative intensity, expressed in an original style of elliptical impressionism galvanised by sudden realistic shocks, Derek Beaven uses an austere background to dramatise a story of the rivalry of young love, the rivalry of ton-up motorcycle gangs, and the rivalry of international industrial espionage of military urgency . . . An ingenious, multi-layered novel' *Sunday Telegraph*

'A cold-weather, Cold War thriller' *Daily Telegraph*

'One of our most uncompromisingly individual novelists' *Guardian*

'An oblique, suggestive, estranging book that knits together sex, treachery, Cold War politics and hard science' *Literary Review*

'Gripping' *Sunday Express*

'A wonderful book . . . very moving' ROSIE BOYCOTT

'A master of evoking atmosphere . . . Beaven writes about physical surroundings and physical sensations with absolute clarity and a poetically oblique manner' *Sunday Business Post*

'A profoundly go NA SHAW

D1461010

By the same author

Newton's Niece
Acts of Mutiny
If the Invader Comes

DEREK BEAVEN

His Coldest Winter

HARPER PERENNIAL
London, New York, Toronto and Sydney

Harper Perennial
An imprint of HarperCollins*Publishers*
77–85 Fulham Palace Road
Hammersmith
London w6 8jb

www.harperperennial.co.uk

This edition published by Harper Perennial 2006

First published in Great Britain in 2005 by Fourth Estate

A catalogue record for this book is
available from the British Library

ISBN-13 978-0-00-715110-3

Typeset in Stempel Garamond by
Palimpsest Book Production Ltd, Polmont, Stirlingshire

For Sue
with love

And to Laura with many thanks

I

FIRST SIGHT

THE NIGHT AIR was like broken glass, a black rush that crammed his mouth, cut his cheeks. Snow from the headlight sliced up at his eyes and splintered past his ears. He was seventeen – it was his first time on a motorbike and he'd just driven straight across London. His back ached, his arms ached, his shins ached. The rest of him was numb.

He was on his way home from the family Christmas at his aunt's. At last, the capital was behind him, its High Streets ended, its festive, undrawn curtains done with. He'd struggled through Child's Hill, pressed on past Hendon Central. Apex Corner had been a snarl, a ring of trade names and used cars for sale, a jostle for inches by neon signs or tinselled star-buys. Everyone in town had seemed to be elbowing a way out of it before the weather turned. Now, with the traffic thinned almost to nothing and snow falling in earnest, he was on his own.

His bike hammered under him. Two miles passed without a waymark, three ... A rise foreshadowed the Chiltern hills, and he stared up the dual carriageway, waiting for detail. None came. A chain of red dots glimmered far ahead, then vanished. Oncoming headlamps swung once through his line of vision, and were gone. Some winter conspiracy seemed to have swapped the city for a void, in which the merest extra throttle caused a gale to drag his face as though he were a rocket pilot being tested.

Then a roundabout showed at the crest. Alan braked hard, his fingers half-frozen in the glove. He could hardly feel the pedal against the tread of his left shoe; he nudged the gear change with the toe of his right, sending an icy vibration up through his knees and backbone. The big machine whined and slowed as the frame shook to the cog. Two other riders buzzed by him out of nowhere, their stop lights scoring arcs this way, now that, into the bends.

They were racing. It was the bypass already, and they'd just shown him up. Too powerful for its rig, his own Triumph made him wait for each line to straighten before he dared accelerate, and the awkward sidecar – which the law required, and which his father and uncle had helped him bolt to the frame just that Boxing Day morning – felt like a child's stabiliser. He tried to hurry, but the pair were out of sight before he was halfway round, leaving only their tyre tracks on the whitening ground.

A flurry blew without warning. Torn flock seemed to swoop across the central hummock, flying up in wads against the headlight. There was a car half-blocking the exit, the driver climbing out to clear his windscreen; Alan skirted him. But the bike hit ice and his whole rig kicked sideways. He wasn't spooked. Spurred on by the racers, he flung a challenge to the elements, bit back whatever pain he could still feel and opened up the throttle. The power was breathtaking, the flurry just turbulence left behind him as he shot like an arrow into the darkness.

The Watford Bypass gave him his bearings. He'd been along it countless times – with his parents on their visits to London, or on theatre trips with various teachers. From here, he reckoned he knew the lie of the land. The road heads exactly north-west, giving the merest flick to either side, then tilts slightly downhill. After that, it lies true as a whip in a wound for three and a half miles, tree-lined, across fields and thickets and former country lanes. It used to come into its own about nine every night: the bike boys fancied themselves creatures of darkness. They gave the strip its mythology, and its ghosts.

Rain or shine, this was the routine. When they'd finished at Oddhams the printers, or Metal Box, or the Rolls-Royce aero-engine factory at Leavesden, when they'd wolfed their suppers and tinkered with their bikes, they'd put on their jeans and black USAF leather jackets and ride over to the Busy Bee, the transport café in the dip, next to the Red Lion. And there, to Elvis records on the jukebox, they'd suck fizzy orangeade through straws until the summer sun went down; or, while the winter moon scuttled family men off to their wives, they'd sit and drink cup after cup of hot, sweet tea, waiting.

Others would arrive in packs, from the Ace on the North Circular, from the Dugout, or the Cellar by the bridge at Eton. Once it was night, they'd improvise illicit races along the black main road. They'd burn it up, in twos or threes or whole packs, trying for the ton, the machines shuddering, the engines thrashing under the cold stars. The bypass was all for racing. It took, on average, one lad per week.

The straight was the lure, flawless but for an extra roundabout that lets the little Elstree Road cross down to the film studios just behind a row of trees. That one scrubby oblong leads a gradual left into a right chicane. It's a test of skill. Regulars could have reminded Alan – you need to watch out for the kink. But he was untutored that night, and if ever he'd made a note of the Elstree through the back window of his parents' car he didn't recall it. What with the bike and the weather thickening, he had no idea what was coming.

Two dim red lights glowed in front before he even reached it. He swerved, barely in time to overtake a doddering pre-war saloon, and, all at once, he couldn't make out the tarmac. No use to slap at his goggles. Only when he reached down to swipe the snow from his head-lamp did he see the fugitive island, its reflective black-and-white zigzags brilliantly revealed against shadowy, onrushing vegetation. He dug into the pedal far too late and yanked once more with the fingers of his right hand.

The brakes hardly registered. He clung on blindly while the kink wooed and pocketed him, tightening all the time, racing him in until there was nothing for it – he was forced to steer right. For a second, the handlebar was muscled like a snake. Then it went limp, and he was skidding. Only just in time, the tyres gripped and the brakes bit and he felt his wheel miraculously cheat the kerb.

But a shape filled the beam, an oncoming rush of wagon-side and big wheels. He glimpsed a painted trade name, heard the blaring of a horn already past. The one chance, pulling left, was the direction that could flip him and his sidecar like a tossed coin.

He was sure he was about to die, watching the artic's rusted girder go on for ever along that terrible curve, until somehow, by another stroke of fate, the tailbolt missed him. Still everything remained cruelly drawn out, and all he could feel in one broken moment of night and ice and careering snowscape was that his father, whom he loved, was somehow waiting to gather him out there, to receive him and hide him in his coat as he'd done against the cold, years before. In a kind of dream he saw him, on a dark snowy plain, trackless under the moon – in Russia would it be, far off, or America – a figure growing ever larger under the birches, his coat warm and protective, his arms stretched to embrace his son. Half out of the saddle, Alan lunged his whole weight over to bring the sidecar down.

He found himself on the wrong side of a clear road. It was so strange. He was completely unharmed and the straight lay ahead. All that remained was a drench of fear, like the secret thawing of his bones. As though nothing had happened, he let the bike drift back across the tarmac, then screwed open the throttle. The snow thinned into shards again, and cold air jagged his lips and cheeks. At sixty-five the Triumph began a front-wheel shudder; at seventy, it calmed. He was exalted, untouchable.

SCRAWLED ON THE angled, space-age frontage, the neon spelled a challenge: *The Busy Bee*. Why not? He'd won his spurs. Enough glare came from the café's windows to shine up the row of bikes outside – choice specimens, glinting, spotless, with their clip-on handlebars and alloy tanks, their racing seats and TT silencers. He drove nearer, jolting on the rutted car park. A Norton Dominator and a BSA Gold Star with a cut-away fairing were still hot, their cylinder fins hissing in the snowfall. He let his engine die beside them, dragged off his goggles and dismounted.

The cold sleeve he wiped across his forehead undid his elation. Trying to shrug off the pain in his back and get the blood moving in his fingers, he was checked by a flash of the fate he'd so narrowly avoided. It left him momentarily gauche, a jumped-up kid who ought not to have stopped at all, should rather have pressed on home and put himself to bed. The Bee, of all places ... He searched his pockets for a comb, imagining the stares as he walked in; though merely slicking his soaked hair into a Teddy-boy quiff would hardly do the trick, hardly make him one of the lads.

Yet he'd done it, hadn't he, that whole journey through the capital, his first time on a bike, in the dark and in a snowstorm? The family had tried to talk him out of it, but he'd been determined, and if this didn't vindicate him he'd like to know what would. Once he'd passed his test and got rid of the sidecar, he'd pull some cash together, do his own modifications.

The wind seemed altogether different now. A snowflake melted on the newly exposed skin under his eye. Two truck drivers approached from the other side of the car park, and one of them nodded to him. As they filed through the slamming doorway, a snatch of rock-and-roll music leaked from the Bee's interior. Alan thrust back his fears and followed them.

Scratched plywood tables set in ranks, tube-framed chairs bolted to a scuffed, grimy floor, steam under paper chains mingling with the strains of Eddie Cochrane – the legend had never laid claim to smartness, but the inside was a let-down. It was cavernous, yellow-tiled, strip-lit, and for all the cowboy hats beside the Christmas tree, for all the automobile posters dreaming of sunshine free-ways, there was a very English air of fag-ends and fly papers. A kicked panel disfigured the serving counter. Behind it, a man in a vest tapped boiling water from a huge tin urn. The woman next to him chatted to the truckers, elbows raised, pinning up her hair. Her ciga-rette wagged between her lips as she flicked a glance in Alan's direction.

The bike boys were almost lost in the emptiness. About a dozen of them sat at the far side, marked out by their leather jackets and winkle-picker shoes. One lad had his feet up on the table; another's shoulders still glistened with melted snow. There were a few girls with them. Alan looked down at his own fake suede windcheater, baggy and snow-stained, with only a thin, synthetic sheepskin showing at the lapel. The silk college scarf he'd comman-deered from his father was ridiculous with maroon stripes. His ruined black shoes were chiselled, not pointed. In his oil-stained sweater, he might just pass for a down-on-his-luck grease monkey. All the tube lights seemed to sting the damp folds in his jeans.

9

He bought tea and sat at a table near one of the front windows, but the agonised curve of his near miss began instantly replaying in his head. He'd nearly been smashed to pieces. If he hadn't lurched himself over to slam the wheel back on the tar... Suddenly, his legs were trembling so much he half-wondered how he was ever going to climb back on the bike. Shivering despite the fug of the café, sipping his tea and cradling the heat in his hands, he tried to think of home. His house was only another half-hour away. But there was the lorry again, racing into his mind's eye. It came on and on. He clutched hard at the white china mug, recalled that dazed vision of his dad, like God, like Father Christmas, waiting to take him. For Christ's sake, he'd looked death in the face and it had been almost soothing! He forced his arms against the edge of the table, feeling faint, rickety, remembering a dark pool he'd seen once under the water mill at Gaddesden. A girl went over to the jukebox. 'Teenangel' played to the smell of frying bacon.

His tea was nearly cold before he got a grip on himself. Then he saw how foolish he'd been, how puffed up and vainglorious. He'd persuaded his parents he could handle the bike and manage the long drive. He'd assured them he'd be fine on his own in the empty house for a day or so. Now he wished he'd never set out. He thought of the dinner the day before, the lighted fires, the reflections in the Christmas tree baubles. He smelled the smells of his aunt's terraced house, pictured the cramped conviviality, and tried to nestle back into the family atmosphere.

He tried and failed. To his surprise, what *wouldn't* hold now was the idea that his family quite belonged to him at all. How disorientated he felt, as though the night had already changed him and lent a cold regard he'd never known. The feeling stole over him that he could travel neither back, nor forward, and he wondered exactly what it was that had just happened, precisely what kind of experience his almost-accident had been.

There they'd all gathered – as so often on Christmas Day – in the house on Wickham Lane, just over Shooters Hill, where London fringed into Kent. There they'd all met, the ten of them at the festive table, his aunt with drops of perspiration on her brow, his uncle, the mechanic, sucking at his new false teeth as he carved the bird, his grandfather sitting stoical with that Edwardian watch-chain stretched across his best brown waistcoat, his nan, his cousins, their gran. He and his parents were the unwelcome guests.

Unwelcome, that was it. He wondered how on earth he'd always failed to notice such tension under the pleasant surface of things. Had he been blind? Why, if ever he'd stopped to think, it was obvious. Feelings simply bristled between the two sides of the family; they barely tolerated each other. To tell the truth, it was as clear as daylight: he and his mother and father weren't liked, they didn't fit in, never had done.

He knew the cause of it immediately. That stood out a mile. It was his father, of course. But he'd never have guessed it in the normal run of events, never in a million years got such a dispassionate angle on his own kith and kin. He was seventeen, sacrificial, entranced – only something like the crisis at the Elstree roundabout could have shaken the awkward truth out of him. It was his dad.

LIONEL. ALAN HAD watched him, between the gravy-boat and the tureen of sprouts. Lionel – he savoured the slight unfamiliarity of his father's Christian name ... Lionel had worn the yellow paper crown out of his cracker in a spirit of pure misrule. The slim, Nordic face of the wedding photograph, that innocent face, not so much handsome as candid, the face which at home in the brown album tied up with fine cord once used to remind Alan of royalty, had grown ill-defined. And what suddenly showed through wasn't the loved father at all, but some aspect of clown, jester, agent provocateur. Lionel's hair contrived to stick up in odd spikes through the paper hat. His clothes! Shrunk and over-ironed by Alan's mother, his striped pullover hung round him like a smock. The tie, the shirt-sleeves ... Lionel was *bizarre*.

It wasn't just the squeamishness of youth. Alan's vision was immaculate. A kind of hypnosis had genuinely ended, an illusion peeled off, for his legs no longer shook and he felt calm and focused – on his father. Lionel was a spectacle of contradictions. He lacked any authentic shape. He was plump and he was puny, he was muscular and he was effete. Like some gigantic baby, he told his subversive jokes to himself, ate his turkey with a strange expression of exaggerated innocence. Catching Alan's eye, as he *would* do, he made a pretence at being drunk, even though the one bottle of Sauternes between ten was regarded as daring, and quite celebratory enough. His behaviour was a local chaos, masked with abstruse, science-couched observations. It was a flagrant *naughtiness* that subtly, yet emphatically, disrupted the good intentions of the dinner. And all the while grandparents, aunt, uncle and cousins conspired to pass no comment at all.

The single-sash window framed the winter grey. The pink glass bowl chained overhead supplied the little dining room with an electric glow. A blazing coal fire scorched the back of Alan's uncle's mother, who would always deny discomfort. The party took their meal and put up with Lionel, the problematic star in their midst, the clever working-class child made so prodigiously good. In turn, Lionel, who'd travelled the world, who'd flown first class in Boeing Stratocruisers and had seen so many things that everyday folk never would, seemed to insist on remaining that child.

He *was* a star – government work. But the family never asked Lionel Rae about it, nor responded to his permanent, self-absorbed pantomime. They tolerated his dogmatic outbursts. Warily, they observed the formalities, praised the aunt's labour and the uncle's skill with the knife. They avoided any subject that smacked of politics, let alone of religion, lest the fault that ran through the little clan should widen and engulf them.

Lionel *was* clever. His was a frightening, almost artificial intelligence. He'd lightly remark to Alan that he was a soft, bloody machine for designing bloody hard ones.

And Alan loved the complicated wit he shared with his father. All these years Lionel's creature, his sense of *possession* left him bucked, even exalted. A couple of winters before, Lionel had been De Havilland's senior telemetry engineer, when the big aerospace firm had been developing Blue Streak. Had the missile ever come to fruition, each warhead would have been targeted on Moscow, Leningrad, Novosibirsk. It *was* rocket science.

But his genius was of the cankered kind, as Lionel himself wryly acknowledged. Fate had targeted *him*, he said, because he refused to believe in her. Rockets had sent him on his travels, and Alan had the postcards to prove it: incredible images of tropical beaches with sand and palm trees, Californian scenes with fin-tail Cadillacs in sun-drenched streets, the lush greens and impossibly quaint temples of the Far East. In Alan's sock drawer at home there were still pairs of pale blue-and-white chaussettes, issued by PanAm Airlines against the cold of altitude and brought back by his dad as trophies. Somewhere in his long-untouched toy box, he kept the miniature plastic cruets made by Americans for air meals simply to throw away. Lionel had been in Nevada, he'd been at Cape Canaveral. He'd seen the Yanks put their man in orbit. When others in the family had never risen twenty feet above the ground, the magician Lionel had placed a foot on the threshold of space. Then the Ministry axed Blue Streak, and suddenly rockets had let him down, they'd jilted him. Now, he sat here at the Christmas dinner, claiming only half in jest to be a Martian.

He wasn't drunk. Lionel hardly touched alcohol, never

smoked. He didn't sing or dance, read novels, listen to music. He had no time for art, less for films. He hated churches, the sun in summer, the rain in winter. He hated vicissitude, the Victorians, God, history, the city, the country, winding lanes, other drivers. He loathed the class system, the Tories, Labour, nature. But Alan had never minded these foibles of malediction so long as he could bask in their astringent, apparent comedy.

At the previous dinner, Lionel had invoked the death of Schrödinger – whom he'd actually met, but no one else had heard of – with the story of the cat that was alive and dead at the same time. Until you opened the box! It was the bones of a joke. As for his own death, he suggested, nothing would do but a perfectly controlled space capsule, a warhead womb stamped 'Made in England' and primed to fall right back on London. Neither would he stay in one job long enough to put down roots. Nor could he touch anything, he grinned, darkly, without it either going wrong or going down – including, so it seemed, the British Independent Nuclear Deterrent. And he was proud that no one had ever come up with a name for what might be the matter with him. He was too clever to be anything so ordinary as insane.

They lived in extraordinary times. Alan had no idea of it; then again he knew it well enough. Lionel had done no more than carry on the family tradition, hadn't he, preparing to bandy shell fire? His own dad had been an artilleryman, and *his* father before him. The uncle had been in the Engineers. Lionel hadn't. What better way to outdo them than with these intercontinental ballistics? His hubris

had left the family little profit, though: Alan's parents were
hardly well enough off to lord it – they'd shifted ground
too often to accumulate capital. Now Lionel was a mere
circuit designer with a company called Lidlock.

Alan bit his lip. Something else filled his thoughts. No,
it was outrageous, though there was dazzle in it, perfec-
tion. It seemed, for a fleeting second, to explain everything. But it was shocking, out of the question – the very
notion of treachery and spying far too melodramatic, and
Lionel wasn't a melodramatic man. Steam hissed in the
urn. A burst of laughter came from the bike boys. Lionel
had no time for drama of any kind, and besides, Alan was
the tainted one, the depressive, blotched soul of the family.
But for the luck of old Harry, he should have died back
there. And spies in the news were far too sensational, such
very public curiosities: George Blake, Greville Wynne,
William Vassall. It was far too *convenient*, in a way, to
attach the notion of 'working for the enemy' to Lionel's
real life.

The café owner shouted to his wife. Alan let go his
breath through his nostrils; he was losing his grasp,
couldn't trust himself. Some thrust of cold had always been
inside him, whose tip he could only just feel. He'd been
wretched the last couple of months, since the girl in the
school choir had turned him down, since the world had
been just hours from wiping itself out. Kruschev had
backed down and ordered the ships around. But hadn't
the way his dad looked at him then made him complicit,
somehow, in the whole performance? Once more, he
shoved the thought away. No, and he still loved him.

Though when his mother was around he hated him for her sake, loathed him both for his looks and his manners.

He licked his lips guiltily, and stole a glance to either side, because he'd put on Lionel's brainy nonsense, and been taken up as if into a flying saucer. Father and son were bound together, partners in brilliance, hero and villain, doctor and patient, hurtling round a planet that couldn't touch them, peering down every so often at his aunt's simple family in the house on Wickham Lane, who gawped back and admired. He licked his lips again. That had been the sci-fi story of his life. No rival version had occurred, until, on the Watford Bypass, in the Busy Bee café, when his hand shook as he tried to hold his tea and his feet burned as they thawed back to life, some scale fell from his eyes. The rest of the family couldn't stand Lionel, and, by extension, they couldn't stand him.

There was an exhaust roar outside. Another. He looked up, startled. Headlights flashed through the window and sparked the dribs of tinsel hanging down. Bikes were arriving, maybe twenty of them, revving and thundering in the car park. They wove in and out of each other, accelerating and braking, turning this way, now that, in an intricate dance. The din was shattering.

SHOUTS AND IRONIC Christmas greetings came from the door. Young men were unknotting scarves from their faces, combing quiffs, primping their damp leather, brushing at snow. They laughed, jeered, lit up fags. They strutted in tight jeans and tight shoes, catcalled at the owner behind the counter, punched buttons on the jukebox. Alan kept his head down over his tea, but a group of four or five were heading straight towards him, shouting their orders to friends in the queue.

'Mind if we join you?'

He fixed his attention on a smear in the rim of his cup.

'Oi! Got a tongue in your head?' Immediately, they clustered round.

'What? Sorry. Sure.' He gestured. 'Take a seat.'

Three lads sat down at his table. 'All right, mate? How you doing, then?'

Involuntarily, Alan glanced at his watch. It was too early for trouble, tonight of all nights when everyone was still supposed to be at home pulling crackers. 'Fine, thanks.'

'Nice watch. What time is it?'

'Half seven.' 'Hound Dog' came banging out of the record machine.

'Not thinking of going, were you?'

'No. No, I wasn't.'

The young man opposite him grinned knowingly. He had a narrow face beneath his blond, fifties, Teddy-boy wave, the skin pale, except where cold had turned the spots under his cheekbones a raw red. He shot a glance at Alan's goggles and gloves on the table. 'What bike you got, mate?'

' '59 Bonnie.'

'Fuck off. How old are you, then?'

'Seventeen.'

'Yeah? Santa come down the chimney, did he?'

'My uncle's a mechanic. Works with bikes down in Kent. He knew I was looking and sorted me one out.'

The newcomer sniffed and eyed him. 'Not Watford, then, you?' he enquired, as though idly.

'Me? No. Stopped off for a cup of tea. I've got a few miles to go yet. Mate.'

'Got a few miles to go, have you?' The lad mimicked Alan's speech and grinned at the other two. 'That's lucky for you, son. See . . . ,' he spread his hands like the crooked charmer in a cowboy film, 'we've come looking for Watford boys. Got a bone to pick with Watford. Haven't we, men?'

The others laughed. Alan felt his own cheeks crease. 'Where are you lot from, then?' he said.

The rider beside him spoke for the first time. 'Fucking Stanmore, ain't we.' Then he laughed again, and swore, breathing out his cigarette smoke. His teeth were irregular. They showed like points beneath his top lip. 'Yours that sidecar rig out there?' he said.

The crease stuck in Alan's face. He forced a chuckle. 'Bloody thing just nearly killed me.'

His neighbour leaned towards him. 'Why don't you tell us your name?'

'Alan.' He could smell the breath. It was heavy, slightly tarry. 'What's yours?'

'I'm Mac. Mr Macbride to you.' His friends laughed. 'See Nobby there?' Mac pointed behind him to a tall figure standing at the counter. 'Nob got banned, didn't he. Doing eighty down fucking Clamp Hill. Oi! Nob! Has to ride up behind ever since. Or in a sidecar. Don't you, Nob!'

Alan looked. A tall figure was staring back at them. He was older, grimmer than the rest, seeming to stoop slightly in his black, fringed jacket, the black hair straggling on the collar at either side. But the face . . . Nob's pock-marked skin had been slashed. The scars ran in meaty weals on both cheeks, as though someone had played noughts and crosses on him.

'Over here, Nob. This kid says he'll give you a lift in his chair if you want one.' Mac turned back extravagantly to Alan. 'Where was it you said you was going?'

'Over past Hemel.' Alan pulled his gaze from the scars. 'Hemel, Nob. Any use?'

Nob was just coming over, a bottle of Pepsi in his huge dirty hand, when a ruckus started in the far corner. It was with the boys who'd been there all the time. They were the locals, Watford. Alan swung round again, but his view was screened by the rows of leather backs. He heard threats and counter-threats, then a short, winded scream, a boy's – or maybe a girl's. For when a torrent of swearing rose over the jukebox guitars, and the crowd seemed to sigh, it was a girl who answered back, her voice spirited, her words unexpectedly eloquent. Someone shouted her name, Cynthia, and the scuffle began again, because she was the fucking cause of it all. A cup smashed against a wall.

Presley's last chords clanged on the hush. Then the lads round Alan were on their feet, half-sneering, half-cheering, and he stood, too, relieved. He let himself be swept up in the action, even became part of it, shouting with the rest. Only the two lorry drivers remained unconcerned, their sports pages propped in front of their fry-ups. A round-

faced Ted from the far side of the room stood on a table:
'Fight! Fight! Fight!'

The man in the vest called from behind the counter, 'If
you bloody lot want a bloody punch-up you can bloody
do it outside. Go on! Get out of it! All of you!' With his
cleaning cloth over his shoulder, he stood unmoved at his
urn. The mood hung for a second, steamy, and Alan felt
his neck prickle. One instant could ruin another face. He
clutched his goggles and gloves, alert for the click of the
first knife. Then, as if at a signal, everyone crowded for
the door. And Alan Rae went with them, thrust by the
night into the thick of things.

VIOLENCE WAS A chimera – no one quite believed in it. That
was a quirk left by the war: Alan's mother had walked to
work over broken glass, his uncle had seen a Normandy
hedge trimmed by machine-gun bullets, the A-bomb had
blown the Japs out of the fight. Violence lacked shape.
Teds and bike boys seemed its only ministers.
Wisecracking, fire-cracking, they were ambiguous as devils
in an old pageant.

Light flared from the café windows. The car park was
white where the bikes made a natural arena. They seemed
to herd the rival gangs together, closing in with their
welded angles and shimmering chrome. A ring had already
formed, and Alan glanced to where his Triumph was
parked, fifty yards from the exit. He heard the wind sough,
felt the snow fall as cars passed by in the road, their engines

muffled, the swish of their tyres powdery. The flecked gust, slicing through the trees at the far side, began to sting his cheek.

Two figures stood primed in the bleak little space, champions of Cynthia – whoever she was. They were identically clad, both the same height, but the Watford boy was thinner, and his face looked desperate in the harsh light. People were calling out his name. 'Go, Pete!' 'You can get him, Pete!' Pete's eyes were hooded, his shoulders hunched too soon, defensive. He looked out from behind his fists, shifting his weight nervously from foot to foot. The other lad was chunkier, more robust, and his mates flanked him, egging him on. His hook-nosed profile was caught in silhouette as he quipped confidently to one of them.

One of the girls was crying, and people craned to see. The sobbing rose to a wail until a puffy, high-heeled creature wearing only thin slacks and a jumper broke from the ranks opposite and entered the ring. 'You don't have to, Jimmy!' she called. 'She don't mean nothing! Just leave it, Jimmy, why don't you!' The snow fluttered at her heaped-up hair.

'I ain't fucking leaving it.' A great laugh went up. 'Stupid tart.'

Alan watched the girl turn away. He scanned the faces, saw Nob, caught a glimpse of Macbride. The names echoed grimly in his head. He'd already spotted a length of chain hanging from someone's hand. His heart pounded softly as the two boys at the centre began to circle each other.

The initial blows were feints. Fists skidded off leather, grazing a sleeve or missing a shoulder. Then Pete took a punch to the face and rocked back. The Stanmore gang roared as he rubbed his cheek, and Jimmy paraded in the applause. But Pete was canny, seized the moment to dart in, and came up under the other boy's guard with a smack that glanced his eye. The sound was like fabric tearing. Instantly, the two were clutching one another, wrestling and sliding amongst the flakes while the crowd swayed. People ran this way and that to the rough shove and rhythm of the fight, and Alan moved with them in a wild, weird ballet. Whenever the combatants lurched towards him, he heard their breath as though it were his own, and watched the sharp, committed gusts snatched out of their mouths by the wind.

Now there was a lull, and the fighters were locked, resting on each other's grip. A different girl was across from him, framed momentarily in a gap. Fair-haired, she wore a blue scarf at her neck and a pale blue coat over her jeans. Their eyes met, and it was she who dropped her gaze first. Then the crowd swirled, and when he looked again she was nowhere to be seen, and the two fighters were tangling, kicking each other's legs. It was Pete who slipped. He hit the icy gravel so hard it forced a noise out of him. The chants went up for Jim-my! Jim-my! Jimmy raised his arm and made to drop down with a finisher; but his victim rolled clear and was instantly, spiritedly, back on his feet, half-crouched, coming on with both fists, with the Watford lads yelling for him and Alan yelling, too, until the pair of them spun away and the ring broke up.

Now it was all a whirl of limbs and faces in the slip and slide. Alan elbowed himself to the front. Two heads still bobbed and ducked in a fierce exchange, two bodies were still grappling. One flailed, the other got heaved up. One lost his footing and they were both scrabbling on the ground, here the point of a thin shoe, there a hand trying to get a hold on leather or fleece. But the hand went limp at the sound of a body blow, and another cry went up, and suddenly the figures were apart. It was a chase.

The gangs cheered and surged after them, two forms reeling and stumbling in the dark between the bikes. Alan slid and fell himself in the rush. As he got to his feet, a shape came skipping past him with an outlandish, mocking step, turning first this way, now that – like a matador, the leather jacket open like waistcoat wings. It stopped in front of the café window and waited. The other caught up, floundered, lunged, slipped, and skidded front first into the snow.

Something was spattering out of its face, dark drops falling faster than snowflakes, and it was Jimmy, staggering up, twisting away now and gasping, his hands on his thighs. Still more of the dark stuff was spilling down in the wind, leaving black garlands in the bright, fluorescent white.

He tried to straighten, not in time. Pete came in hard, gave him three punishing jabs to the body, one more to the cut face, and a vicious dead leg with his knee. Jimmy screamed and dropped where he stood. He cringed in the white scuff, covering his head with his arms. 'OK!' His voice was thin. 'OK!' A couple of his mates went over to him. Pete stepped back, and looked away, dusting the snow off his sleeves and the backs of his jeans.

Nobody in the car park moved or spoke. The mere exchange of a look seemed the riskiest thing in the world.

Even the wind died, the fat snowflakes coming straight down while the cold plucked once more at the exposed skin of Alan's throat and neck. A lorry from the main road revved in low gear and began lumbering in at the gate, its lights flashing and sweeping the rows of bikes.

Then the mood broke. Someone from Stanmore cracked on at Jimmy that he was a fucking useless cunt. The insult was buoyant, the relief almost palpable. A roar of merriment went up. Alan felt drunk with events as some great wave of generosity and good humour threatened to make them all lifelong friends. Christ, it was a fucking good dust-up, a fucking good Christmas, because that Pete had a few tricks up his sleeve and he bloody gave Jimmy Chapman something to fucking think about. Yes, he fucking did.

JOSHING AND LAUGHING, the two gangs were returning inside to drink tea and talk bikes. Alan was at the doorway when he heard a voice at his shoulder.

It was the fair girl again. She was adjusting her scarf over her head. He could see by the neon flicker and the snow-glaze from the café window her heavily made-up eyes, and her hair under the fabric, fashionably back-combed. Quite tall, she was handsome rather than pretty, seemingly preoccupied with tying the two ends under her chin. Her pale blue mac hung open to reveal her sloppy-Joe jumper, and the tight fit of her jeans. 'They said you were going to Hemel.' She brushed at the flakes just settling on her shoulders.

'Sort of.' He stared at her, then briefly down at his hands.

But she was matter-of-fact, still glancing round, as though unconcernedly. 'You couldn't give me a lift, could you? It's getting worse, isn't it?'

'What, Hemel? D'you mean now?' It was illegal for him to take a passenger.

'I told my parents I'd be back before ten. You needn't if you don't want.' She spoke with an unexpected formality. Then she suddenly smiled straight at him, and the smile and her eyes – another blue – brought him back to that moment he'd first seen her during the fight. 'Except that my . . . Except that no one in there . . .' Her voice was disarming, musical. She gestured towards the café, and shrugged again at the weather. Her hair clustered at her brow inside the scarf. She was too attractive.

He nodded. 'OK.' All at once, they were walking together through the bikes towards his own snow-powdered machine. He snatched a look back at the Bee. The only figure watching them was tall and ragged-looking, the one they'd called Nob. He was standing at the entrance under the sign, his scars catching the fitful glow like lines on a mask.

She took no notice of the sidecar, but brushed off the pillion and seated herself, while he tore off the L-plates. Once he'd lowered himself into the saddle in front of her, he felt a warmth despite the icy wind. It was like the heat of a fantasy – but one suddenly sanctioned, and given approval.

Three times he bobbed up and down on the kick-start before the engine fired. As he nudged the rig cautiously out on to the road, she put her hands in the pockets of his jacket and drew her arms tight around his waist. He could feel her fingertips. He looked down and saw her thin red shoes on the footrests, and her parted thighs. He felt her tuck her knees into the crooks of his and nudge her cheek close against the back of his neck. Her body on his was the one warm thing, and he thought he'd always known her, that she'd lain next to him since the start of things.

The full storm had crept up on them. Now it matted the air and blotted out the road. The few cars crawled in each other's tracks, the snow piling up in ridges either side. Drivers peered through freezing slots scraped in their windscreens; lights narrowed and swung. He guessed at the chaos on the low road and took his chance along the motorway. Five minutes later they were slogging up past Bricket Wood with the snow sweeping at them from over the hills, and the cold so intense he kept calling back just to make sure she was alive. Each time, she gripped more tightly and pressed herself more closely against him.

At last, he took the exit and cut down past Hemel new town, driving under its hard sodium lights, beside its rows of council terraces, until she called out where she lived – in Boxmoor, she said, near the Fishery pub. He took her down towards the canal, and from there along a lane to a cottage which backed right on to the tow-path. And he was sure her family had lived there for centuries. And for ever, he reckoned, he'd known about them and longed for the girl in the pale blue coat.

She got off the bike. He sat still, keeping the Triumph idling.

'Thanks for the lift.' She was halfway to her door.

'Wait!' He let the bike fall and went after her, his shoe skating on the path. He thought she looked frightened for a moment. 'Will I see you again?'

'Do you want to?'

'What do you think?'

She hesitated.

'For Christ's sake,' he said. 'I don't even know your name.'

'It's Cynthia. Didn't I tell you? But everyone calls me Cynth.'

'Jesus! I mean . . . sorry.' He was alarmed. 'I'm Alan. I suppose I'd better . . .' His voice dropped, suspicious. 'Why did you ask me for a lift?'

She shrugged. 'It was a hunch. I needed to get away. Didn't I?' She looked down. Then she said again, 'Didn't I?' as though he must understand.

'Can I see you?'

'All right,' she murmured.

'What was that?'

'I said all right.'

'When? I don't live round here. Tell me!'

'I don't know. Come when the snow clears away. If you want to.'

'You mean that?'

'If you want to.'

'Of course I do!' On an impulse, he put his gloved hands on either side of her shoulders. Before he knew it she was close up against his chest, her arms clutching on to him. She didn't let go.

The embrace lasted a minute, long enough for her warmth to seep into him again. When they broke apart, she lifted her face and allowed her open lips to touch his. For a second, he tasted her mouth. Then, before he could respond, she'd turned away and was at her door, the key already in her hand, the lock already clicking. 'Cynthia!'

Her door was open. He took a step towards her.

She raised her hand once, swinging round in the frame. 'I'll see you, then, Alan. Come when the snow clears away.' She smiled.

He raised his own hand. The door closed behind her. He called out softly, wary of rousing the house, 'OK. I'll do that. When the snow clears away!'

He kick-started the bike. 'I'll see you, then, Cynth. I'll see you!' Revving the engine, he turned the machine around in the road and drove out by Two Waters.

All along the valley road, picking his way in the wheel-marked drifts through little Bourne End, steering the last two miles by pub signs or gate lanterns, skidding kerbless and guideless in the white-out between farms, he felt her kiss still on his lips and her name still on his tongue. He felt her embrace still behind his own back. And he knew somehow, somewhere, it was behind his father's back, too, and he was betraying him.

A SOUND SLICED through a dream. Geoffrey Fairhurst opened his eyes enough to aim the flat of his hand at the stud on his alarm clock. Broad daylight was seeping from the curtain edges. He cursed the clock for making him late for work, because, as the simplest fool knew, at twenty past seven in the tail end of December nothing half so bright was supposed to occur. And what mocking brightness it was – a sweet limpidity that washed pearl the moulded ridges in the ceiling's plaster and stole almost a yard along the papered walls. Wearily, he raised himself.

His wife, Louisa, began to stir. 'Louie?' He put a hand to her shoulder, and she made a series of indefinable noises before turning over and huddling further into the blankets.

He didn't blame her. The room was even colder than the past few mornings, and, as he groped on the bedside table for his watch, the air bit wickedly at his ears and nostrils. It reminded him there'd been a snowstorm. In the same breath, it explained the light outside.

His spirits lifted. An uncomplicated man in a plainer tale – so he'd have described himself – he felt a childhood excitement that made him throw off the covers and climb out of bed. He grabbed his dressing gown around him, tiptoed shivering across the rug to the window and parted the curtains.

A radiance from the frostwork on the glass bathed him from every angle. It was like the illumination of some white rock, exuberant, cleansing, touching his good-natured, standard-English profile, probing his already slightly receding hairline. It lit up the stubble under his chin. But the panes were so scribbled over and spangled he could see nothing of the world outside. And the ice was so coarse that when he rubbed at it with the heel of his hand it stung his skin and cost him seconds of a delicate tingling pain before he'd melted a patch large enough to squint through.

The effort was worth it. The fall had been as heavy as any child could have wished. He remembered looking out over the Vale of Aylesbury from the tied cottage on the Waddesdon Estate, where he'd been born twenty-three years previously. Now, he lived only a dozen miles away – in a self-possessed little Chiltern town suddenly buried under snow. From the window of his house on Cowper Road, through the dip and up the slope to the new so-called chalets opposite, each roof was laden a foot thick, every branch above the blanketed ridges was freighted with finely balanced icing, and each smoking chimney exhaled almost clandestinely from an overcoat of slow grey white – that brightened even as he watched. All fuss and detail of things was covered. Even the bristly woods on the crown of the far hill were mere smudges, nothing but white heaps under the sky. Snow was still falling.

Then Louisa was standing beside him. She'd bundled herself in the eiderdown, and was melting her own view-hole. He waited for her to share the moment, but she made no comment on what she saw, only turned away after a few seconds to crouch at the paraffin heater. He watched her open the stove, light a match and touch it to the wick, until the flame spread around the rim of the burner. 'Wonderful isn't it, the snow?' He put a hand on her hair.

She glanced back at him in the way that so confused him. 'Yes, it is, isn't it,' she said, flatly, and began putting the flue back together.

He picked up the flannel trousers he wore for work and

made his way across the landing, feeling angry and bewildered in ways he didn't understand. He trod quietly on the bare boards, as though there were sleeping children in the next room, but it struck him that he didn't quite belong any more in his own home.

A more mundane problem nagged him while he was shaving. It was his week to drive, and exactly how he was going to get his car across the other side of the valley to pick up Lionel Rae, who worked in the same lab, he couldn't tell. Dressed and breakfasted, he remembered Rae was staying a couple of extra days at his sister's somewhere down in Kent. So he was let off tackling the steep slopes round the chalets where Lionel and Judith lived.

It was odd he should feel so relieved, because as a rule he enjoyed Rae's company. He felt lucky to have found someone he could get on with. Rae didn't stand on ceremony, didn't preen in his former glory, but was informal and approachable. Geoffrey already saw himself as something of a protégé. Rae encouraged him to question everything dusty or old-fashioned, and he liked the attention. To tell the truth, he liked Lionel better than his own equally brilliant, but rather remote and punctilious boss, Dr Raj Gill.

He didn't reach the lab until ten thirty. The drive to St Albans was infinitely slow, pretty but dangerous, and there were abandoned cars all along the way. The snow would melt under the tyres of the little convoys, then freeze again in their tracks. His brisk white Mini did better than most, but still slid about badly, and a crawl was the best he could manage. By the time he turned into the factory car park, his nerves were jangled. Few of his colleagues appeared to have made it. His half-finished, makeshift lab space was entirely empty.

GEOFFREY STOOD AMONGST the electronic paraphernalia and metallic grey cabinets that defined his days. The lab was both futuristic and foetal: there were ducts and pipes, and cables angled across the walls like rationalised veins. It was warm. There was an audible mains hum, combined with an intermittent buzzing sound. Something was switching in and out. It made him think of Louisa again. A threat hung in the air between them, so recent and out of the blue that he couldn't see why it should be, or exactly what he might have done wrong. Of course he loved her. He filled a glass beaker with water and placed it in the specimen kiln to heat up, then closed the snug steel door and paced about.

He went downstairs to the basement where the big new electron microscope was set up beyond the clean-room barriers. Just short of the airlock, he paused. He knew the machine intimately, felt its function almost in his own body. It had its own hums and whispers, the heating and refrigerant drives for its diffusion pumps, the sense of its own electronic life. In a climate of science and specialisation, he'd specialised – and been hired here at Lidlock. Though he was young and very much the new boy, the microprobe was 'his baby'.

He felt his body shiver in spite of the warmth. As a

great telescope observed the past, so perhaps the electron beam looked into the future. Threat was writ large enough there. It was a threat that had been engineered by men just like himself and Lionel – intelligent people, scientists. Since the Missile Crisis, there was no getting away from it, no hope of keeping the rival megatonnage at some intellectual arm's length. What was one actually supposed to do before hail and fire scorched the grass, and burning mountains toppled into the sea? The question wasn't rhetorical. No wonder he'd shivered. Sooner or later, someone would press the button; people were even savvy about it.

At least Rae had left his warheads behind him; at least both of them were out of all that. He compressed his lips and cast an eye over the schedule of tasks pinned up before the holiday. Lidlock Ltd had been a backwater until quite recently. The company made safety systems for rotating machinery, and that was still its stock in trade – a more benign manufacture it was hard to imagine. St Albans itself had somehow remained 'saintly' and aloof, squeezed between the Hatfield defence complex and the Handley Page airstrip at Frogmore. And if Lidlock seemed to have done exceptionally well, with two recent units put up like glass boxes, and a lab section – the section Geoffrey had been recruited to join – hastily erected and tooled up to poke into fresh possibilities, well, what of it? Technology was expanding everywhere. The company was starting to diversify.

Technology was more than expanding. Four years previously, an engineer in Dallas, Texas, had built the first integrated circuit: virtually on his kitchen table, Jack Kilby, a self-effacing back-room boy with a knack for DIY, had etched the equivalent of a transistor, a capacitor and three resistors into a sliver of germanium. With its sticking-out wires sealed crudely in celluloid, Kilby's finger-sized mock-up represented a breakthrough. Robert Noyce, a rival American, had made a similar invention using silicon. In only months, Texas Instruments had Kilby's device down near the size of a pencil point; and Fairchild Corporation likewise with Noyce's. Soon enough, there was the race to write entire textual machines on to microscopic wafers of single-crystal silicon. To those who *knew*, technology was about to exceed itself.

Miles away across the Atlantic, struggling with hastily adapted equipment, settling into half-finished premises and sharing temporary desk space with 'Design', Geoffrey's colleagues didn't *know* officially. When they saw their precocious junior fitted for his 'clean suit', however, and were asked to prepare him ever smaller samples of grit, they mostly guessed the drift – and the source of the funding.

Geoffrey himself didn't, quite. That is, he guessed and didn't guess. A country lad, snapped up on graduation at nearly a thousand pounds a year, soon married – wedded also to Apollonian notions of the common good – he still couldn't quite let two and two make four. At school, he'd been taught by a charismatic science master. At UCL, a professor had uncovered his extraordinary flair for microscopy. Now, his bright start at Lidlock had thrust him to the very edge of the new, but he was still wet behind the ears, and his brain was fully stretched piloting his incredible new instrument over sub-miniature horizons. So the leap of dimension was too great. Computers were still adding machines the size of houses: he'd seen the immense ACE at the National Physical Laboratory in Bushy Park. It was the leading device in a country that led the world, and it could just about tackle the school timetable problem, the freeze-cooling of fish, and the simplest Fourier analyses.

No, in his conscious mind, he failed to join the dots. His research was pure, and the company – with an eye to the commercial future only – was just speculating in semiconductor techniques thrown up by the Americans. Nor was it remotely possible that this micro-calligraphy on grains of frosted rock could have summoned his fellow traveller, Lionel Rae, appearing from De Havilland's barely a month after his own arrival.

Geoffrey returned upstairs without yet confronting the electron probe, and went to sit at the section of bench which was his office space. On the pad in front of him lay a stencilled notice that must have been circulated during the holiday. He took the biro from his jacket and idly clicked the button at the end. Hardly noticing what he was doing, he wrote the letters 'C.S.' at the top of the page. Then he sighed, because those two telltale initials let slip the person who was really on his mind. He glanced down at the memo.

To all Lab staff: The Requirements of the Official Secrets Act 1911, Section 2. A Reminder...

He felt his face redden, and hastily scrubbed out the two jottings. He picked up the sheet to read it.

The several recent and gravely troubling spy scandals in the news ... a heightened state of alert ... on our guard against any species of conduct which might render us liable to ...

At the end of its three paragraphs was the signature of Bob Butterfield, the company's managing director.

He glanced around nervously, until he saw that there was a copy for everyone. He relaxed. It was nothing. In fact, when he read it again, the memo cheered him immensely. It wasn't like Butterfield to dream of Reds under the bed. The likely case, surely, was that some civil servant on high had got into a flap and issued a directive to every boss in the region with a government contract. It was certainly no secret that Lidlock supplied a minor safety device for Victor jets. Butterfield was just passing the flap down.

Geoffrey pictured the Yorkshire engineer's bottled fury at the risk to his pension from sexual goings-on. Amused, he vaguely remembered having signed something when he'd joined. But the idea of anyone at Lidlock having the inclination to sidle off in search of a Russian – for the sake of one military component – was surely far-fetched. He crumpled the memo between his palms just as Lance O'Neill burst into the lab.

'GOOD CHRISTMAS, GEOFF?' Hat in hand, overcoat unbuttoned, Lance was a kindred spirit. He was tall, dark-haired,

only a few years older. His school-hero face glowed, and
the cold had heightened the scrum injuries it catalogued:
the broken nose, the notched eyebrow, the resculpted right
ear. 'Well?' He flung his scarf on to the extraction unit and
leaned back against the pipework to slap snow off his
trouser bottoms.

'Good enough, thanks,' Geoffrey laughed. 'And you?'

'The usual,' said O'Neill. 'Kids enjoyed it, I suppose.
Brass monkeys, wasn't it? We ran out of coal. Can't say
I'm sorry to be back.' He looked about him as he peeled
off his coat. 'Bugger of a job getting in. Trains no go. Buses
no go. Half an hour to get the bloody car started.'

'Don't tell me,' Geoffrey said. 'Still,' he put on a radio
voice, 'we must all do our duty and keep our spirits up.'
He tossed his ball of paper into the air and caught it. 'So
take a look at this, why don't you? Better still . . .' Rather
than trying to salvage his own, he got up and fetched
Lance's memo from the corner where he worked. 'Bobby's
got the wind up about spies and sex. We've all been sent
one.' Grinning, he held it out for him, and indicated Lionel
Rae's empty desk by the window. 'His nibs as well.'

'Hang on. Let me thaw out a bit first. Made the coffee,
have you?'

Geoffrey took the beaker from the kiln. 'Sorry.'

Finally ensconced on a high stool next to the radiator,
with his pipe alight and his cup delicately balanced on the
slatted top of a small, but very expensive, oscilloscope,
Lance cast an eye over the memo. He seemed to miss the
joke. 'Well, it was on the cards, wasn't it?'

'What was?'

'We're being designated, aren't we. Dedicated. Whatever you want to call it. Especially you and your Dr Gill.'

'Me and Raj?' Geoffrey perched on the edge of his bench and began once more to click his pen. His Dr Gill could hardly be dragged away from the silicon, or the clean rooms where it was aligned, cut into discs, polished, oxidised, doped, baked, masked and etched. Dr Gill's empathy with the whole mysterious process, and with the quantum values of semiconductor atoms themselves, was such that Geoffrey often strove to understand quite what his boss required of him.

'It's a measure of your success, Geoff. They're upping the stakes.'

'What stakes, for God's sake?'

'Oh, come on. Haven't you got the hang of it? It's the MOD. I worry for you. They're not pissing around, matey. Why do you think Rae's here? Work it out, *for God's sake.*'

A technician came in with a batch of perspex cases, each bound with surgical tape. They were old samples, and had to be archived. He put the cases down, pointedly removed Lance's cup from the oscilloscope and handed it back to him.

'Thanks, Terry.' Lance drained the cup and tapped his pipe into a large meniscus glass he kept for the purpose. 'Message received. Here we go, then.' He got off his stool, glanced first at Terry, and then back to Geoffrey. 'Enough said, I think. We'll speak later. There's stuff here I'd better be getting straight on with.'

Geoffrey stood blinking as Lance's words sank in. It took him several seconds to lose his pastoral innocence: if

Lance was right, his whole life had shifted gear. He stared at his colleague, now bent over an optical device for classifying the specimens. Everything belatedly added up. What if the buildings, the expansion, the investment were *all* military? Once the old man retired, the factory premises could be painlessly rejigged – to make pocket-sized guidance systems for missiles. A technology was about to take off, but its production was already earmarked by the government. He, the well-meaning Geoff Fairhurst, was about to become absorbed into the armaments and aerospace frenzy that occupied the lee of the Chilterns from Stevenage right down to Aldermaston.

What a simpleton he'd been. His body gave that shiver again. The agricultural landscape he'd grown up in – the fertile plain, the windy chalk hills and sloping beechwoods, the ancient estates with their cottages, brakes and streams – was taking on a seamy side, a sense of underworld. For it might not be coincidence that the big V-bombers flew slowly and protectively over the factory like great grey bats. And maybe British intelligence already had a strong presence in the area. There might really be enemy agents, sympathisers, potential traitors somewhere out there. Eyes and ears might even now be sending details of his own life, his own name, directly to London . . . or to Moscow.

And suddenly, the pompous 'any species of conduct' *did* apply to him. His heart thumped. 'C.S.' He unscrewed the ball of paper, smoothed it with the side of his hand and scratched again with his pen at the initials he'd written at the top. Cynthia Somers was nothing real, nothing tangible. There'd been no furtive fumblings in corridors.

Assignations had not been made. It was all pure as the driven snow, and he was a happily married man. No substantial alteration would occur if he never saw Cynthia again. Yet he wasn't being honest with himself. In truth, she was a gamble with his deepest feelings, Cynthia, the missing term of an equation. His cover seemed almost blown, the sense of threat sharpening itself to a point.

Down in the basement, the microscope preserved its vacuum and waited. It was indeed a tool that could scry into the invisible. Before long, dressed in his special space-suit, he'd be approaching it once again. A bead of sweat moistened the armpit of his shirt.

Now he had to see her, simply to reassure himself. He needed to be certain it was all in his own mind, this infatuation, that it was his *own* fire he was playing with, that he wasn't at risk of making a complete and dangerous fool of himself.

LANCE WAS ABSORBED with the specimens; Terry was labelling them. Geoffrey went over to the lab window. A flake or two spiralled in the airstream against a dull hurry of clouds. Track-marked snow covered the car park a foot deep. Snow lay upon the pavements and window sills of the old quarter, above whose fairy-tale roofs towered the Norman abbey of St Alban the Martyr. The great building shimmered at the heart of things. He understood nothing of women – no one understood them, not even themselves.

There were pencilled circuit diagrams on Lionel Rae's

desk. He picked a few up, complex, hurriedly sketched logic gates with their spiky symbols and jotted values – emblems, he thought in passing, of Rae's extraordinary mind. The man calculated like a machine, as fluent in electronics as ordinary people were in English. But the pages would do to cloak his mission. He held the sheaf out purposefully in front of him. 'I'm going up to the drawing office,' he said.

The drawing office lay at the far end of the block. Just before it, he could contrive to pass the room where the six girl typists sat at their desks. All down the ground-floor corridor with its run of identical newly painted flush-panel doors he was amazed at the lengths to which his emotions were taking him. The large, metal-framed windows looked over crystallised rose beds to whitened, wooded parkland. Children in the distance were sledging down a bank.

'Morning, Geoff.' Someone barged past his shoulder, and he turned, startled, uncertain to whom the retreating back belonged. Others were arriving ahead of him, scarfed up in greatcoats, disappearing into offices. He nodded to one or two as he passed; the place was filling up, coming to life. For form's sake, he put his head in to exchange a few words with Clive Powell, the production manager, and again felt he had no outer shell, that his thoughts were leaking out somehow to betray him, and that was why Louisa . . .

But with Cynthia Somers it was *not* sex. It was precisely because his feeling for her would not 'render any one of us liable' that there was nothing to feel ashamed of.

Blushing again, he made his way on through the double doors and up the main staircase. It led straight to photo-litho on the second floor. But a narrow passage on the first led to the test shop stair at the far end, and, half-way along, there was a glass partition which looked into the typists' room. Once he reached it, Geoffrey allowed himself to hesitate and glance sideways. Four of the girls were there under the strip lighting, rattling away at their machines, pausing every now and then, elbows in, to flick the carriage levers across in that upright, female way they had. Cynthia's chair was empty.

Someone was working the Roneo. He craned his neck to see. At the same moment, the girl gave over cranking the handle, turned and stared back at him – not Cynthia but the freckly redhead from accounts, June Something-or-other. His spirits plummeted as he looked hastily away, shocked at the extent of his disappointment, at how much he'd anticipated seeing her again. Then another girl caught his eye, and he retreated, diagrams in hand.

They'd spoken several times, Cynthia and he. Once in the spring, she'd come with some files for Lionel Rae, and had stopped by Geoffrey's piece of bench to look over his shoulder. He'd been examining photographic results, swirling iridescent images and beautiful sliced forms that could sometimes take on all kinds of impressions. They could almost stand as pictures in their own right. He'd got up in his white coat to explain them to her, though words had seemed only to mar a shared sense of wonder. Then he'd even taken her down to show her where the probe was, outlined its principles as simply as he could, chattered on at times too freely – at others with a formality that verged on the tongue-tied – about the semi-magical properties of silicon, and about his own scanning electron beam. It could penetrate, he'd said, more deeply into nature's enigma than anything before it.

A flicker of a smile had crossed her face. But she'd seemed genuinely interested; and it was flattering, since she was so attractive. That was when he'd first felt the understanding between them, a meeting of minds. Most definitely, he wasn't sexually in love with her. In fact he'd have liked to protect her from the sexual tide coming in, an intelligent girl who might all too easily be damaged. She was younger, and he was married. She had her own life, of which he could, and should, know nothing.

It scared him to feel quite so devastated at her absence from the typing room. He stuffed the papers into his jacket pocket. *She* scared him, even as she thrilled him with her sense of difference, of selfhood, the crisp, faintly provocative way she wore her clothes, the cut of her hair, the tightness of her skirt.

THERE WAS NO thaw overnight. More snow fell. On the next day, a Friday, the earth had another new beginning, without smutch or stain. Then a wind got up from the east that set ranks of silver-grey clouds streaming in the middle air. It plucked the traceries from stalks and wires, dislodged the frosting of empty boughs, and brought great swags of snow from shifting evergreens thudding down on to the white carpet below. Any wakeful creatures hoping to scavenge food it sent back to their burrows.

The roads were more perilous than ever. Driving off from his house, Geoffrey skidded most of the way down Cowper Road. The only visible patches of tarmac showed on the High Street, the long straight road which neatly bisected his home town along the valley floor. Attempts had been made to put down salt and grit. He watched the market people while he waited behind a van at the traffic lights. The fishmonger had shovelled up two huge sugary pyramids on the wide pavement in front of the old Town Hall. He was setting out his stock under the arches, wearing fingerless gloves and an Arsenal bobble-hat, and whistling at the favour of sub-zero temperatures. The packed fish lay incalculably cooled, head to tail in their propped-up boxes.

Few other people were on foot. A dark-coated City commuter was starting down King's Road towards the station, his bowler resolute, his rolled umbrella held out to the side like a ski stick. The market boys by WH Smith's were larking round their trailer with handfuls of snow. A woman pushed a pram in the direction of Woolworths.

The lights changed to green and Geoffrey's wheels slipped as he accelerated behind the van. Then the old road bottlenecked between Victorian shopfronts and the fine eighteenth-century houses with discreet brass plates of solicitors and accountants. He nose-to-tailed it past the medieval church on the left and the modest cinema on the right.

Five ancient routes converge towards London through

the chalk knuckles of the Chilterns. The small market town that was home to both Geoffrey and Alan was on the middle one of these, its fold the Roman Akeman Street. A canal and a mainline railway ran in addition, hidden by the tangled lanes yet squeezed to within almost touching distance of the road. Somehow, the valley accommodated a ruined castle, a ruined gasworks, an aerosol factory and a Tudor public school. Most of the houses were old and higgledy-piggledy, though there was nothing outrageously quaint, nor very ugly, nor very remarkable. Geoffrey had grown fiercely fond of the place. He'd imagined it would be a home for a family. He believed it still could be.

The cars in front of him crept past the Eagle and Child. Run-down timbered cottages marked the town's end by Swing Gate Lane. Then the hedges after Bankmill were all but covered, and the road seemed one ruck in a stark white bedsheet, along which Geoffrey crawled for three interminable miles. When he turned off at Two Waters to cross the Grand Union, the canal appeared oddly to craze and steam in the shelter of its bridge.

There was another queue right into Hemel Hempstead new town and up through the housing estate. The hill was steep. On one side, the local boys had made a strip of ice and were taking turns to slide down; on the other, a stream of younger children were dragging toboggans up towards Jarman's Field, their progress mostly faster than the cars. He turned off at the crest to cross the bridge over the motorway, but St Albans Abbey only came into view after another five-mile slog against the grain of the landscape.

Built from the stone slabs of Watling Street, it marked the next Roman route around the capital.

But at Lidlock there was still no sign of Cynthia, even though he found pretexts enough to pass the typists' room, to check post and reception, to roam the stores and the workshops. He gained no more than enquiring looks, and was left to deal with a sense of loss he hadn't bargained for. It had been, he ruefully acknowledged, in the nature of an experiment.

More staff had made it into the lab: Bill Hollingworth, Royston Gaines, Millicent Throssel, the female metallurgist. Lance was there, of course. Geoffrey stood beside Rae's empty desk looking out of the window at the white expanse between himself and the parked cars. He felt strangely old and set up for life. In his sports jacket and flannels, with his honest looks – the sandy hair just a little unruly, the blue eyes engaging, the smile a fraction too ready and disarming – he'd tried to pull this masculine world around him. He had slide-rule and praxis at work, his good wife at home. He drew a promising salary.

So he stared at the featureless white outside, as at a screen on which his past life could be projected. A village youth, he'd courted Merriam, from the prefabs. She'd caught the same bus to school. As it jolted towards Aylesbury Grammar, she'd seemed so perfect, two rows in front, half-obscured by the rail at the back of her seat. Her sleeve, her shoulder, the line of her neck, the clusters of her auburn hair – he'd been struck to the quick when she'd turned round to look at him.

One day, he'd encountered her, and there was nothing

for it but to ask her out. They'd been to the Gaumont matinee, and for cycle rides together. They'd lain in the long grass at the edge of Lodge Hill and he'd kissed her romantically. So far, so good. But the lips of an unknown girl he kissed at a party game suddenly tasted far sweeter, and filled his sexual imagination to bursting for more than a week. He was flummoxed. Shortly afterwards, the illusion collapsed and he hadn't loved Merriam at all.

A similar disenchantment happened a year later. He was left thinking he'd misunderstood the whole business, and this was exactly when his intellectual engagement had been caught by the inspired science master. Science was manly, and above all hectic fictions of his heart. He'd met Louisa while they were both students in London, and married her, on the basis that what he'd felt before was infatuation, not love at all. He *loved* Louisa.

IT WAS CYNTHIA who woke those first feelings again, still stranger and more knowing. She focused him, as if one of the electromagnetic lenses he worked with had been switched on. Her skin, her eyes, the colours she wore, the weave of her clothes, things she'd touched assumed a special quality – but he couldn't imagine sleeping with her as he slept with Louisa. Neither could he fancy her privately, as he fancied any number of women rather more than his wife.

This time, however, he knew what was happening. He'd read of Huxley's experiments with mescalin. Vision was chemical; the lucid phenomenon of the girl at work was some brainstorm of illusion. The mind was a frontier, and there was a secret gambler in him. He'd elected to observe himself 'falling in love'.

He was paying a price, of sorts. Now the lab had its own alteration. Its metallic surfaces, lit oddly from the whiteness outside, were too smooth, too grey, their edges too hard. It was suddenly a barren place. Nor could he lose himself in the work. Dr Gill was being cryptic, full of nods and winks, but seemingly producing nothing for his attention. Geoffrey could only attend to a backlog of routine tasks: on the microscope, he checked supply voltages, performed unnecessary recalibrations. He couldn't run the electron beam itself because he lacked any detailed brief.

Lance took him to a pub in the cattle market for lunch. They sat by the fire with beer and sandwiches, surrounded by the smoke and backchat of stockmen. 'Things all right, Geoff? You were looking a bit down in the mouth this morning.'

'Was I? Yes. Fine, thanks.'

'Not your normal chatty self.'

'Haven't been sleeping too well. Maybe it's a bug. There's one going around, isn't there? Louie's been a bit off colour this last week or so.'

'Oh, well, that explains it. Not getting enough. That's your problem, old son.'

'It's nothing like that.' Geoffrey laughed uncomfortably.

In the afternoon, morbid thoughts of Cynthia crowded in on him: she'd left the firm; she was seriously ill; some

Brylcreemed boyfriend with a car had smashed her up in an accident on the ice, her legs, her spine, her face; some thug in leather and jeans had lured her on to his motor-bike.

There came a point where he managed to tell himself these imaginings were false, and that, as a true researcher, he should be taking note of them. He reached for a pad. But pen on paper would leave a trail of evidence. With Butterfield's memo still in his mind, he paused, biro unclicked. Again, it was as though his thoughts were on display, as though his skull had been can-openered and the brain laid bare.

At last, with darkness beginning to fall, the frenzy seemed to drain away. Cynthia Somers was just a nice girl, nothing more – maybe not even a nice girl. Perhaps he really had been fighting off a bug of some kind. Maybe it was something he'd eaten.

With great relief he worked on for two hours, setting up a control programme of silica-film deposit tests for the following week. And he felt reconciled to the firm. Government patronage needn't just be military. In any case, someone had to invest in initial research. Great bene-fits had come out of the hectic experimentation of the war years – nuclear power, for one. Lionel Rae hadn't neces-sarily been hired to steer the firm into dark waters, no matter what Lance believed. Rae was all right, he thought. Rae would look after him. On his way home, he'd stop and buy Louie something nice.

Lance looked up at him. 'That's more like it, Geoff,' he said.

There was permission to leave early. Geoffrey quit the building at four thirty, and the freezing crust in the car park crunched under his feet. But the Mini started first time. He set the electric heater, and the demisters, and turned on the lights. Gloved and scarfed, he nudged his way out of the gates and crept along the skirt of town. There was the frailest early sunset: strips of pale yellow were brushed on the cloud cover just above the horizon. He crossed the Verulam Road, where slush churned up by the day's traffic had frozen into brown heaps. The car struck one of them. It made a dull sound against the bodywork.

Then, at the bus-stop on Bluehouse Hill, just beside the tract of ground that covered the Roman town and the site of the martyrdom, he saw Cynthia in the queue. He was sure he did. She was wearing calf-length boots, black, quite breathtaking. He braked involuntarily, and the wheels locked. The car slithered to a halt five yards past the stop, stalling the engine as his foot slipped off the clutch. In the mirror, he saw the six or so people in the queue staring at him.

PLATITUDES SPILLED FROM his mouth as he stepped through the foot-deep kerbside snow towards her: 'Thought I recognised you . . . too cold to be hanging about for a bus that might never come . . . wondered whether I was going your way.' He felt they would do, in front of the onlookers. She had that smile on her face.

Now she was next to him in the car, and they were

heading off along the Hempstead road. He drove in silence, horrified at himself, and intrigued. He could see out of the corner of his eye the tight grey pencil skirt that folded over her knees, the tops of her boots.

She seemed to read his mind. 'Kinky boots,' she said. She lifted the right one as far as the skirt would allow and angled it towards him.

He pretended to take his first look. The boots were soft leather that hugged her calves, wrinkled at the ankle and stretched smoothly, sexily, over a high heel. 'They're lovely.' He looked back at the road.

'When the bus didn't turn up yesterday, I took the day off and bought them with my Christmas money.' She seemed completely natural. 'Aren't they fabulous? They've just come in. Everyone wants a pair.'

'I didn't know they were allowed,' he said.

She laughed. 'Oh, yes.' She was delightful.

'So yesterday the bus didn't show up?'

'I nearly froze to death waiting.'

'But today?'

She seemed once again to know what prompted his questions. 'Oh, today Butterfield's Doreen was off and they couldn't find anyone to take his shorthand, except me. So I was drafted queen bee for the day. Makes a change, I suppose.'

Geoffrey believed he might have heard an apology in her tone. He stole a glance at her face. She was gazing straight ahead through the windscreen, at the landscape. Then she smiled and turned to meet his eye. 'I like the snow,' she said. 'Don't you?'

'Yes. Yes, I do, actually. I like it, too.'

'I taught myself shorthand when I was still at school. My mum helped. It makes a difference. What about you? You've been working on all that hush-hush integrated-circuit stuff I was typing up for old Butterfield. You have, haven't you?'

He was silent for a moment. The snow in the headlights glistened. 'I'm not really supposed to say. Cynthia.' Her name.

'Oh come on, Geoff.' She'd spoken his. 'I probably know more about it than you.'

'Do you?'

'We work for the same outfit, don't we? Do you like records? Do you like the Beatles?'

'I don't know,' he said. 'Should I?'

'Only the group everyone's talking about.'

'Were they the ones who made "Walk Right In"?'

She spluttered. 'Not likely.'

'Oh.'

He thought the subject closed.

'Love me, do,' she said.

Geoffrey's foot flapped down on to the accelerator just when he should have been braking for a bend. Luckily, the wheels spun at the low speed, and the car simply skidded sideways. He brought it under control, unnerved.

'It's been in the charts for weeks.'

'Oh,' he said. 'Yes.'

'I thought we were going into the hedge, then.'

The earth was silver. The farms and woodlands stretched

away to either side under a darkening sky, supernaturally luminous.

'Sorry about that,' he said.

'We'd have been in a pickle, wouldn't we, stuck out here?'

Geoffrey trained his eyes on the road. He could feel her face turned towards his. He believed her eyes were amused, her lips slightly parted. He could see her without looking, knew her already. He felt the blush creep up from his collar and into his cheeks, and he cleared his throat. 'Now. Where am I supposed to be taking you?'

'Boxmoor. You go by there, don't you? I've seen you a few times. Sure I have.'

'Have you?'

'You must have seen me, too. At the bus-stop. Blackbirds Moor, by the cut.'

'No. Never.' He took a risk. 'Wish I had, though.'

Cynthia made no reply. They crossed the motorway and came to the heights of the new town. His heart thumped. She'd dealt him a card: he could offer to take her in to work. Something would begin whose end it was impossible to foresee. Perhaps, just while the snow lay, there was a brief dispensation, an angel of *mise-en-scène* under whose wings they were allowed to meet. How easy she seemed with the flirtation – for flirtation it undoubtedly was. He flicked an eye sideways again at the skirt over her knees, and at her boots.

They drove down the hill from Adeyfield. Hemel Hempstead shopping centre raised its modernist blocks, and lights blazed from the strict mathematical forms. Geoffrey negotiated the roundabout named Paradise, felt it apt and ebbing. The Mini nosed towards Boxmoor under the very faintest western glow.

'Now. Whereabouts am I to drop you?'

'Oh, anywhere will do. It's an easy walk from here. I don't want to put you to any trouble.'

'Honestly, it's no trouble. No trouble at all. It'll save you a bit of time. After all, Friday night, a girl like you ... I expect the boys'll be queuing up to take you out. And women always need ages to get ready, don't they?' He was crass. But he continued, because he was doing nothing wrong, 'Take my wife, for example ...'

She crossed and uncrossed her ankles. 'The boys I knock about with,' she said, 'you'd call them rough and ready. Till you get to know them, that is. Teds, really. We go out on the bikes. That's what I like.'

'On the bikes?'

'Yes. There's nothing like it. When you're on the back and the world's coming at you and you're going faster and faster and there's nothing you could ever do. So you just hang on. And all at once there's a moment when you're not afraid any more, you're not left out, or alone, or different, and it's like ... I don't know. Like you're winning.' Her voice was animated. 'Like that's the only time, the only chance you've ever got. When any second ... the next second, you might die and you don't care. You just don't care. Blokes think they own you. One kiss and you're property, you don't exist any more. But on the bikes you come back to life.'

Geoffrey's throat was tight. He tried to swallow. 'I've never ridden a motorbike,' he said.

'You should try it.' She sounded sincere. 'You might like it.'

She showed him the turn-off. It took him to the road behind the pub called the Fishery, a snow-blank lane with only tyre tracks between the cottages. 'Just here. Next to that lamppost. Thank you ever so much. I'm really grateful.'

He stopped, and she opened the door her side. And he watched her swing her boots away and lever herself lightly out of the car. Her feet sank deep into the white drift. She turned and looked in at him. 'Thanks again, then.' Her voice seemed suddenly serious, a little sad.

He heard himself say, 'This weather's so awkward if you haven't got transport. Tell you what. If I see you Monday morning and it's still like this, I'll stop. How about that?'

'Oh,' she said. He saw her hesitate. 'All right. That would be nice.'

'Could be any time between eight and half past. I can't guarantee . . .'

'Till Monday, then. Perhaps.' She smiled and shut the car door. 'Thanks, Geoff.'

He watched her go up to the little house. She turned once more and waved briefly before disappearing inside.

All along the valley road, between the occluded farms and the occasional pubs, he felt such elation, and such guilt. His blood pumped. His legs shook so that he could hardly manage the pedals. Almost, he wished there'd be a thaw over the weekend – for by that the deed would be undone.

But there was no thaw. Instead, most unusually for temperate southern England, the mercury dropped like a stone, and the winds got up again. The weather was about to strut and ad lib. On the Saturday night blizzards west of the Malverns would drift twenty feet deep. By the Sunday, cars and houses not so very far from Geoffrey's home would be completely buried, with never a train able to move. Sheep on the Welsh hills would disappear along with their shepherds. Birds in mid-flight would fall lifeless from the air.

II

PARALLEL COURSES

THE PHONE RANG. Cynth had got hold of his number. Alan hurried downstairs into the hall to pick up the receiver. He stood barefoot on the floor tiles in his pyjamas, the memory of her lips still touching his.

It was his mother. She sounded strained, far more distant than his aunt's house in Kent, her voice almost scrambled. His father had been called away, unexpectedly, on business, and she'd be returning home alone. But not until the weather eased. Travelling just now was next to nigh impossible. Was Alan coping? Would he pass on the message about Lionel to the Fairhursts, as their phone line seemed to be down?

'Called away?'

'Yes. On business.'

'What business?' He could hardly hide his disappointment.

'You know, dear. The firm.'

'Oh. Just like that? Out of the blue?'

'Sometimes it isn't for us to ask ... Apparently, there's an emergency. He *is* still important, Alan, in spite of what you seem to think. They're sending a car to take him to the airfield at Northolt. I'm only worried he won't have enough to wear.' His mother sighed; the sound was crackly, metallic. 'So can you manage to go up to the Fairhursts for us? About getting to work. Geoffrey and . . . Louise, I think her name is. You know who I mean, don't you?'

'More or less. Give me the address, then.'

He heard her calling to his father. The name of the road was indistinct.

'What was that?'

'Cowper.'

'Oh, right,' he said. 'Up past the almshouses.'

'That's it, dear. Your dad says it's on a corner. The point is he doesn't remember the exact number. But my address book should be on my dressing table. You'll keep the boiler going, won't you? We don't want burst pipes. And you've got enough to eat?'

'Sure,' he said. 'Bye.' He put the phone down.

He had to pull himself together to attend to his mother's message. Of course it wouldn't have been Cynth. His father had been called away, and he was to tell the Fairhursts. He bit his lip and turned back to the stair. Then he stopped. *Called away*.

He'd paid no heed to the spy theory since the Busy Bee. The absurd notion of Lionel in the pay of the Kremlin had simply bobbed up in the wake of his scare, and, with equal facility, it had bobbed down again. All his imagination had been taken up with the girl in blue. *Come when the snow clears away*. The snow this morning lay deeper than ever. It was four days since he'd seen her.

Still, there was a grainy, B-movie quality to his mother's news. He noted how on edge she'd been. He recalled her sideswipe for his lack of respect. And the scene she'd evoked was open to interpretation. Under the cover of darkness, later that afternoon, an unmarked car would appear out of the murky, snow-covered backstreets of south-east London. It would halt before the house in Wickham Lane, engine running, headlights flaring. A peremptory knock at the door would be followed by the emergence of his father, and an awkward farewell would take place in the presence of two men in raincoats, who would then whisk Lionel off – to Northolt, she claimed. Taken with a dose of Harry Lime, it had all the elements of an arrest by MI6, or even a lift-out by the Russians. At the very least it was a coincidence: as if his own lurid suspicions had already exposed his dad, as if a weird mirror life of his whole family had started to materialise.

He went to the sitting room. The grey-white glare struck up through the undrawn curtains. It scoured the hastily textured ceiling, exposed the jazzy walls, the geometric light fittings, the scratch-resistant wood-block floor, the teak-style sideboard. It clung to the one beauty, the polished piano, where Alan and his mother found a degree of sympathy. The Rayburn in the fireplace had gone out. He switched on the electric heater in the dining area and stood over it, shivering, holding his breath.

Then he switched it off. Four days – because of the snow. Or was that merely an excuse? Cynth could hardly have predicted the weather. All he had to do was swap brooding for action. And there was no need to take the bike. All he had to do was get over to her door somehow and knock, while the snow kept the gangs away. He'd walk if he had to, set off as soon as he'd run his mother's errand.

He must simply get dressed, snatch something to eat, wrap up. Four days. There was only the Fairhursts' address. Only that one thing. He went up to his parents' bedroom.

The address book lay on her dressing table, exactly where she'd said. He found the house number and closed it again. His fingertips rested on the cover. The book was right next to her lipsticks, her powder jars and sprays. Her scent still lingered in the air; her dresses filled the cupboard. Fastened to tangled nylons in her drawer was an elasticated garment she wore next to her skin. Before he knew it, before he even knew why, he was wavering. Cynth would never know, neither would his mother. It was just a game. He could give it up when he liked. Four days was long enough – a good stint, even.

Now he was remote, almost an onlooker. Someone had said there was a tart in the fourth year, if you gave her a quid ... Tarts with Teds, bike boys with painted girls, grubby, trodden articles from *Tit Bits*, *The People*, *Reveille* – some women liked it, were insatiable. There was a place you could touch them and they'd do anything. The complicated female clothes fastened awkwardly here, zipped clumsily there, and soon Cynth was queen of the bypass. After that, in his mother's threefold mirror, it didn't take him long. A few minutes, and it was all over.

But the feeling afterwards was bitter as ever. Poor boy, he hated himself. He wished he *had* been killed at the Elstree. It wasn't the deed – trivial, a pantomime – but the shame. Why did this shitty side of things always have to show through, this script of a dirty planet, hurriedly made-up, abruptly shoved in, scrawled across unsullied teenage love? His life was worthless. He was paralysed, crippled, because his father so respected his mother, cared so assiduously for her, showed nothing the least sexual in his approaches to her. Lionel in this so triumphed over his oddities – while *he*, Alan, was the sick, perverted one. He alone wore the family's missing sexuality.

ALAN CLEANED HIS face and put the garments back, still covering his traces. He thought of the bike death he'd escaped and Cynth picking him out, and he tried not to cry. She was real and waiting for him, and he'd just disqualified himself from ever going near her. He'd let her and everyone down, because of what he *was*.

He stood for a moment on the stair, oblivious to the cold. *Called away. Come when the snow clears away.* As his hand strayed over the splodgy, embossed wallpaper, a peculiar train of thought struck him: Cynth and the disappearance of his father were somehow connected. He snorted and carried on down. But there was a logic to it so perfect and tempting – just as at the Bee – that he stopped once again to let the idea sink in. It was like one of those flip-flop circuits his father went on about. If he let Cynth go, Lionel would be back in a day or two. If, on the other hand, Alan went after Cynth – as he still longed to, as she herself had invited him to – the eerie conviction grew that his Commie dad would never show up again. The hairs stood up on the back of his neck as he recognised exactly the quantum condition his father had joked about. Lionel, just like the cat in the story, was in two situations at once, and the determining factor was Alan himself.

He laughed out loud and dismissed the whole notion. It was a thought experiment, the sort of ridiculous parlour game Lionel himself might have dreamed up – if he'd ever played parlour games. No one could shape things *retrospectively*. The bells of St Peter's began in the town.

His mother had been concerned about the heating. The so-called chalet was deceptively spacious; two of its four bedrooms were tucked like polar caves under the ground-floor eaves. In one was a huge cast-iron boiler, which Lionel had found in *Exchange and Mart*, its pieces so heavy they'd almost crushed the car's suspension. His father, fired up himself, had assembled it, persisting with calculation and design.

The other bedroom he'd already turned into a workshop for his projects, installing a bench and a Gothic, industrial lathe. For the boiler, he'd burst forth to rip the home apart, tunnelling through walls, wrenching up floorboards, creating ventages and installing thermostats, wiring and cursing again. Flung hammers had missed Alan, the dutiful apprentice, by inches. For all this sweat and telemetry, the heating system had failed to heat. A fault lay at its heart so basic as to be childlike – a complete mis-imagination of the heat transfer from copper to ducted air. Prime Lionel, of course, unworldly and bitterly funny; but an image came to Alan before he could stop it, of his father already under interrogation, his face bloodied, his legs jerking. He hooked an iron handle into the boiler's lid, lifted it and peered inside.

Only embers remained from the night. He opened the draught as far as it would go, before dumping in fresh coke from the scuttle. Then he prowled for food. Back in his bedroom, he dressed himself beside one of Lionel's grilles, and the breeze raised goose pimples on his legs.

He hitched up his jeans. Sadly, he scooped Brylcreem on to the palm of each hand, and swept it through his thick dark hair. He had to stoop to see in his own mirror – quite *like* his mother as it happened, sultry, maybe a GI's kid, even. He combed his quiff, checked this profile, now that, touched at definite sideburns with his razor. The good looks were a cruel irony; it was a cold hard world. Lionel had said so often enough – and Lionel should know.

Listlessly, he zipped his suede jacket, picked up his gloves and silk scarf. He went down to run his drab errand – all that was left of an impulse so hopeful only minutes before. A pair of his dad's wellingtons stood by the door to the boiler room. He plunged his feet in them, because there were no others to fit him.

CRYSTALLINE BETWEEN CHALET and garage, the snow was chest high. He kicked a path. The slot of sky was leaden. The frontages, all open-plan, were mapped into one steep slope by the overnight fall. A neighbour was clearing a drive; a child, wrapped up in coats and scarves, patted a snowman. The church bells began again, echoing back from the opposite side of the muffled town, and the sound touched him – strident, so public.

He screwed the key and swung the garage door up from
its white wedge. His Triumph stood on the oil-stained
cement gleaming dimly, its mudguards spotless, the chrome
of its two silencers lustrous from his efforts. He sat astride
the tangerine-and-cream petrol tank and the big twin
wafted up its greased-burnt metal smell. He squeezed at
the clutch and clicked the gear change with his toe. The
handlebars swerved in his grip when he twisted the
throttle.

He turned round to where Cynth had been and touched
the pillion seat. Just there her thighs had opened, just there
she'd melted herself against him in the icy night. He pulled
himself away, strode out and yanked down the garage door.
It made a split-second dissonance with the bells as it grated
in its runners and clanged shut.

There was a footpath over the road, and he shoved his
way down between the shrouded fences. Fifty yards, and
his boots thumped in the foot tunnel. Its exit was blocked.
Its leaks were miniature stalactites, the air noisome under
the railway. A powdery shower broke him out to where,
in a snow-bright paddock, the last barge horse waited at
the end of its chain. The animal was up to its knees in the
drift, clad in a canvas coat on which the fall remained an
inch thick. Alan petted the nose. 'Not going anywhere,
either, are you, Charlie? Except the knacker's.' The old
horse tossed its head languidly.

The canal lock was just a rise in the whiteness away to
Alan's right, its two wooden gate-arms barely visible. He
searched for the path where stalks of old nettles and bram-
bles poked up, his feet plunging when he missed his

ground. At last, he stamped footholds in the brick steps, beat the flakes off his jeans, and looked back. The horse had followed his progress with weary concern. The canal, attended by bare, freighted willows, curved into the distance under a milky sky, to thread the King's Road Bridge beside the station. Grey-green water showed through where the ice was smashed in a broad central swathe, still, reflective with a ragged edge. Barges must have come up that morning.

Sure enough, the lock was full, and there were the floating, transparent shards the boats had left. A crush of footprints trod all around the wooden arms as far as the winding gear. Countless times he'd seen the barges. Often, he walked to school beside them, as they chugged in midstream with their cargoes of coke or anthracite, the man in the first boat, his wife at the helm of the second, the black stove-pipes smoking, the grimy tarpaulins draped from the plank along the top, a snotty kid pedalling suddenly past on the tow-path to prepare the next lock.

And he knew by heart the manoeuvre by which the narrow-boats were drawn side by side into the lock, so that there was only the merest nudge to shut the down-side gate behind them, or a rope's tail to pull the upside pair together. Today, he'd just missed them, going on up towards the high point at Tring. And only four miles back, they'd have passed the back of Cynthia's cottage.

He climbed on to the gate, breathing in as though the boats had picked up some infinitesimal scent of her. Her taste lay on his tongue. The air held it. But there hadn't been a train all morning, no chance of a bus from the town.

The one movement in the frozen landscape had already passed, in the wrong direction. It all made the same point. She'd picked him out for his detachment; she was beyond him for his deviance.

He worked his way along the beam, the iron handrail under his glove, his boots in the scuff of the bargeman's. He balanced past the paddle rack where the rail ran out. The water was deep to his right, and forbidding, the drop less than the height of a man. One slip to his left would send him smashing through the drench from the bad fit of the gates into the canal twenty feet below. The church bells stopped abruptly, and he looked up over the town. Then he stepped purposefully across the posts, grabbed hold of the second rail, and shuffled along the further gate. Jumping off, he skirted the mooring bollard and took the downward slope of the tow-path.

The drifts were shallower, the hedge protective, and soon, past a pollarded willow, he was back level with the tunnel and the barge horse. Only the Bulbourne stream lay between himself and the High Street. It ran ten feet below the bank, shallow-flooded into watercress beds – half an acre of green tangle with white eyes and pearls and ice-curlicues.

Bright water trickled on gravel. He reached the stile, picked his way down the dyke, and then the footbridge was no more than one snow-covered plank above the stream and the green cress, to the next, and the next with just a flimsy wooden handrail, and on into the lane that emerged by the post office. A short step to cross the main road, and he was trudging up Cowper Road past the almshouses. Hardly anyone was about. He had no trouble finding the Fairhursts' address near the corner of Charles Street.

LOUISA FAIRHURST LOOKED at him from the sofa. 'Called away?' The morning glare sprang from the window, and Alan noted her neat, slim shape, her dark eyes glinting behind spectacles, her brown hair gathered back except for the ringlets she'd allowed to straggle next to her ears. She wore a black V-neck jumper and a pleated grey skirt, which she kept arranging over her knees.

He perched on his armchair, set his brimming cup on the fender. 'Dad goes off places.' He felt himself blush, as though she'd caught him staring. 'At least he always used to.' He picked up his coffee, and sipped.

But her eyes widened dramatically. 'What sort of emergency? Has it been on the news? Berlin?'

'Just business, I expect.'

She leaned back and stroked her hair. The room was stiflingly hot. The Fairhursts' furnishings were dark wood with thick, well-worn fabrics. And there were modern touches: a copper bowl, a Picasso reproduction, an unusual potted plant with some decorations. A finch on its twig in a glass dome wore a tiny Santa bonnet. Between the fireplace and the sash window a music stand was hemmed in by the sofa, and behind that stood a cello, its belly out, its scrolled neck propped against the wall.

'You're on your own over there?' Mrs Fairhurst gestured in the direction of his home.

'I rode back on the bike. My motorbike. Through London.'

'Heavens,' she said. She had her hand at her collar-bone, lingering, seeming pensive. He lowered his gaze. An empty tumbler with a twist of lemon in it had been left on the floor beside the chair.

The front door opened and someone in the hallway stamped snow off his boots. 'Couldn't get any! Louie?'

'I'm in here!'

'Weren't any papers. Wasn't any milk. And as for kindling . . .' Then Geoffrey was with them, coat open, still wearing a scarf. Alan recognised the man who sometimes dropped off his father after work. 'Hello there,' said Mr Fairhurst.

'This is Alan. Rae's son. Apparently, Lionel's been spirited away.'

'I think the firm . . .' Alan said, hesitantly.

Geoffrey unwound the scarf from his neck. 'Strange.'

'He had to come because of our phone,' Louisa said.

'I see,' Geoffrey said. He peeled off his coat. 'Hot in here. Coffee for me?'

'In the kitchen. Where it always is.'

Mr Fairhurst spoke directly to Alan. 'Chap comes back from slaughtering mammoths on the tundra and his wife won't even make him coffee.'

'It's not as though you caught one,' Louisa said, coldly.

Alan half-rose from his chair.

Louisa lifted a hand. 'If only we'd known!' she said. 'At

72

least you must stay to lunch. Of course you will, all on your own. You'd be very welcome. Wouldn't he, Geoff?' She called after her husband.

'It'll clear up soon enough, I expect,' Alan said. 'Then I can get the bike out.'

All at once, she wagged her finger, her eyes roguish, her voice with a hectic, over-bright tone. 'Come along, Alan.' Yet she seemed unaware. 'And it's such a trudge back, through town,' she said.

'I go over the cut.'

'The canal?'

'Over the lock gates. It's nothing.'

'In this weather! You'll fall in. Have you seen anyone at all?'

'Couple of school friends called for me yesterday. Took some airguns up the common.' The coals shifted. His cheek burned. '*We* didn't get anything, either.'

'My God!' Louisa cried. 'Did you think you'd shoot rabbits? Do you really have proper food over there? I insist you stay. It's no trouble. We're only having soup and bread.'

'I thought . . .'

'That's settled, then.'

They sat on in front of the fire, in a conversation of Louisa's choosing, and lunch was far later than Alan could have imagined. They took it formally, in the dining room, which looked out on to the snow-covered garden at the back of the house. Two robins and a coal tit pecked at the bacon rind hung out.

'I've heard a great deal about your father, Alan. Geoffrey

tells me everything. Except the official secrets, of course.'
Louisa shook her ringlets, her laugh on the edge of some
other emotion. 'We all have to be careful of official secrets.'
She glanced at her husband. 'Don't we, Geoff?'

Geoffrey buttered his bread.

'Especially if there's an *emergency*!' She looked directly
into Alan's eyes. 'It's so *Kafkaesque*. Everything, don't you
think? And now I keep imagining you out on the common
with your friends, guns at the ready. Like an old print.'
She finished eating, set her chair back and crossed her legs.
'Or like the end of the bloody world.' She removed her
spectacles and placed them on the cloth, her other hand
clearly stroking her knee, just under the table where he
could see. But her face was all earnest enquiry. 'So what's
Lionel Rae like to live with, I wonder?' she said. 'I only
hear the stories. Such a brain, Geoff says. Ghastly to live
with, I'd have thought. Is he?'

'Louie!' Geoffrey said.

'Well, to me he's just a name.'

'And my colleague.' Her husband looked to Alan as if
in apology. 'And Alan's father.'

'Not mine, though,' she flared, with sudden passion. 'Is
he? Nor my . . . buddy.'

'It's OK.' Alan was guarded. 'He's all right.'

Geoffrey washed up after the meal. Louisa took Alan
back to the sitting room and brought them both lemonade,
in which the twists of lemon floated. Then she reached a
different bottle from the shelf and offered to lace his, too.
'Keeps the cold out,' she said with a wink.

He declined, and she raised an eyebrow. He felt himself

smile, and an understanding between them made Cynth blur and fall away. They resumed their places; the afternoon slipped by. Geoffrey was busy somewhere else in the house. Louisa kept Alan talking – about his father and the Missile Crisis and the state of the world, and when she leaned forward to poke the coals her jumper fell away from her neckline. This time she saw him looking, and smiled as he glanced aside, at the cello.

'You want to hear?'

'Yes. That is . . .'

She lifted the instrument from its corner. Then she seated herself facing him on the upright chair, and took the cello's body between her knees. She picked up the bow, tightened it and began suddenly. He was amazed at the force of her attack, at the beautiful, astonishing sound that came out, like three instruments at once.

'But no.' She broke off theatrically, looking flushed, her head thrown a little back, the body of the instrument filling the scoop of her skirt and its scroll over her shoulder. 'You must come another time. You like Bach? When's your mother returning? The TV said there was going to be a thaw. Come tomorrow evening, and I'll play then. Oh! It's New Year's Eve. Of course you'll have parties to go to; and won't the girls be queuing up for you, now that you've got this bike?'

He smiled again, but she appeared downcast. 'I don't know what *we*'ll be doing. Geoff hasn't said. Come tomorrow for tea! Honestly, we can't just leave you alone over there to freeze.' She stood and returned the cello to its place, adjusted too girlishly her pleats and sat once again on the sofa. Then she too smiled. 'And I'm secretly dying to see this mighty machine,' she said. 'You can bring it, if this long-awaited thaw ever begins. Oh, it must, mustn't it? Because it can't go on much longer, can it, like this . . . Geoff will be at work.'

So much later than Alan had intended, he eventually stood up to go. 'Thanks,' he said, 'for everything.'

Geoffrey entered the room, holding some buff envelopes. 'Paid these,' he said. 'Chance to catch up.'

'Alan's coming up to tea with me tomorrow,' Louisa blinked the information at her husband like a challenge. 'If he can, he's going to bring the bike. To show me.'

'Good, then.' Geoffrey cleared his throat. 'What kind is it, Alan?'

'Triumph. '59 Bonneville. You keen, then, Mr Fairhurst?'

'Not me. Trouble keeping the car going. Only . . .' Geoffrey hesitated. He darted a glance towards Louisa. 'Friday evening I gave someone a lift. Someone who does know about them. Motorbikes.' He fiddled with the unsealed flap of one of the bills. 'What with the weather, and everything, it's the least one can do. We got talking, you know.' He paused.

'Was he anyone I know?' Louisa said.

'No.' Geoffrey stood still looking down, his free hand now at his belt, the other out near the door handle. 'No one you'd know. It was a she, actually. One of the typist girls, freezing at the bus-stop, wanting to be delivered home. Down Hemel way. Waiting for a bus that wasn't going to come. Apparently her . . . her friends ride bikes.'

He laughed apologetically. 'You know the sort. Nice enough girl, don't get me wrong. You wouldn't catch me on one, though. Motorbike, I mean.' Geoffrey laughed again. 'Especially not in this weather.' Alan heard Louisa make some sound in her throat. But he was too taken up with her, lulled by the way her hand strayed to her breast and smoothed her clothes, by the messages she'd been sending him, perhaps, all along. He could hardly take his eyes off her, while Geoffrey's voice continued softly: 'Down near that pub you can see, just before Two Waters, the other side of the canal.'

So brief the days; the light was long gone as he edged his way across the lock gates. The pent-up water lay black and troubling, the shadowy handrail stuck to his gloves, and the sluice splashed noisily into the broken canal far beneath. Only as he prepared to reach out across the central gap did he realise just what it was he'd heard Geoffrey say.

THERE WAS NO time to lose. He got himself down off the lock and began hurrying back towards the stile. But the shortest route to Cynth's lay along the tow-path itself, and the sky was just clearing in patches; there was already a moon. What a fool he'd been.

He set out immediately beside the crazing, murkily breathing cut. *That pub you can see, just before Two Waters, the other side of the canal.* It was the Fishery. Gold letters broadcast the name across the open meadow. No other canal-side pub could be seen from the road. He recalled the tension between the Fairhurst couple. He remembered Louisa's sudden sharpnesses, the almost inaudible sound in her throat.

He passed the stile, one thought sparking another. Geoffrey had come home with Cynth, and the forced ease in his voice betrayed that giving her a lift was nothing casual at all. Louisa already suspected something. His own news would remove Lionel, Geoffrey's regular travelling companion, from the front seat in his car. Cynth worked at Lidlock. She worked in the same factory as his father – she might even know him. Cynthia might know Lionel. The moon swam.

Where the snow would let him, he tried almost to run. It wasn't fair. It was too coincidental, like something of his father's devising, some invention, spinning with secrets. Now he had to be careful where he stepped, for the wash of barges had taken bites from the bank. Still he forced his pace, risking pitching headlong, or breaking a shin against an iron reinforcement. The blizzards had bent canes down; Alan thrust them aside. A cold thorn drew blood from his face. He felt the trickle, smelt the tip of his glove. But he hardly checked his stride. Tomorrow was a Monday. Cynth wouldn't be at home like himself, at draughty leisure until the schools reopened; she'd be standing in the dawn, waiting for a bus – or a white Mini Minor – to pick her up. Tomorrow evening, New Year's Eve, she'd be out for sure. If *he* didn't contact her straight away, Geoffrey Fairhurst would surely have every chance to 'get talking' with her again. To say nothing of anyone else.

He reached the King's Road lock. Iced willows hung glimmering threads over the far bank, and there were dark sounds under the iron girders that supported the road: a car was stuck in snow, a motorbike revved far off. Now the canal swung right-handed between the bricked railway embankment and the boys' school park. He made himself hurry.

The path at the Crystal Palace pub threw a loop over the bridge for the horses to change sides. He crossed and met drifts and had to plough a way beside the dark walls of old houses. The canal glistened, and the merest ripples showed moony on the central swathe, where the roof of Alsford's timber yard kept the smash in the ice just a hint above zero. He heard no one, saw no one, but the drifts were bad, and his feet grew numb in his borrowed boots. When he stamped them down, he heard their owner's grim chuckle. 'You can't get something for nothing, and what you do get is precious little – second law of thermo-dynamics,' his dad's voice at his shoulder. 'You know what the third is? Never trust anybody, not even your own father.'

Half an hour later, the path swapped sides again, and he was chilled to the bone. The canal was pastoral in summer, its greens landscape oils, its browns varnished as an old master. In summer the only blue streak was the kingfisher. Couples courted, hedgerow birds chattered in the briars, gnats whined above the faint hum of traffic, and dragonflies lingered by heated odours. In summer, roach and minnows rose out of the gravy-coloured water to a surface that dappled and basked.

Midwinter dark brings up other things. When Lionel was a boy, so Alan's aunt had told him, they'd given him a pet dog which the budding genius loved, then spurned out of hand when he found it was a bitch. Alan glimpsed the minutest corner of some fairy story where good sat at dice with evil, saw himself small, sleepless, following the family's trek from location to location. Always Lionel had an answer, knew a remedy for this terror or that nightmare. Always Lionel, the all-mocking, the all-condoning, had been the one he went to, his friend, his comforter, his confessor.

Then he'd become a teenager, and they'd settled in the Chiltern valley town, and he'd put away childish things. He, too, believed in science and not God, because Lionel was good, and hadn't science completely demolished that old myth of a loving creation? Entropy, Evolution and the English Sunday pointed only to some brilliant sadist in charge, Lionel would grin. And if all this set Alan's family apart from the dull and worshipping burghers, still, at the school, he'd joined in and done well, and his life in the chalk hills seemed secure, even authentic – until Cynth had appeared. Now he was here on the canal bank, and his father, too, had a morbid eye for difference, and his cast-iron thermodynamic world was crumbling by the minute. It was. Too many guesses were coming through, too many details were related. Too many homely ground rules were starting to alter.

For he saw what would happen and it wasn't a game. A heave of the ice crust beside him, every second hardening and thickening, locked in some fate he'd force to occur. He would. News items sketched themselves: a reporter to camera, sombre studio discussions, the heads, caught in grainy stills, of other recent traitors, the black-and-white image of a departing plane in whose wake trailed personal obloquy and prurient interest. Each step he took, collapsing the distance between himself and a girl he hardly knew, made it so.

Now the hedge was a clew that grudged its unravelling, and the path stretched between pitch black and phosphor-escence. Stars prickled and disappeared; his footsteps squeaked ominously in the snow. He pressed on. For about a mile and a half, he made progress. Then, when he'd just reached the third lock at Bourne End, a great swatch of cloud caught the moon in a ragged fringe. He hesitated and looked round. Behind him was a hump bridge and a lone building. One window was alight, silent in a gabled silhouette, but ahead was only darkness. He could just remember how the way had seemed to plunge down abruptly.

He tried careful, exploratory steps. The sluice splashed from unknown gates. Before he realised it, he was knee deep in snow, then waist deep, then breasting a mound like a breakless wave in a shelving sea. He was lifting his arms to keep them clear. He was struggling blindly to his right, hoping it was away from the real water's edge.

NOW THE MOON dodged out, and he climbed out of a drift far deeper than any he'd encountered. It filled the whole drop and stretched off into the lustrous distance. Now the moon was gone, and he stood shivering under a hedge he couldn't see, swinging his arms to beat the snow from his clothes. His slaps rang like shots, his heart thumped. He half-expected Nob and the Stanmore boys to roar up the deserted lane on to the bridge behind him.

So near home yet so far from it, the way forward was blocked. Blundering on, he could even die of exposure. He could pitch headlong into the canal. That was the reality; Cynth was a folly. He saw himself trapped under the ice, or clambering out, freezing and smothered, unable to go for help. No one would *know* if he gave up now; nothing about his life would actually have been disturbed. His mother would come home, and after a while his father – because he'd always returned before. There'd be other girls, ordinary girls – because just now he was out on a limb, compromised, sullied. But he could taste her lips, hear her voice, just as she'd been outside her house. *Come when the snow clears away.* She could save him. He wanted her.

The sluice echoed; the dark above him was almost palpable, the canal a presence. Witch lights twinkled from the estates above Chaulden. The only true marker was behind, the upstairs window next to the bridge. He set his back to it and stared ahead. Then, as he watched, the merest glimmer seemed to shape itself on the drift, like a faint serpentine cord.

He edged forward. The sheen vanished the instant his boot sank through it, but he took another step, and another. Twigs and thorns scratched at his face. He realised he was hugging the hedge, and that it grew up from a narrow ridge that sloped to the tow-path. Barely a foot beneath the surface, there was a strip of firm ground.

He trod again. There came the glimmer, maybe some natural warmth, maybe the snow's reflectivity. Transient, it was just enough to guide him, and he carried on, clutching for handholds among the stems and branches, fending off the thorny brushwood. Undergrowth crackled, frost crunched, and he was a climber on a rock face, shuffling endlessly sideways. He kept on. Sometimes a groove or a cross-ditch took him up to his thighs and he had to launch himself to traverse it. Inch by inch, foot by foot, he made ground, guessing by elf light the hedge's roots.

The wrong side of the water, the cut cunningly curving in, a false path with only the blank wall of the railway ahead ... He stilled his fears in the effort, because there was no going back. In a journey so short, but a peril so genuine, he lost sense of blind minutes, or hours. His father's son, he even tried to work out what had caused such a drift – some fluke around the bridge during the previous night's blow, some aerofoil effect of the adjacent meadows heaping snow into the sudden hollow.

At last the rack of cloud that had so bamboozled him began to break up, and ragged strips revealed the hidden moon. Territory began to reassemble, along with an ease and quiet he hadn't expected. There was the tow-path again, like an old friend. He stepped down and took tentative steps. The ground was firm.

Almost before he knew it, the drift was behind him and he was speeding along. Brightness flooded the sky and the

going was no worse than before Bourne End; and if the
cut did duck under the railway and swerve to the right,
still he could follow the track as though born to it. The
street lights of Hemel were strung on the Adeyfield rise.
Beside him, low in the mead, lay a glistening ice sheet
where the Bulbourne stream made yet more watercress
beds. And it was hardly a step to her door. If she were
visiting, babysitting, if ever something so mundane, or if
the bike gang had managed to get out on the roads and
carry her away to the Busy Bee . . .

She'd be there, in the cottage on the opposite bank. She
had to be.

THE WOMAN WORE a pink dressing gown and slippers,
curlers in her wet blonde hair. Framed by the lit hall, she
regarded Alan blankly, with fear, even. It *was* mundane,
banal – but her features held a perfect echo of the face that
had been four days in his thoughts.

'Yes?'

'I was wondering . . .' He sounded gruff. A riff of television came from one of the rooms. He had no idea what
time it was. Seven o'clock, eight . . .? 'I was looking for
Cynth. My name's Alan. If it's a bad time to call . . . Is she
in at all, please?'

The woman took in his suede jacket and blue jeans. She
called over her shoulder. 'Cynthia! Someone for you!' Her
speech had an unEnglish lilt; it took him aback. He remembered Cynth's clear tones in the café, her unexpected

formality. 'She'll be down in a minute.' The woman's eyes narrowed. 'Have we seen you before?'

'I met her Boxing Day. Brought her home.' He spread a gloved hand. 'She said to call, but . . .' His right knee shook whenever he put his weight on it.

'So,' she said.

There were footfalls on the stair, and Cynthia was beside her mother. She wore a clinging high-necked jumper, a wide red belt cinched to her waist, grey slacks tight to her body. But her blue eyes seemed without recognition, and his heart sank. The kiss at this same doorway had meant nothing. The fierce embrace on the back of his bike had been only to keep herself out of the airstream. He was just a teenage kid, just a set of wheels she'd used and thrown away. He should never have come. He looked at her as if for the last time – her face as compelling, her gaze proud and intelligent, her blonde hair shaped exactly as he remembered it. His voice stuck in his throat.

Cynth turned to her mother. 'This is Alan. It's fine, Mum. The one I told you about. No, really. You don't have to worry all the time.' She leaned towards him. 'Your face is scratched.' She licked a handkerchief from her sleeve, dabbed at his cheeks. 'What on earth have you been doing? Honestly! How did this all happen?'

He found himself grinning. 'You said when the snow cleared away. I couldn't wait that long.'

Her mother left them, and Cynth stood back, smiling herself. His knee still shook. From somewhere inside, the same accented voice made a comment about the cold, and there was a glimpse of a bright kitchen beyond the halo of Cynth's hair.

'Wait,' she said. 'Just wait there. All right, Mum! I told you . . .'

The door closed tight on him, a flush door with a spangled glass panel in it and a dull bronze letter-box, like the door to a council house. The cheek she'd touched stung again. He put a hand up to it and stood back. There were lace nets in the windows. On the sill behind the drawn downstairs curtains, knick-knacks were faintly illumined: a bowl, a glass vase, glass animals and a painted wooden horse. Upstairs, in what looked like a child's bedroom, was the outline of a toy globe. He stepped further into the road and looked up again, saw the chimney stack, a smoking silhouette above the snow-covered roof. And beside the usual television aerial was a separate mast, stubbed and spiky against the streaking, moonlit sky. He recognised the short-wave radio antenna.

The door opened again. She wore a padded duffel coat and a thick scarf around her neck. She was just pressing her feet into a pair of wellingtons beside the mat. 'All right?' she said, looking up. Her eyes were hastily lined. There was a touch of lipstick to her mouth.

He nodded.

'Come on, then,' she smiled. 'Your poor face, Alan! Where's the bike? I don't know how you managed it. Getting over here, I mean.'

'The bike's at home,' he said. 'I walked.'

'Walked! I thought you weren't from round here.'

He told her where he lived. 'I came along the canal.'

'Heavens!'

'I had to see you.'

'Oh!' She looked moved, and seemed to pause for thought. 'We'd better just walk some more, then.'

They began towards the new town. At the end of her lane he took her gloved hand. She didn't pull away.

THE PAVEMENT SNOW lay trampled. A wider street looked across the flat white Blackbirds Moor, and the line of the canal disappeared under the road bridge. They were walking beside a run of little Victorian terraces. He turned to her, and it was as though she'd been expecting him. He thought of how he'd met her, what he knew of her, the threads of her life that were quite beyond him, yet curiously linked to his own. He gripped her hand. 'I don't know why you asked me,' he said at length. 'Someone like you.'

'What?'

'At the Busy Bee. I don't get why you asked me to give you a lift.'

'It was a hunch.' She looked down and kicked at a parcel of snow which sprayed up in the street light. 'I told you.'

'And why you kissed me,' he said. 'Straight away. I don't get that, either.'

'Complaining?'

'No. No, I'm not.' He studied her hair, the way it fell like a blonde cap, the fashionable wisps cut to a point against her cheek. Everything was almost too iced and right. 'Would you kiss anyone who gave you a lift?'

'No.'

'You mean that?'

She spoke firmly. 'Of course.'

A solitary car nursed the kerb of the big roundabout. Two others crawled, far off, their headlights carving a pale track. He led her across the heaps and ruts in the road. In the deserted shopping precinct, he put his arm around her. They stopped only a few paces further on, and he kissed her for the second time, lingeringly. He was scared. 'What about the lads. I mean the Watford boys ... and the others?'

'The lads? They're all right. Once you get to know them.'

'But, you and me ...' They walked on. He looked all around him, keeping his arm tightly about her waist. Their footfalls crunched. The precinct was mantled between tall blocks – by day a showpiece of the New Jerusalem, by night fantastical. The concrete awnings were snow-heaped, the ledges blind. Twenty yards away on the empty concourse, a tailor's fluorescent light flickered on and off, and the postured dummies flashed and jumped.

'Yes,' she said at last. 'You and me.'

'I've thought of you ever since. I didn't know ... I couldn't get you out of my head. Did you think of me?'

'Yes.'

'You remembered my name.' His breath hung in a shape when he let it go.

'Yes, I did, Alan. And you remembered mine.'

'The fight, it was all about you. I had no idea. And then you ...'

She kissed him again, impulsively, and he clasped her to him.

'Don't you believe in hunches, then?' she said, her cheek against his.

'They'll want you back.'

'I'm not scared. Are you?'

Something in his shoulders melted and a plume of feeling came up his spine. It was like guitar chords, like a jukebox already playing in the abandoned square. He pressed his gloved hands down her back. He could feel the swell of her hips.

'Alan?'

'Yes?'

'I'm not . . . I wouldn't . . . I don't do this all the time.'

'I thought . . .'

'Don't think. And, all right, I *was* frightened at the Bee. That ruck nearly got out of hand. It's hard to keep pretending. That everything's fine, I mean. If you're a girl, you . . . put on a face. You look like you're having fun and you tell your mum and dad . . . But you get in too deep, and then you can't get away. People won't let you. That's why . . .'

'That's why you picked me?'

She put a hand on the collar of his coat. 'When you back a hunch . . . When you look, and there really is someone there, you're given a moment, a chance. You know in your heart. I hoped you'd come. Before . . .'

'Before what?'

'No. It's nothing. Before nothing.'

Instantly he was suspicious, half-glad of the voice in his

head: *Never trust anyone*. Yes, it was too romantic, almost too easy. Was she thinking of Geoffrey, and covering up? Women were like that. She was insatiable, liked it too much, couldn't get enough of it. There was some cruel trick and she was merely playing with him. Then he felt his own shame again, his reflection, just that morning, in the mirror. He let go of her.

They walked on. Even as he stole glances at her, at her shape, at her real presence, there were unknown eyes peering from upper floors, and he knew himself tranced, like an insect landed inadvertently on a great four-dimensional flower, an unknown orchid, infinitely female, exquisitely perilous, whose petals shone weirdly, whose perfumed tendrils just touched him.

They turned out at the end of the shops into the ornamental gardens. Modern lamps on stalks cast circles. A fountain's arrested jets marked where, under blanketed ice, the little River Gade ran back towards the roundabout. Her hip just nudged against his, and he couldn't resist. 'All right, then. But I don't care,' he said, grandiose and boyish, mismanaged words almost for other ears than hers. 'It doesn't matter. It's just you I really want, Cynth. I really do.'

'Do you? A nice boy like you?'

He stopped and pulled her to him once more. 'Of course I do. More than anything.' This time he kissed her forcefully, but when his tongue touched hers, she put her hand against his chest. 'I told Mum I wouldn't be long,' she said, and moved on.

She cradled herself against him all along the walkway.

She talked of the ride in the dark in the snowstorm and how she'd felt when she'd clung to him on the pillion. Then, suddenly, she halted and was listening, and he could hear a dark sound, like a cello – or a bike. Or many bikes.

Sure enough, from the Adeyfield rise came a subdued roar of engines. She hurried him across the Paradise roundabout, over the wide verge and into the protection of the Kodak building. Drawn back, pressed against an indentation in the space-age concrete, they stood, waiting and watching.

THE HEADLIGHTS SHOWED first. Wavering down the hill at the far side came the finger-beam lanterns of a line of motorbikes, picking their way impossibly until, one by one, they crawled under the shadow of buildings and were lost to view. They reappeared from behind the ornamental walls, the leaders negotiating gingerly the car tracks of the roundabout, the others manifesting in turn, their engines at low revs, taking exaggerated care in the unridable conditions, keeping their file, about twenty of them. One near the front was fitted with a sidecar.

'Look!' Cynth said, pointing.

By frosty street light, quite clear amongst the USAF fleece jackets and scarfed faces, a shape in the sidecar seat rose, tall and sombre. Who could it be but Nob? Alan scanned the tributary roads, unnerved. No other traffic was in sight. One of the front riders swept round in a tight circle, daringly. His headlamp blazed across the Kodak façade, and the beam flashed in their faces. They must have been seen. Too late, Alan huddled Cynth back.

But the riders gave no hint. Instead, they jostled and gathered their machines, edging a wheel here, revving and nudging forward until they made an unearthly-looking posse by the sign to the station. Slowly, and with surpassing care, they turned off in the direction of the Moor.

'They're going to my house,' she whispered. 'It's *me*. They want me, Alan!' She clung on to his coat.

'No,' he said. 'Surely, it's just . . .'

'I'm telling you.'

'We can't be sure.' He stroked her hair. 'We don't know.'

But she started off after them, half-running, half-sliding. He followed, and the path seemed far longer and more treacherous than it had before. By the terraces, they both had to stop, getting their breath. But they heard all too clearly the menace of throttles being flipped at idle, a random growl that seemed to swell out from the houses and over the flat white lea that led to the canal. They hurried on past the Three Blackbirds, growing more circumspect as they went, avoiding the lamps, shrinking now and then against the house fronts. The noise filled the air. There was a blank wall at the corner of Cynth's lane. They crept along it and peered round.

A mêlée of bikes filled the little roadway. Exhaust notes echoed off every shrouded surface. Headlights danced, brake lights flashed, masked faces appeared and disappeared. Right in front of Cynth's house, there was shouting, and two booted, flying-jacketed figures were bathed by the street lamp in an odd milky light. Cynth put her hands up to her face. 'I knew they'd come,' she said. 'If I stepped out of line. If I wanted something just for me. What if they start on Dad? What if Mum tells them about you?'

'Have you seen any of them since . . .' He tried to make sense of it. 'Since the Bee?'

'What?'

'The Stanmore lads. Will they have realised you . . . that we . . . ?'

She was crying, shaking. 'I thought . . . What are we going to do?' She clutched at his coat.

'We have to get you away.' He put his arm around her, trying to lead her, starting to drag her, almost. 'Don't you see?'

A car appeared before they could move. It skidded past them and entered the lane, an old-style, khaki-coloured Standard Vanguard with the distinctive humped back. But there was a faded Stars and Stripes on the side, and on the rear a Confederate flag, once crudely painted, now only half-visible. They stared after it from the shelter of the wall, and the bikes made way as it drew up in the midst of the pack. Lights appeared in the neighbouring houses; windows were thrown open. Then came more shouts above the din. Three young men got out of the car. Cynth gripped Alan's arm. 'What are we going to do?' she repeated. Her voice was pinched, agonised. 'Alan!'

'Hide,' he said. He began to pull her away again. 'We must. Till they go.'

'What if they don't?'

'They'll have to. Once they find out you're not there.'

'How will they, Alan?' She turned her face to his. 'Eh? What if they break in! My mum and dad – I'll have to go to them. You don't know what they're like.' The bikes roared in sudden unison. 'Let me go!' She started forward.

He kept hold of her. The scene that confronted him was nightmarish, lawless, like something in a film. 'They'll give up in a minute. They wouldn't ... Maybe they've been drinking. Maybe ...' He was nonplussed. 'You're sure it's them?'

'I've got to show them I'm here.'

He held on to her.

But she began breathing too quickly. 'Let me, Alan! I *must* – there's no way out!' Some of the bikes were beginning to mill and weave, just as he remembered at the Bee.

'I'm calling the police.'

She twisted in his grip and stared at him. 'Don't be daft.' She was shivering.

They were both so young. He looked around. 'Is there a phone box?'

Another volley of shouts came from the street, and the car was turning round. It came racing towards them accompanied by two of the bikes, drew level, braked, then nosed out. The rear wheels skidded on the packed snow as it headed back towards the new town centre.

Now several bikes were right in the neck of the street, and one of them lost grip almost exactly where Alan and Cynth were standing. The machine swung and went down awkwardly; its rider tried to wrestle it back up while it roared and slipped like a live thing. The figure staggered round: the more he fought, the more the bike's light seemed to search at them. Alan flinched against the corner house. He could feel Cynth trembling. The next moment, the light blazed in their faces, and they stood paralysed until a second bike made a precarious circle in the rutted ice. Then it, too, was pointing its headlamp beam straight at them.

'Run!' Alan pulled her after him.

A throttle revved open. Too suddenly – there was a splintering sound. Alan gave one quick glance back as, slipping, holding on to each other, they tried to escape: the second bike was flat in the snow just where they'd been standing, its rear light glowing, its back wheel whirring. Then he and Cynth were dashing into a side street.

They were in a warren of lanes. They took this sudden turn, now that, leaving the criss-cross of lights and the din of engines, hurrying past the house fronts in a desperate scramble. When a machine came up behind them, they hid in a doorway. Another passed the street's end just ahead. Now the sidecar combination was coming straight towards them, its light full on and its engine roaring. With the instinct of the hunted, they dived into an alley. It led to a modern estate. They stumbled past a shuttered chemist's shop, around a corrugated-iron chapel, beside a run of identical council houses. Seemingly out of nowhere, a rider appeared and growled between the snow-blank fronts. Alan stood stock-still, then chose the opposite direction, conscious only of Cynth half-walking, half-running beside him.

A steep rise climbed past a school. They took it without hesitation, slogging up a deserted white slope between more council terraces, until the noise of the searchers began to fade. The lines of the houses were stark, the roofs, with their uniform chimneys, almost one bare ridge. Snow-covered cars were parked precariously on the incline, some pre-war, others with toy-town shapes glowing like marzipan under the sodium lights. Treeless side roads led blind or seemed to turn back down again. Continually, Alan expected to hear the big bikes scaling the ice, and he hurried Cynth upwards, not daring to look back.

At last, the road narrowed sharply and began to level off, and they turned exhausted after the long ascent. The same moon that had lit the canal now glared from the ridge, and the valley below them was a folded sheen spread out. Strings of light glittered. They could hear the bikes still down in the warren. From somewhere to the left, a hammering bell drew out a long line of sound.

'I can't go home, can I?' She said it simply. 'How can we tell when they'll . . . ? Alan, I don't know what to do.'

He pulled her to him, her breath against his. 'We'd better keep moving.' He tried to sound practical. 'Otherwise we'll freeze.'

'We'll freeze anyway,' she said. 'With nowhere to go.'

There were no more houses. They were standing on one of the many little kerbless roads that traversed the high waste ground of the common. He turned towards the dark. Towering black trees stood out against the sky. 'My house is empty,' he said. He saw no alternative. 'If we can just keep going along the top here, it'll take about an hour.'

She stared at him, then took his arm. Under the moon, they walked hand in hand. Only later did Alan reflect that he was rescuing her for the second time in his life. It was the last thing he'd expected when he'd set out.

GEOFF FAIRHURST WENT out alone, with a heavy brown carrying case strapped across his back. Flurries of snow had come all morning; the sky was a ship running aground, a bruised underside. Nearly a week had passed. Louisa had decamped to her friend's a couple of miles away.

She'd sent a telegram, then a letter saying she needed 'time to think'. She'd posted an afterthought: would he bring her cello? There was no rush – the weekend would do, preferably Saturday afternoon. He hurried upwards, away from the town, walking as fast as the instrument would allow.

He went over in his mind yet again, all along Doctors Commons Road, the events of the previous Sunday. He couldn't account for them. Lionel's boy had turned up and Louisa had welcomed him with open arms – a shade too open. All he, Geoffrey, had done was to tell the truth about a conversation with a girl at work, to whom, in exceptional circumstances, he'd given a lift. So he put it in an effort of detachment, because everything else, unless he'd somehow blurted it in his sleep, had been bottled hermetically within himself.

Once Alan had left, Louisa had worked herself into a state. 'Some doe-eyed little secretary' had been mentioned. Finally beyond reason, she'd thrown clothes into a duffel bag and run off into the night. She'd done as much once, twice before. This time, however, it was dark, and the temperature was below zero. After searching the town fruitlessly for three hours, he'd gone to the King's Road police station. They'd promised to 'keep an eye out' and advised him to phone the hospitals later in the night. He'd gone back to look further afield until he was so tired and cold he could hardly put one foot in front of the other.

Sleepless and desolate the next morning, he'd tried the police again. No news. He hadn't been able to go in to work, much less pick up Cynthia Somers at the bus-stop on the road through Boxmoor. Instead, he'd spent the best part of New Year's Eve helplessly distraught, tramping yet more widely the snows and glassy drifts in search of Louisa, her tracks – or her frozen corpse. On returning, he'd found the telegram at last. She was at the house of the pianist woman with whom she regularly played, and he was 'not to worry'.

Out of breath in the lee of one of the grander residences halfway along Graemsdyke, he wrenched his thoughts from his wife and turned towards the far side of the valley. Eyes slitted, he tried to identify exactly which modern gabled box contained Rae's catalytic son. Was he still slumming it over there? At least no jumped-up young tearaway on a Triumph Bonneville had come visiting this afternoon; but then the roads had grown even more treacherous, if that were possible.

He located Rae's house. Two micro-miniature figures were just visible, poised at the top of the drive. Perhaps Judith, perhaps even Lionel had come back. His spirits lifted. And then fell: the garage door was up, and he was almost certain there was no car. Besides, the figures were hesitant on the slope. They might simply be canvassers, Jehovah's Witnesses, neighbours. He wondered why he was even bothering to speculate. He wondered why the boy, now for ever coupled by the fateful subject of motorbikes with Cynthia Somers, continued to intrude on his bewilderment.

In summer, a gang of lads had commandeered the stretch of kerb outside the tea shop in the High Street, sitting sideways on their machines and trying to look threatening. Half the time, they made their girls stand between their knees – girls of the kind whose jeans did up at the front. It probably *had* been a little disruptive, right next to Woolworths. Geoffrey bit his lip. He'd imagined Cynth to be different. Yet when *she*'d spoken of bikes, her voice had been animated with a passion, and a kind of horror. He looked about him. His unrazored cheeks were already flushed and raw in the wind. He clapped his gloves together, imagining Alan Rae on his journey back across London that first night of the blizzard, the rough music of the Triumph, the sawtooth gale.

A row of icicles hung along the gutters of someone's breeze-block garage, thick glassy spikes almost bending in the air stream. He reached up to snap them off, one after the other, and heard them chime and fracture in the carpeted concrete below, except for the last, which he carried in his glove like a dagger. All right, he'd done a kind of wrong to Louisa. In his heart, or more chastely in his head, he'd committed adultery. But since when was it a crime to have private thoughts, fantasies? He'd even owned up: 'It was a she, actually. Just one of the typist girls.' Louisa had immediately jumped to conclusions, and used them to enact something that perhaps had long lain waiting at the back of her mind. He knew her weird anger. Now he caught a glimpse of his own.

He stood to one side of the pavement. A mother shepherded her morose, overcoated twins with one hand, and struggled to push a toddler with the other. He let her pass. Louisa *would* take things to a kind of brink, but never so far as this. And her regular plea of hormones annoyed him, for all he was a scientist. Louie's pact with her blood seemed to justify any excess. Was he secretly glad, then, that she'd gone? What with the cello, there seemed little prospect of her speedy return. Making him walk over to deliver it merely added insult to injury. He heard the mother behind him shout to her twins to watch where they were putting their feet or they'd have that pushchair over! A car climbed slowly by in the ruts.

On the Tuesday, when Geoffrey *had* eventually got back to Lidlock, Cynthia, too, had been missing. That was New Year, but she'd hardly be one of the hangover brigade. Some genuine climate of absence seemed to have set in along with the meteorological mayhem. He checked himself. Once again, as a scientist, he rejected the pathetic fallacy; he rejected all that woolly ragbag of rhetorical knitting the English master at school had seemed so pleased about. Yes, coincidences happened; but connections were strictly causal. Simply, as Lionel Rae would have put it, it was a cold hard world out there. He threw his icicle at it.

The weather was certainly a phenomenon. Conditions

more proper to the Russian steppes had migrated, and were staying put. Toiling up Cross Oak until there was nothing left to shield him, Geoffrey almost didn't care if the unkind wind blew for ever. A blast tugged at the damned cello. It threatened to spin him round. His scarf was useless; he had to hold his lapels across his throat with a glove. Another gust caught him as he was crossing the top road. It scouted him, and he almost slipped, and when he faced round to stare accusingly into the eye of the blast, it stabbed right back, an aerial corkscrew, steel-bright. The cistern tower beside the black barn appeared to buckle, while the cello across his shoulders, her priceless Vuillaume, was pulled this way and that. He could hear the wind in its strings, despite the thick canvas case, and now the blast groped under him, belling his coat out like a woman's skirt, gripping his bare legs through his trousers with icy fingers. It pestered him even after he'd crossed the ridge.

There was respite once the road plunged down. Here, he took slow mountaineer's steps, careful of ice. Pancake Wood dropped to the new valley floor, and finally, while the sky streamed overhead, Hockeridge Bottom was calm and quiet under the trees. It was only a mile along lovely, transfigured paths to the house of Louisa's friend, Astraea. Geoffrey might have enjoyed the lace edgings on the trees or the still unblemished mantle underfoot, but today his feelings competed in a tormenting round. Just now, it was the bitterness of passion unachieved – as though he could never have sufficient time any more for what he wanted to accomplish.

All week, he'd thrown himself into his work in order to cope. Dr Gill, inscrutably close to making channels in buried silicon layers, was suddenly at the other extreme, suddenly in a hurry for tests. Lionel Rae had once said human intelligence was already artificial; they, and countless others in America – in fact, all across the free world – were merely attempting to replicate it. Rae said both Descartes and science fiction claimed all animals were machines. Weren't humans animals? Rae said silicon life, not carbon life, could equally have evolved. Everything was just molecular chance. Two gulls, far inland, drifted on the wind. Temporarily drained, Geoffrey could see no prospect of future rest, or peace. His legs carried him forward mechanically along the snows, as though he himself were already some prototype.

ASTRAEA AND BENJAMIN Hawke had done up a farmhouse at the edge of the wood – from which Astraea affected at dinner parties to despise the country, 'carried off to the wilds like bloody Kate the shrew'. The house did have some medieval brickwork. It even had traces of a moat. Geoffrey reached the clearing to find the white roofs sagging quaintly between gables. Snow-laden trees arched on one side; outbuildings gaped derelict on the other. It was a winter scene by Bruegel or Van der Neer, authentically rustic. Chickens ought to have scattered as he approached, geese hissed. Freezing dogs should have barked, dragging their chains.

Instead, from every pore of the brickwork leaked the alternating bass of 'Under the Moon of Love'. Geoffrey knocked and pushed open the kitchen door. A deafening sax riff snorted at him from the sudden warmth. Astraea Hawke stood between her long pine table and her blacked range, irôning – *à la* Shrimpton – her long blonde hair.

Another figure was disclosed as the door swung wider. Louisa, seated at the far side of the table, was reading a magazine.

'Louie!'

Astraea lifted her head a fraction. 'Hullo, Geoff! Ah, you've brought it. Come in, why don't you.'

Louisa looked up and got to her feet. 'Oh,' she said. She lifted her magazine and put it down again. The air boomed and thumped.

'Hello, Astraea.' Geoffrey stepped on to the kitchen flagstones and swung the instrument off his shoulder. He looked around guiltily for a place to stand it and found the corner of a dresser. 'I got your letters, Louie,' he said, eventually getting his wife to meet his eye.

Louisa came towards him. But she didn't greet or kiss him. She swerved pointedly aside and picked up the strap of the carrying case. 'Thank you,' she said. Turning her back, she walked, and then almost ran with her cello out of the room. Geoffrey stared after her. Then he regarded her friend, still bent over, her ear pressed once more to the ironing board.

Astraea was much of his own age, already a housewife. Willowy, debby in any contortion, she'd once given concerts. Ben, her older husband, worked for the Foreign

Office, and was frequently abroad. Today, Astraea wore jodhpurs for effect, teamed with a vile Swiss jumper of bright blue. Her insouciance dismayed him: 'I shouldn't bother going after her. Shut the back door and sit down.' She spoke from board level, steering the iron blindly towards her forehead. There was a smell of burning protein. 'Go on. She's a bit overwrought. Don't gawp! I'll be with you in a minute.'

Geoffrey did as he was bid. He rested his elbows on the table. The door his wife had vanished through remained open, and the sound that blared from it vibrated the heavy pine.

'Ben's home. But he's gone off to see if he can get supplies of anything. Milk, for example. No one has any, so don't expect tea, or coffee. We've resorted to booze. Why don't you help yourself?'

There were some used glasses beside an opened bottle of red wine. Geoffrey filled one, then stared at the old-fashioned range under the chimney. The record concluded its invitation to walk and talk, but the obviously new and very high-fidelity radiogram in the adjacent sitting room clunked, and the next disc from its stack pumped sound along the passage, as though directly into his eardrums.

'You musn't think I'm taking sides, Geoff.' Astraea stood up and ran the back of her hand under a fall of hair. 'Ben was here when Louisa arrived. Of course he tried to phone you straight away, but your line's down, isn't it. It was the least we could do to take her in – for a few days.' She studied the flat strands for a moment longer, caught his eye, then unplugged the iron and dismantled the ironing board.

'Yes, of course. Thanks,' he said, raising his voice.

The wine was sour. He knocked it back and poured himself another, looking over the dirty dishes in the sink and out through the sash window. A few crows hung on the wind above gaunt trees, black shapes crinkled by faults in the old glass. 'I'd hoped we might be able to talk,' he said.

'She might need a little longer. She's been hurt, hasn't she.'

'Has she?'

'It's none of my business, Geoff, but . . .'

'What's she been telling you?'

'Well, it wouldn't do for me to get involved. As I say, it's none of my business. But if you went home and had maybe a shave and some humble pie . . .' She seemed to fix him with an accusing eye. 'You see, I think Louie's going to need a good deal of winning round.' In mawkish falsetto, 'Oh Carol!' echoed the point.

'I haven't done anything.' Geoffrey held his drink to his lips, and the anger rose up in him again. He almost didn't know why he was bothering.

'You know best, Geoff. Look, I'd better go and see to her. Maybe wait till Benjamin gets back and you can have a talk with him, man to man. Have you been listening to the news? How people can dream of going on strike just now! The dustmen haven't been for three weeks. No one can get coal into the power stations, or, so it seems, vegetables out of the ground. Without a pneumatic drill!' She looked at herself in a mirror, then flickered briefly at the door in the full turbulence of the music. 'Help yourself, won't you?' she said, as she disappeared.

Geoffrey preserved Astraea's figure in his head and, just for that moment, stopped hating her, because he'd had the ghost of an impression she was trying to keep a straight face. Just for that moment, he let himself imagine how instead of Louie he might have married someone capable of humour. The thought passed. Far more likely some new and complicated female accusation was being hatched around him by the two girls. He looked out again at the white, distorted landscape and wanted to throw his red drink at it.

His people, landless agricultural poor, weren't given to rumination. His whole modus vivendi, he told himself, was just an extension of rural practicality – natural science. As for knowledge of the arts, he was self-taught. To folk who'd followed the horse plough or finished rabbits, there seemed something effeminate about the table talk the Hawkes took for granted. He'd attempted for Louie's sake to trust and get to like Astraea and the smooth-faced Ben. It hadn't been easy. They had the knack, probably without meaning to, of making him the peasant. So he felt.

But he wasn't so green as he seemed, nor so unsophisticated as to let himself be taken advantage of. A new record began, full of 'lips', 'heart', and 'close to you'. Cliché and innuendo – and how cluttered was the rest of the arrangement with fiddly orchestral licks, session violins to hide the offence. He wished it would stop: such a mockery, so commercial, like dud American space rockets

and hula hoops. These boys with rubber hips, some virtually castrati, whining about love. Sex was everywhere these
days; the people were claiming it. Sex had somehow so
offended his wife that she'd left him. Another spasm of
emotional pain went through him like a shrapnel wound
– like his father's, for that matter. He cast an eye again
over the domestic muddle by which the Hawkes asserted
their class. He could make no sense of ironed hair and a
stomping full-volume set alongside the Brahms or Debussy
that Astraea and Louie played together.

And now everything that had offered his wife refuge
began to disapprove of him: the saddle in the corner, the
basket of logs, the pile of *Tatler*s on the shelf of the dresser.
Louisa hadn't run just to her friend, but to her own. She
was 'well brought up'. Her flight, and perhaps his febrile
candour about a girl at work, showed him once again as
something unfinished, in clay.

He wasn't used to alcohol. He'd bought a bottle of
Scotch after he'd received Louisa's telegram, back on New
Year's Eve. To the endless highland dancing on the television he'd forced the anaesthetic down, and gone to bed
and dreamed Lionel Rae came knocking at his door, calling
out. When he'd got up to be sick, the dream was still going
on, with bells pealing, and showers of pebbles, or was it
flurries of hail, hurled at his window, a car slip-sliding on
the slope outside, revving, Lionel calling his name.

He helped himself. And another. He could hear an
engine noise now, under the infernal music. Maybe it was
Ben coming back. Maybe it was just the growling wind
stirring the tops of the trees outside, knocking snow off.

He wished Lionel hadn't been 'called away' from Kent. Lionel and he, they understood each other. There was even something oddly familiar about the world on its four-minute warning, his marriage, his all-absorbing work, his mind seemingly about to collapse. He drank again. The radiogram clicked. It was the record Cynthia had mentioned – 'Love Me Do'. Witty torture. Actually, he really quite fancied Astraea. He poured the last dribs. Astray. Astray-*er*. He was losing it.

IT WAS GLOAMING, but the deep snowfall brightened his way. Geoffrey almost threw himself along, shrugging his arms without feeling the cold. Trees loomed and avoided him at the last moment. Once, a fox turned and stared. They linked eyes and the animal stayed stock-still, it seemed for minutes, with one paw raised above the snow, before it sloped off.

Ben Hawke had indeed come back and genially opened another bottle. His wife had appeared and confronted him – Geoffrey hadn't caught about what. Seemingly out of nowhere, a domestic scene had erupted, and Ben had driven off again. The black Rover's emphatic rear still sped across a window frame in Geoffrey's mind's eye – just the corner of his eye, because he'd been left to comfort Astraea in her own kitchen, stunned at the curious role reversal. Private lives were so often a closed book. Divorce was an upper-class matter, separation a rarity. He didn't actually know anyone who'd left his wife, nor any woman who'd left her husband – other than Louisa, of course.

If it hadn't been for the wine, he'd never have embraced Astraea at all. His comfort had been scrupulous; at least, he was pretty sure it had. But she'd responded as though it hadn't; at least, he was almost certain she had. It left an intriguing thought with him, along with the imprint of her breasts, but he brushed it away. Still, with something of an erection, he had 'Love Me Do' playing over and over in his head. A pigeon clattered from a bare branch.

He fell in with some footprints, panting up the steep, and stooped to peer at them, as he wouldn't have done sober. The prints were of a man, wearing shoes, not boots. The tracks stretched ahead, unequivocal signs that someone had turned abruptly out of the undergrowth to share the route. At once, the absurd feeling crept over Geoffrey that just as he stood to examine the spoor, so the other fellow was watching him. It was amusing; he even half-wanted to meet the chap. The wind soughed in the treetops. Snow fell from a branch. He tried to think about Louisa but found her replaced – by Cynthia, by Merriam, by generalised womanhood, by a tart in a doorway in London. Principally by Astraea. It might have been wiser to find a path no one had trodden first.

Nevertheless, he was soon striding up under the canopied twilight, and most likely the man had passed hours before. Yet the prints remained clear, and his own rhythm worked against the fellow traveller's, the sputnik's. He laughed out loud. There was no way he could avoid stepping in and out of the neat, crisp shapes.

He came to the road. A car passed, slithering in the heaps at the corner. Opposite were the playing fields that belonged to the Tudor boys' school, with their rugby posts, and quaint, snow-capped pavilion. Half-cut, he'd missed his route and come out too far to the east. He could see the state school – Alan's, he presumed – in a flat expanse beyond the trees in the distance. Without knowing quite why, he turned right towards it instead of taking the direct way home.

The vast building was an architectural prodigy not quite included in the town's wizened, olde-worlde view of itself. More stately than state, rather a chateau than a council school, it was set on the ridge in its own far vaster park. No, he thought, its style was English, of Wren and the Enlightenment, and so unexpectedly provident. The scale *was* extraordinary: harmonies, proportions from another age had been landed here on a hilltop, and the magnificence grew as he approached the lodge gates, a grandeur from which endless white lawns seemed to fluoresce off towards the valley slopes. At the end of a long straight drive, a Romanesque temple spread colonnades and classical wings. Geoffrey could see capitals and pediments and the shapes of great ice-clad cedar trees in a quadrangle beyond. Smoke from the high chimneys drifted dark on dark.

A car came along the drive towards him, its headlamps blazing. Shadowy boys in football kit were leaving the scuffed pitches to his right. There'd been some tournament. A light snapped on in the block, and the place flickered, semi-dormant. He let himself approach, drink-emboldened. With slightly self-correcting feet, he passed the chapel and entered the quadrangle. He came right up to the pillared main entrance. The doors were unlocked. He was standing in a high, oak-panelled vestibule. He could just see an indeterminate male, ghostlike, himself, in the ball of a polished brass chandelier. A carved staircase rose up behind an arch, two portals led off to high-ceilinged corridors, but directly in front of him a pair of doors, glazed and half-curtained, stood inviting. No one was about. Pushing gently at one of them, he slipped in. His boots thumped softly on the parquet.

IT WAS A LARGE salon, almost a ballroom, oak-panelled to well over shoulder height. The plasterwork above was pure Wedgwood, the ceiling an elegant, coffered vault. The semi-darkness left him feeling he'd stumbled into a less war-weary century, and he was jealous, a little bemused. A velvet-curtained stage was topped with an art-deco clock face, perhaps the one incongruous touch. But the grand piano beneath it made him think once more of Astraea.

He opened the polished lid and touched a key, as lightly as he could. The sound was clear and sweet. He played a triad, as he'd seen Louisa do often enough when passing a keyboard at the Royal College – E major. Then, unbuttoning his overcoat, he attempted several huge two-handed chords. The empty space applauded. He stepped back, bowed and turned around, smiling to himself. Over the entrance ran a pretty, railed musician's gallery, to be reached, he guessed, by the fine staircase he'd passed. The dying day still cast a hint of grey light from the high windows to his left. He smoothed his lapel – where Astraea had pressed herself.

Then he heard the draped doors creak. He kept quite still, but he was conspicuous even in the gloom, standing there in his overcoat and gloves. A face was peering in at him. A woman was coming towards him, her movement staid, her heeled court shoes clicking.

'I probably shouldn't be here,' he announced. 'Couldn't resist looking.'

The woman stopped. She wore a tweed skirt suit, over which her large, faded face floated like a moon. The string of beads on the full bosom of her twin set held his eye a touch too long. 'It's all so . . . big,' he forced a laugh. 'So unusual. I was just passing.' His voice echoed.

The woman was looking at him. 'We're an unusual school. Experimental, even, Mr . . . ? Any child is welcome. Term starts on Monday, of course, and there are things to see to. You must tell me your name. I want to know your name, please.'

'Fairhurst. Geoff. Fairhurst. I live in the town. Cowper Road, actually. But I've never . . .' He put his hand inadvertently into his jacket pocket and fumbled with the edges of some paper there.

'I'm sorry, Mr Fairhurst, but you've no business to be here. I'm afraid I must ask you to leave immediately.'

'Course. Was just going, anyway.' The words came out slurred.

'One can't be too careful,' she said, keeping her distance. 'I'm sure you understand. Especially in view of the . . . You say you're local. You'll have read the *Gazette*, then?'

'No.'

'I shall be telling our girls on Monday, as soon as they arrive. Straight after assembly, in fact.'

'Telling them . . . ?'

'Warning them.' Her voice rose slightly in pitch.

'What of?'

'Of the man. You didn't know?' The woman touched her beads.

'A man, eh? Where?'

'In the woods, of course.' She gestured beyond the walls and grounds. 'To the left as you go out. Two attacks have so far been reported.' She sounded strained.

'But I was walking there just now.'

'I really would prefer it if you left, Mr . . . Fairhurst.' She said his name very clearly. 'Straight away.'

'Yes, of course. Sorry.'

The woman stood her ground as he passed. Her tongue licked the top lip, her breath just caught in her throat. She followed him out to the front doors. Four bolts slid home firmly behind him.

From the gates, the long midwinter twilight left the school barely visible. It was reduced to a statement, almost a symbol between the symmetrical lodge cottages. He filled it full of all the children of the town, and of the neighbouring hills. He thought of Alan. He saw a cradle for the mind and the bright souls awaiting birth in it, at risk from all manner of evils and dangers. He turned to the last red stroke of sunset and imagined it swelling with fire.

The narrow lane plunged down to the town, overclad with branches. Geoffrey looked behind him slightly too often. An occasional gaslight glimmered, still warming up. Snow lay treacherous on the steep banks, but eventually, the road came out beside the boys' school houses and the fourteenth-century coffee-rooms. He hadn't gone far along the High Street when six bike riders in a pack streaked by in the direction of Watford, their headlights flaring on the partially cleared tarmac. The roar rattled the windows of the coaching inn beside him.

He stared while the lads disappeared beyond the church. Then a sidecar combination came the other way out of the dark, the driver wearing goggles. In the street light Geoffrey couldn't help thinking of Alan Rae. And, huddled against the boy's back, was Cynthia, her face turned towards him. He was sure of it. His kid brother was stealing his girl. He was imagining things. He had no brother.

Late in the night he awoke. He felt sick, but his body was sexually charged. A double heat swaddled Louisa and himself in the ice-cold bedroom – until he put out a hand into the emptiness beside him. His head was filled with confused and tumbling images: of a pure, white, tented landscape that roared and vibrated to the spectral hunt of folklore, of a Minuteman about to burst from its under-ground silo, of the controversial double-slit experiment somehow interfused with all these fragments. A young man's face lingered, Alan's, but nothing like him. Unanswered questions from his visit to Astraea circled him, like crows around a farmhouse.

His head hurt. He realised how his marriage had begun to go wrong with little signs, and didn't know which had come first, his feelings for Cynthia or the growing distance between himself and Louisa. He switched on the bedside light. In Louisa's cabinet drawer, the Dutch cap lay next to the tube of spermicidal jelly, half-clamped by its own white plastic box. He pictured her squatting beside the bed, shunting the indignity in. Hard, ice-cold tears were behind his eyes as he stumbled out of bed, grabbing his jacket from where he'd thrown it on the chair, thrusting his arms into the sleeves and hugging it round him.

Bare-legged, he returned from the toilet. Reaching automatically into the jacket pocket, his hand touched paper edges again, and he pulled the fold out. He held it under the glow from the lamp: the sheaf of diagrams he'd taken from Rae's desk to go looking for Cynthia, the characters and voltages scattered across them.

With a mental note to return them, he was about to thrust the pages back in his pocket when he noticed a name pencilled at the margin. He held it higher under the light, mildly intrigued. The name was Planck, with a telephone exchange and number beneath it. Another sheet showed up Bohr, Einstein, and one more he didn't recognise, Turing. Each had a Greater London code and number. He blinked and tried to make sense of it. There were other terms as well: 'M switching.' 'C.S.' His throat constricted. Lionel had written the same initials as he, and in the same crowded lab. Close under the letters was the phrase 'amenable to voltage'. He put the papers down and found himself shivering.

The woman in the school hall had been afraid, too. She'd thought he was the bogeyman, the wicked Russian spy, the fairy-tale fiend in the woods ... He got back into bed. Then he remembered she'd asked his name. Perhaps she'd informed the police. He saw himself taken and interrogated for a series of attacks he hadn't committed, the questions turning rougher, his innocence crumbling as the fists went in. He looked again at the diagrams: surely Rae's perfectly innocent working notes. Panic drew a tight band across his chest, as though his heart were about to stop.

III

HONOUR

ALAN WOKE TOO. There might have been a thud at the window, like a snowball hitting the pane. Gusts outside made a vibration in the darkness as he lifted his head and pressed back the covers. He went to the window mindful of childhood stories, parting the curtains, half-expecting to find some vampire face at the glass. He saw only the white slope of the back garden and the glaring hillside above. Racks of scudding, moonlit cloud grazed the tall trees on the crest.

The wind dropped. The heating fan clicked in, a motorised hum coming up in the dark behind his chair from the duct Lionel had installed. Chilled in his thin pyjamas, he edged his way to the door and tiptoed as stealthily as he could across the brief landing to his parents' bedroom.

He could just hear Cynth beyond the door panel, her breathing a soft note at last, peaceful at the back of her throat. He was glad. She'd spent much of the week muffled in his parents' bed, shivering and sweating with fever, at times a little delirious. He'd nursed her. He'd wanted to call the doctor, but she'd said no, and laughed. All she needed was him. It was just a bit of flu, she'd said. So it had turned out.

He'd suggested a letter to her parents, though: how she

and Alan had seen the bike gang's antics and made their escape. It said she'd had no means of getting in touch, just wanted them to know she was safe at Alan's house – till she was well enough to come back. How complicated the persistent snow and the freezing temperatures made everything! She gave them the number to ring. All her mum and dad needed to do was go down to the phone box in the new town.

Alan had called his own mother. Judith Rae had no news of Lionel, but repeated frost had cracked the car's cylinder head, and now she was having to wait for someone to come out, remove the block and fit a new one – it would all be hugely expensive. In fact, his mother was at her wits' end. And the garages were fully stretched, of course. His uncle was going to help if he could, but Len was tied up with his other work. Alan had assured her he'd been managing perfectly well, and she'd sounded both cross and apologetic at that. She'd even threatened to come straight home by train, because Christmas wasn't supposed to have been like this. But, well, Alan *was* old enough to get himself to school. He'd need extra money, of course. She supposed she'd just have to arrange something with Vera next door.

It had left him the whole week with Cynth. He might almost have watered the car's anti-freeze himself, for now he was man of the house, ordering matters, ranging out for food and medications, keeping the fires in and the cold rooms as warm as he could. Cynth had curled in his arm and they'd sung songs together, 'Love Me Do', 'Can't Help Falling in Love'. At the piano, they'd picked out 'The Three Ravens' and 'The Trees They Do Grow High'.

But from *her* parents nothing had been heard. The phone hadn't rung, nor any reply come in the post. All one afternoon Cynth tried to remember the surname of the new neighbours a few doors down who did have a phone. She'd tried calling relatives in London to no avail. For three hectic days she'd urged Alan to take her back, there and then. But, frankly, she'd been too ill to go, and she'd admitted as much.

Only on the Saturday had she seemed well enough. He'd made her wait most of the day and wrapped her in some of his own clothes. Then he'd driven over with her. But her parents had been out, and hadn't returned, though Alan and Cynth had waited around until it grew dusk. The risky exposure had all been for nothing, and their return through the dark so dispiriting.

He stood a moment longer at her bedroom door and heard her turn over. The night gusts still prowled; the chill still threatened her. In the morning, they might try her parents again. He crept downstairs in his pyjamas, just to make sure all was secure.

It was as well he did. Another gibbous and westering moon stabbed through the undrawn drapes of the room housing the boiler, but, when he brushed the enamel, the grey cast iron was nearly as cool. He peered inside. Lionel's fire was mere embers, and the tall plastic scuttle stood empty. Outside, the wind thrummed. Alan looked about him. Nothing was clear yet, nothing settled. In a world that was not as he'd thought, she made everything magical, sentient, and the cold that had brought her set him a challenge. It asked a price. He wanted so much to pay it, but couldn't see how. On an impulse, he stripped naked and moved through the house.

The kitchen, never curtained, was lit by the sheen from outside. He skirted the table with the scuttle in his hand, took down the back-door key from its hook and twisted it in the lock. As softly as he could, he yanked the door loose from its frame and stepped out. The cold snatched his breath. The air struck at his ribs, his joints; the ice on the concrete was like knives under his feet.

A cinder path led up the slope between banks, with a spoil of white and earth under the snow – where Lionel and he had terraced an ugly lawn out of the chalk, and the land held flint like silica hunches. Biting his lips and cheeks, he raised his fists, unclasped his fingers, stretched out his shaking hands. The trees on the ridge bent in the hilltop gale. He waited as long as he could bear, hardly knowing why, praying almost. The pain intensified, for her sake. He was trying to soak it up, for her sake.

At last he turned away, foolish and uncertain. The bunker's hatch grated as he lifted it. Now against the back wall of the house the wind attacked in earnest, and gusts swept over his bare back as he crouched with the shovel, jabbing at invisible coke in the thwarted hole, shifting his feet back and forth. When the wind fell, the dinging, scraping metal threatened to wake the neighbourhood, and the coals came in miserly morsels, thumping and clattering into the scuttle. It sounded mocking, like laughter. He gave an involuntary cry, turned around. But there was no one else. He made sure of it, standing up, peering again across the terraced white lawn to the snow-bonneted brassicas in the vegetable patch.

The back door rattled as he shoved it shut. He set the scuttle down and huddled himself in a ball on the floor, shuddering violently, his knees against his chest. Then he forced himself to go and feed the frozen pieces one by one into the boiler, watching them warm and catch. Only after the lid's clang and the door's soft clicket behind him did he let himself think of his bed. One tingling foot set on the first step of the stairs made the landing light suddenly blaze on. A pent scream launched from his mouth. Both knees buckled under him.

BLINDED, HE THOUGHT it was his mother. The figure shook fire from its hair. His eyes adjusted and it was Cynth coming down laughing towards him, her hair exalted by the light, her body silhouetted in his mother's filmy slip. Then she had her arms about him. 'Silly, sweet boy. What are you doing down here?'

'I had to get the coke in.'

'You're joking. Come here.' She crouched down on the stair next to him and pulled him shivering against her.

'I heard a noise. The boiler was going out.'

Now she held his shoulders to look at him. 'Didn't you even put a coat on?'

His teeth were chattering. 'Didn't want to wake you.'

'Honestly. Come along,' she said.

In his parents' bed he lay curled up with his head on her breast. She stroked his hair, chuckling and whispering in his ear: he deserved to have turned into an icicle out

123

there in the garden, he ought to have been eaten by foxes. 'Alan. Alan. What am I?' she said.

'You're like one of those old tunes,' he said, 'like the folk songs we were singing. Do you remember? Or were you feverish?'

'I remember. Of course I do.'

'Some tunes are so beautiful you think you've always heard them. Do you know?'

'I know,' she said, softly.

'You're the tune, then.'

'You're the words.'

He could see her eyes in the moonlight. 'I think the Stanmore lads . . .'

She put her fingers against his lips.

Then he was kissing her and her warmth was seeping into him. He stretched out, luxuriating, and put his arms round her, feeling her breasts against his chest through the fabric, her thighs pressed to his. He'd never kissed her like this. At once, he was licking the inside of her mouth; her tongue wrote characters on his. The lace at her nipple was against the palm of his hand and there were noises in her throat. The strap slipped from her shoulder. She broke the kiss to help her arm out of it, and he thrust back the covers to see her. Then he was suckling her, grazing her neck.

He stopped to look into her eyes. She was smiling. 'When it's someone you care about.'

'And you care about me?'

'Alan! Can't you tell?'

'All week, I . . .'

'Yes?'

'Before . . . I've been so bloody turned inwards. On myself, I guess.'

'How so?'

'It doesn't matter,' he said. His doubts were swept away. She was sweetly erotic, deliciously close. 'I knew it had to happen,' he whispered. 'I just couldn't think how.'

'Oh, you did, did you.' She scolded him with kisses. 'Knew it had to happen, did you.'

The silky hem of the garment crept above her hips. Her spine, her belly, the taper of her waist made him gasp. She sat up and lifted her arms and threw the slip away. Now, her thighs lay parted, his hand between them. But she caught his arm, checking him, and he was relieved that she was like him, his own tremulous age, shy in her own way. It made sense that she was real, that neither knew how far to go, nor what was being asked of them. They lay unsatisfied, stroking and embracing, until the sexual passion ebbed and both were drowsy.

In the morning, the room was pale, and he was scared of Lionel. The wind had died. There was no sound but her breathing beside him, and the faint hum of the heating fan. The moisture at the corner of the window made frozen stars and glinting streaks, but his father's wardrobe stood a sinister presence against the far wall, and his mother's triple mirror gave weird angles to the edge of her bed, the window, part of the ceiling. He turned to Cynth just as she opened her eyes.

She was instantly smiling and pulling him towards her. He was happy beyond belief. It wasn't even her blissful looks but her continuing warmth that surprised him the most. Overwhelmed, he shifted away and swung his feet out of the bed on to the flecked bedroom carpet.

'Don't be silly,' she said. She scrambled across the bed and twined herself around him, and he saw how they looked, the two of them, tangled together in the mirror. 'I'll get you some tea,' he said. He was stroking her hair. In the corner of his eye, he caught the gesture reflected.

'Like we're married,' she laughed. 'And you're trying to be in my good books. I did want to.' She looked up at him. 'Last night. I didn't stop you because I didn't like it. You do know that, don't you? I wanted to as much as you did.'

'I never expected,' he said. 'Not really. Wait.' He was darting to the upstairs closet, grabbing his jeans and suede jacket from his own room and running down to the kitchen. Thrilled and terrified, he put the kettle on. He attended to matters. The boiler was still in. Kneeling in the sitting room, he gave the Rayburn fire its rake and opened the curtains. In the kitchen, he measured tea into the china pot and took the last inch of milk from the fridge. The kettle clicked off in a gargle of steam. He was supplanting his father, sleeping in his bed. Cynth was upstairs, queen of the bypass, probably just clambering back into his mother's slip. Outside, the snow had lain for two weeks.

A photograph stood on the fridge top: Lionel in a frame in his ill-fitting suit beside a Boeing Stratocruiser. Deliberately, Alan had kept quiet about his surname. That was a hunch, as though sharing Lionel and Lidlock would be sure to break the spell. But this one picture he'd overlooked, and hiding it face down brought up Lionel's secret kingdom – those circuits he'd sketch, calculating the semi-conductor current here, the oscillation there, dropping voltage across resistance, that paternal private cipher. But the answer to his father was out of reach, however much he tried to make sense of him.

They sat up in bed drinking their tea. In the window there was a brush of pink and a strip of blue sky.

'You outside, naked,' she said. 'How mad is that?'

'My dad's been called away,' he said. 'I told you. My mum stranded. Then the Stanmore boys at your house.'

'Sure, sure. Complaining again, then, are you? Complaining you're my sweetheart?'

'No!' He leaned over to kiss her, and his fear melted.

'You'll spill my tea! Wait till I put it down.'

Now he was kneeling by the beside table, his father's side, rifling through the one drawer he'd never really bothered looking in. That was another hunch. There was a packet of them. He was surprised.

Later, they listened to the church bells. And there were winter birds flying past the eaves.

A BRIGHT CROSSFIRE of guns seemed to echo off the closed shopfronts. Then the tyre gripped, and the bike sprang forward into the neck of the High Street. Alan glanced past Cynth over his shoulder. Two cars left at the lights were still hardly moving. Head down over the instruments, he accelerated between St Peter's and the dignified properties on the other side, toeing through the gears, hearing the thudding note rise and abruptly fall to each twist of the grip.

They loved each other. Cynthia's arms were around his waist, and he was a man. They'd be married. He had prospects. Her mother he'd already met; he'd speak to her father. He imagined their family Sunday beside the still water of the cut, her little brother playing his records, making his plastic models, her parents with their coffee and rolls just as she'd described them. Her mother Austrian – it explained the accent – her father a British Tommy, she said. They'd met after the war, she told him. At this hour, they might all still be lying cosily in bed.

The road was clear each side of a central iced brown ridge. Residue was heaped over gutters and kerbs, and pedestrians flashed by, walled off to right and left, their muffled faces lifted at the noise. He braked behind a Green Line bus, then in a racing growl overtook it by the Eagle and Child. An oncoming car hooted, scour and scurf spewed up from his front wheel and Cynth's voice laughed encouragement.

Then the tarmac was a black channel in a white world, and his girl was tucked invisibly behind him just as she'd been that first night. Alan put aside Lidlock and Lionel and any lingering thoughts of Geoffrey Fairhurst. He forgot the incident with the bikes in the dark. He *dared* the police to find him taking a passenger. But his breath was tight. He brought his left hand off the handlebar to feel hers tucked into the pocket of his jacket. She squeezed back and hugged his waist. He was steering the bends through Bourne End, the sun glaring off the road, the morning ice-blue. He marvelled how his long trek along the drifted canal by moonlight could fold almost into the blinking of an eye. Now he overtook a Ford Zephyr beside the bike garage at Moor End. Virtually before he knew it, he'd found the turn and tucked the Triumph up the narrow back lane that gave access to the Fishery.

The pub was only half-visible, shrouded in a bright mist off the canal. They hit freezing fog without warning, and the air was clammy. The rear wheel slid on the hump bridge over the cut, snow crunched, and there were cold drops of sweat inside Alan's shirt. Between the wall and the watercress beds he had to let a van pass; a man's face appeared at a window; an old woman stared from a kerb. A parked car loomed through the murk at the first corner, significantly black, its engine still running. It was the cops: he saw the silver bell and dark label. Cynth huddled against him, and he tried to look casual while the bike nudged on through the fog, through more turns and down to her house.

There, it was clear again, and sheer winter sun glinted on the ridges in the packed snow. The sky was the exact blue of the coat he'd first seen her in. But there was still no reply at her door, and the house was as cold and unoccupied as the previous evening, though Cynth rapped again and again at the knocker. She tapped on the front windows and called out. She led him to the end of the houses and through the alley to the tow-path, but the little white garden showed no footprints, and the back rooms looked dark and empty through the net curtains. Halfway up the outside wall, there was a twisted growth of ice. 'Burst pipes,' he said. She nodded, biting her lip.

They returned to the front. Cynth stood back in the snowy street and stared up at the windows. She seemed ready to cry with frustration.

'We should try the neighbours,' he suggested.

'Yes,' she sighed. 'Of course.'

'Maybe if they had no water, they . . .'

'Maybe.'

He indicated the house to the left.

'No, this side,' she said. 'They've got a key.'

He brightened. 'Well, then!'

'Yes, but . . .' She looked preoccupied. 'It's not that, is it? Mum and Dad, if they had to leave, why didn't they ring?'

They roused the old couple next door. No, they'd seen nothing, heard nothing since that dreadful rumpus outside. But they didn't hear so well at all these days, Cynthia, dear, neither of them. Oh, yes, they had the spare key, somewhere. It might be in the kitchen drawer, they thought.

She found her letter unopened on the mat. She let it lie and went on into every room. Nothing had been disturbed, but the house was quite empty. She sat down on the stair, then stood up and crossed in front of Alan to where a white fragment some distance from the untouched envelope had caught her eye. Kneeling by the hall-stand, she held up a torn scrap of paper.

In the space next to the words ' . . . of abode', her full name was typed. On the back was official-looking small print. She stood up by the pebbled door glass to scrutinise the lines. Then, as though galvanised by a thought, she pulled the door open and peered outside.

'Cynth?' he said.

'Stupid! I've been stupid! Just hold the latch and keep a lookout.' She brushed past him and ran straight up the stairs. 'Wait! I'll be down in a minute,' she shouted. 'Less than.'

'Look out for what?'

'Anything! Just do it, Alan.'

He called up lamely after her. 'But what about the other neighbours? Shouldn't we ask them if they know what happened?'

'There isn't time!'

'Why not?'

Her voice came from one of the bedrooms. 'Alan!'

His heart was pounding. He'd no idea for what.

HIGH UP ON the Common he was guessing his way. There were glaring white tyre tracks through a criss-cross of routes. The lanes were unhedged. Candescent slopes dropped away to right and left; bare branches arched a silver net high over the bike's roar. The front wheel steered a thin rut of snow through Frithsden Copse, and the sidecar jagged over bumps. Something was dampening the scarf at the back of his neck. He knew it was her tears.

Tumbled together in the sidecar seat were her clothes and her money. One of her skirts was a deep, almost painful red, its pleats flickering constantly at the corner of his eye. A single black leather boot shook and bounced on top of it. He thought of newsreel scenes he'd seen from the war, of refugees carting their possessions away. But this was England, and she was English – half English – and he couldn't see for the life of him why she'd taken the clothes and things from her bedroom, telling him just to get the bike going. She'd slammed the front door behind her, then run back and scrabbled with the key again in order to retrieve her letter from the mat.

A police car, the same one they'd seen before, perhaps, had edged into the lane just as they were leaving. Through those same backstreets they'd used to escape the bike gang he'd dodged again and weaved his way. He couldn't quite believe it. For all the cops knew, he and Cynth could be any young working-class couple, muffled up on their cycle combination, a boy in his goggles, a girl in her scarf. They'd climbed fast up that same long road through the council estate. And the Common was shining with incredible white beauty. But there might, there still might, have been the nose of a black vehicle in the glimpse he'd just snatched behind him, maybe the glint of its radiator chrome at the last bend by the trees.

He hammered along the narrow road under brittle boughs, his stomach awash with fear and excitement, the packed snow too brilliant in the slant, flickering sun. When Ashridge monastery loomed out of a clearing, he gave one more glance back and cut sharply on to a narrow drive between glistening lawns. Packed gravel crunched under the wheel. The buildings raced towards him. Then he was screened from the road by towers and cloisters, hearing his exhaust note clatter back off the stone.

Prim posts stood in the white; chains marked a route. He forced the revs through the college park, slipping the clutch. He coaxed the bike across a treacherous flat, three hundred yards until it bounced and slid off into the woods again and down the track of a dell. He struggled back up and out, smashing through a drift, winding down a lane that ground finally into Gaddesden village.

No car could have followed them. He shared a glance with Cynth, touching his lips once to hers before heading off fast again along the straight clear tar of the village fold, up towards Deer Leap. Words he would say to comfort her queued up in his throat. He wanted to stop and stroke her tear-stained cheeks, smooth her windswept hair.

Once at Ringshall, he motored hard back under the beechwoods in the direction of his own town, until he came to the gap he was looking for. With one last glance behind him, he turned in up the long, tree-lined approach. Far out of sight of the road, he swung round in a circle and stopped the bike. They'd left tracks, but no one would guess they were his.

They were in a flawless white clearing, at its centre a single stone column. The Bridgewater Monument over-topped the tall trees. It finished in a majestic urn a hundred feet from the ground, the sheer fluted column sprouting from a concrete block like a gun emplacement. There was a small green door in it. In winter, Alan knew, it was kept locked. In summer, he'd often climbed the hundreds of stone steps which spiralled past fanciful arrow slots, winding ever higher for the view from the urn's lip. Westward, the Chiltern scarp dropped towards Aldbury and the Vale of Aylesbury; to every other horizon stretched the seemingly endless forest of beech. Now the column seemed to sparkle against the intense sky blue, and he stood next to Cynth looking up, holding her hand.

'They've been taken,' she said, simply.

'Taken?'

'It wasn't me they were after.'

He stared blankly at her.

'That car. The one that came in with the bikes and went out again. That must have been the one.'

'I don't understand.'

She was bleak, keeping her eyes from his.

'Tell me!' He gripped her shoulders. 'You said your mother was Austrian.'

'That's just where she met my dad. I was fibbing, Alan. I had to. They're Czech. Both of them. Yes, he was *with* the British Army, eventually. Not Somers but Simek – that's the truth. From Bratislava. Both DPs after the war – displaced persons – from a few miles over the border. I'm sorry. I didn't want to spoil things.'

'A few miles! Does that make such a difference?'

'Of course. It's behind the Iron Curtain, isn't it.'

'But she's here. There's loads of DPs, Czechs, Poles, and . . . everything. Come on, they're here, they're safe. It doesn't matter about the Iron Curtain. So tell me what's going on, Cynth!'

'My mum, she . . .' Her tears began again. 'You don't know what it's like. It's complicated. About having the right documents. There were question marks, all of a sudden. Irregularities, it seems. No date of naturalisation, no record of registration. Things like that. All these years it wouldn't have mattered, you're right. Except . . . They've been taken, Alan. And my little brother. *They*'ve got them.'

'Who've got them?' He was lost. 'The lads?'

'No.' She stared hard into his eyes. 'Not the lads. It was never the lads, Alan.' She gave a sort of laugh. 'You didn't get it, and I couldn't . . . I was desperate not to tell you. My poor love, it's nothing to do with boys or gangs. Things aren't always what they seem. I wish they were.' Her breath caught. 'The . . . authorities. Maybe ours, maybe theirs.'

He put his arms around her. Her words made no sense. 'Why? Why now?'

'I . . .' She broke away. 'I don't know!'

'I saw the aerial on your chimney.'

She looked up in surprise, almost amused. 'My dad . . . It's nothing. Just his hobby, Alan. Ham radio.' Then her face darkened again. 'But Mum . . . I thought it was only me they were after. How could I have been so . . .' She was silent for a moment. 'Yeah. An army sparks. He's a wizard at that sort of thing, my dad.'

'Mine too.'

'Yours?'

'He works at Lidlock. Like you.'

'He what!'

'I was going to tell you. But you were ill, and we were too wrapped up in each other. Cynth, I didn't want to spoil things, either. Well, then. Our name's Rae. Lionel used to be on Blue Streak. Circuit design . . .'

DEREK BEAVEN

She interrupted him. 'Lionel? Oh, God. Your dad's Lionel Rae. You're Rae's son.'

'You do know him, then?'

'Me!' She hesitated a moment. 'Yes.' Then she looked rapt and thoughtful. 'I'm a junior typist! I know *of* him,' she said, carefully. 'Everyone knows *of* him.' She stammered, 'Or . . . Or maybe after last Saturday they just got scared. Maybe they got scared and left. Just ran. Mum was used to that.' Her tone was bitter. She pulled out a handkerchief and dabbed her eyes.

He kept staring at her. Her voice kindled the night of the first blizzard and the fight at the Bee. It kindled the embrace that ended with his lips brushing hers. He'd thought she was just a girl, but her past twined and grew darker with his own. Something caught his attention as he tried to take her in his arms again. He glanced involuntarily up at the top of the monument. No one could be there. A shaft of sunlight had struck a weld of the rail. No one could be watching.

THE BIKE CLICKED as it cooled. 'We could walk a bit,' he said. 'Shall we?' He put a tentative arm around her waist.

'All right, then.' She was agitated.

They went to the edge of the clearing. The sun flicked through the branches. The snow, deep and untouched, cracked underfoot where its melt had refrozen.

'Why didn't you tell me you were Rae's kid?' Her voice was unsteady.

136

'I was going to. I . . . just didn't want you thinking about me and him at the same time. All the while there was a picture of him in full view – in a frame on top of the fridge. We don't much go in for family photos.'

She managed a smile. 'I suppose I was too busy coughing. It was all a whirl, wasn't it? When I stopped being ill, it was like I'd always known you. It was just us living, just us . . .' She took hold of his hand, then let it go.

'Does Dad make such a difference?'

She looked directly at him again, and then away. The sun caught her hair where the scarf had fallen back. 'I expect it was nothing, back at my house,' she said. 'Most likely just that burst pipe, eh? No water, no coal, so of course they had to decamp. There's some council scheme, I expect. Bound to be. Putting people up. No one thought it was going to carry on like this, did they? They said it was going to thaw. On the telly. That day you came.'

'They keep saying it.'

'It seems so long ago, Alan. All that shouting and commotion. It seems like something I . . . I made up when I was feverish.' She was gazing distractedly into the trees. 'I think maybe we should try going back down there. Give it another chance.' She turned to him. 'I think perhaps I tend to over-dramatise things. You know? Get carried away.' She looked at him, but her eyes seemed remote.

'OK,' he said. 'If that's what you want.'

'D'you mind? The cops will have gone, won't they. Nothing to worry about – driving me, I mean.' She laid a hand on his arm.

They walked back to the bike, and he had a sensation of falling, of everything leaking away from him. He stood for a moment beside her belongings tumbled into the sidecar. Then they both climbed on board and he kicked the machine into life, letting it creep slowly out of the wood down the track-marked avenue. Even the vibration coming up from the engine felt awkward, and her arms around his waist were a stranger's. A party of crows scattered cawing from the topmost branches, and flapped away down the long glade towards the monastery far in the distance.

Not a soul was about when he dropped her at her house. She fished in her pocket for the neighbours' key, then opened the door and came back to the sidecar for her things. Almost without looking at him, she took out some skirts and with them her boots, and he went to help her, picking up another armful of clothes and a carrier bag of knick-nacks, and trudging up the short path after her.

She simply thrust her things inside, then turned to take what he'd brought. 'Thanks, Alan.' Everything was dumped in the heap on the floor. Instead of inviting him in, she placed a hand on his chest. 'I think . . .' she said, hesitating. 'I think I need to be on my own for a while.' Now it was only reluctantly she met his eye. 'You don't mind, do you? Alan? I'm so grateful for you looking after me and everything. You've been fabulous. I really appreciate it. Honestly, I do.' She took his gloved hand and squeezed it. 'Only . . . Only it's all come as something as a shock. Us. You know? This morning. I just need time, eh? Time to digest things. Get myself together again.'

'But your family . . . ?' He was incredulous.

138

'I was jumping to conclusions, I expect. Don't you? Got a bit carried away, didn't we. In all kinds of ways, to tell the truth. I'll scout around. I'm used to fending for myself. I'll ask the neighbours.' She jerked her head to the side. 'Someone'll know something, don't you think? Nobody just disappears!' She laughed. 'There'll be a perfectly ordinary explanation, I'm sure of it.'

He stood dumbfounded on the step, unable to think, even. 'If that's what you want,' he muttered.

'I'm sure it would be best,' she said. 'You do understand, don't you? And I've got your number. I'll give you a call as soon as I find out anything, shall I?'

'Yeah. OK. If you . . .'

She kissed him lightly on the cheek. 'Thanks for everything. Bye, then, Alan.' It was so sudden, so final. 'I'll be in touch.' The door closed.

The mist had gone from the village street. The ice on the watercress beds glittered. He turned to look back from the canal bridge at the shining gold letters across the front of the pub. He felt nothing, a numbness that had little to do with cold. His body gave no other sign of anything amiss than his left wrist shaking uncontrollably on the handlebar. All the way back along the main road her words ran in his head, but they were somehow separate, like the speech of a passenger so evanescent the air stream had snatched her away. He saw only, and with careful attention, the tarmac wet in patches where the sun had warmed it, the stained scuff in the centre snaking ahead, and the dazzle, through the strakes in the hedges, of an unaccustomed light.

He went straight upstairs when he got home and began tidying his parents' bedroom, stretching the sheets and relaying the covers, seeking to hide or remove all trace of Cynth's and his occupation. Every now and then, he caught himself in the glass, a dark, stooping figure, still in his suede coat, clomping mechanically about his business. And he was done not a moment too soon: a car sounded on the steep concrete slope of the drive. He twitched aside the curtain to see his mother just arriving. He was even glad when she came in.

'Well, it's mended at last,' she said. 'It makes a funny noise but it goes. You've been all right, then, Alan, have you?'

'What about Dad?' he said.

'I expect we'll hear soon enough. Don't you?'

That night in his own bed, he thought of what Geoffrey Fairhurst's words had set in train – something whirling and spinning, as he'd conceived it, something of Lionel's design. That was all he could bear to grasp of his disillusion. A vast emptiness prevailed, and his thoughts were far out in space, America and Russia, as though he could see the orbital flight paths of the B52s, and the tips of strategic missiles primed and pointing up out of the earth. Yes, everywhere he looked some sharpened nose-cone prickled up from its underground silo. And each one was either theirs or ours, on a hair-trigger so perfectly engineered that no one could move, or breathe, or tell this from that.

In the morning he dressed automatically in his suit and tie for the new school term. He went down for the breakfast his mother had cooked as though nothing were different, nothing had intervened. And when Paul off the bus from the Cow Roast called for him as usual, he remained fixed in the same state of suspension.

THERE WAS EVEN time before school to open the garage and admire the bike. He pointed out the twin carbs with their flared intakes, the cables and the gauges, the action of the clutch, the movement of the telescopic forks. He showed Paul how the gears were selected and watched him sit astride the machine, exactly as he'd done himself. They were just kids, after all.

The town had quite adjusted to the snow. They could hear all the usual rush-hour traffic as they crossed the lock gates and climbed down. Charlie the barge horse, chewing in his nosebag, lifted his head to stare complacently across at them, and from the station came the thump and judder of a steam train slipping its wheels. But how thick the ice had grown on the cut. Paul put a foot down on a bay in the bank; it bore his weight easily. He even bounced a few times, handing Alan his duffel bag, and there was merely a faint creak from further out.

Thorn stems still hung over the tow-path, yet Alan could barely remember his night journey. Actually, he was amazed how little distress he felt. He was already back in the swing of things, out in the day's brittle air with Paul. And with no recent heavy snow, the trail he'd blazed by moonlight was well-trodden and packed hard from use. It was quite easy to get down under the Lower King's Road bridge and past the station; easy, too, the passage by Alsford's woodyard where he'd first run into drifts. In fact, in the occluded brightness of the morning and the peculiar blankness of his mood, it all felt like nothing very much.

Of course, they'd no need to go this way at all. But the previous summer, Alan and Paul had settled into a routine of walking as far along the canal as they could before turning up towards school. Maybe the chance to talk fishing, maybe the pleasure of watching the water; now it was just frozen brickwork and reed stalks sticking in clumps through the snow-crusted ice. Yes, the bike had acceleration but he hadn't been out much – what with the weather. Yes, pretty hairy on the roads over the Common. Alan bit hard down on his lip, and then on the inside of his cheek.

They left the waterway at Raven's Lane, by the pub called the Boat. They walked up past the aerosol factory and the Baptist church, crossed the High Street and climbed up the steep and slippery rise beside the cinema. There were posters for the new Cliff Richard film, *Summer Holiday*, which made them both laugh. Paul's Christmas had been OK. Alan's too. Clay would challenge Liston for the title. Yeah, but what was Henry Cooper up to? Soon, they got through a gap in the strake fence and fell in with the stream of other teenagers trudging the gravel path that ran from Chesham Road.

Ahead of them, the school rose under streaking clouds, its roofs and palace-like windows at first too large, then set to scale by the snowy lawns at the top of the hill. They passed the broken wicket gate, and Alan felt he might have got away unscathed – emotionally. Thanks to Lionel's wanderlust, he'd been to enough schools. This, with its unexpected magnificence, was unlike the others. Once an orphanage, it had retained its charity, he thought, with its cedars and colonnades, its generous proportions. He forced a smile at something Paul said.

They parted at the door by the changing rooms. Familiar male figures in their dark suits and green ties brushed past Alan in the corridors. He exchanged greetings. He bumped into Marcus Doyle and calmly asked about theatre trips. Marcus was genial. The new Anouilh was booked out, and ditto the Shakespeare at the Old Vic. But there was something coming on at the Mermaid. Sylvia and he were having some of the arts sixth to supper at the lodge, by the way. Would Alan come too?

Alan was flattered, and grateful. They walked together, master and pupil, talking casually of this and that. A bell rang. Fifth-formers were hurrying into classrooms further down the corridor; younger kids milled noisily until a teacher's voice quieted them. A group of girls stood chatting in a doorway, and two from his own year slipped by on flat, silent shoes, their heads held abstracted, their pleated skirts swinging slightly on slim, stockinged calves. He watched them go, as remote and lovely as the ringletted figures in those faded reproductions all along the walls. Up here on the hill, with the sheets of light from the endlessly repeating windows and glazed French doors giving on to the courtyard, everything was secure, and graceful. He registered in his classroom, observed the formalities. He took his place in the choir gallery above the hall, and, from under the white coffered ceiling, looked down at the seated upper school ready to sing hymns to the God Lionel didn't believe in. Mr Flower – Colly – struck chords at the concert grand. And when, after assembly, the girls were asked to stay behind, and some embarrassing sexual note seemed to linger in Mrs Mayhew's voice, he remained aloof.

All morning he worked exercises in maths; all afternoon he sat taking notes in the physics lab, while the headmaster spoke of standing waves in strings and pipes, the Fourier analysis of harmonics. Alan drew the diagrams and did the equations. He wondered briefly what function Lionel might some day have named after him. Then he lost himself in a dance of ideals and constants, because Cynth only existed in a curious separation. Of course she needed time to think things over. She'd ring, probably tonight, and he'd go down and fetch her. She'd meet his mother and they'd discuss their plans.

It was a chance encounter that threw him, just after the last bell of the day. Dubs Davies, the Oxford historian, was striding down the boys' side corridor with a batch of files under his arm. The teacher merely nodded to Alan and swept on at a pace so swift the vast sleeves of his black gown flew out behind him. But a long-forgotten history lesson, still clad in his peculiar dry wit, sneaked back across a year.

Dubs had explained how the cold pillar, under which Alan and Cynth had stood, marked the canal builder.

Francis Egerton, the third Duke of Bridgewater, had renounced womankind and turned his energies to working both the Lancashire coal he owned and the families who dug it up. The countrywide web of coal-carrying canals was the legacy of Brindley, his engineer. So Alan's journeys to school across the lock, and even the retirement pasture of Charlie the barge horse, bore – as Dubs had put it – continuing witness to a duke's dammed desire.

No sooner had he passed than Alan was back on the tow-path that night, caught between Cynth and Lionel. And then the whole week rushed in on him like shards through the dark: Cynth stretching her hand towards him to dab the blood of his scratches, Cynth's eyes pleading with him to let her dash into the milling bikes, Cynth shaking with fever and laughing at his concern, her kisses, her face turned up towards him while they'd made love. Under that wretched monument she'd changed, in a moment, and left him desolate.

HE LOOKED FOR Paul outside, but couldn't find him. He plunged down homeward alone, taking the steep, over-hung lane, feeling himself already sinking like a body in a lock, the surface closing over him, the beloved fingers of current plucking him away. Every turning in the town recalled some detail: the chemist's in the High Street, its flasks glowing red and blue in the window, where he'd come to buy her a bottle of aspirins; the new post office for her letter to her parents; across the road the almshouses, which had led up to Geoffrey and Louisa's, that day he'd gone to find her, the night they'd escaped from the gang. Cynth had walked out of his account, and it wasn't just losing a girlfriend: he *knew* her, she was everything. It was suddenly so tempting to flirt with the figure of death, to stroll beside him in his mind, courting that ultimate pain relief.

Twilight pooled on the plank bridge. He came on to the tow-path and began his detour over the gates. A trail of footsteps in the gathering dark caught his eye, seeming to take a short cut across the ice. Not far from where Paul had stepped out that morning, he stopped and climbed down the bank. Sure enough, a woman, or maybe a child, had made the crossing directly to the paddock and straight to the tunnel, walking over the surface of the canal.

He stepped further out and his shoe crunched the top crust. He listened intently for deeper sounds. The day had nudged above zero, but the temperature was falling fast and the ice surely still thickening. He took a step further. There was a creak. He thought of all the warnings – about the false sense of security, the sudden sickening give. The sunken dark gave back a glimmering emptiness. He took another step. Another. One further, until the ice cracked again. He stood stock-still and looked up. He was almost at the centre. A seagull, far inland, was the fading sky's only movement. The gated sluice fifty yards away to his left splashed noisily into the one patch of moving water.

Only then he remembered the barges. They'd broken this swathe right here under his feet and left just days for a layer to form thick enough to support him. He swung round, equidistant between hedge and paddock. The ice murmured ominously. He dared not move.

He had to. It was the choice again, going on or back. His blood thumping, he inched forward, holding his duffel bag out to the side as though to spread the weight. But each time his shoe even touched the crust it would shatter through, and each time he shifted balance the ice was beginning to groan. All at once it was fracturing, bending, giving way, and he ran ahead blindly, feeling the cold water at his ankles, as he slipped and tumbled on to the further shelf, struggling up when he heard that, too, start to give, scrabbling desperately forward until he fell at last on to the thickened safety of the shallows.

By the bare osiers, he crawled to the bank and hauled himself on to solid ground. It hurt to breathe. When he stood, his left knee was half-crippled, the shin scraped and bleeding under his sodden trousers. His right shoe was full of water. He found his bag among the sedges where he must have thrown it in his panic.

There was fresh snow in the air, tingling at his cheeks by the time he got to his front door, and when he stepped inside he found his soaked and cold-scuffed clothes glistening again with melting specks. He thought of her singing, and how foolish and naive he'd been to imagine her in some country he'd always known:

> *The trees they grow so high,*
> *and the leaves they do grow green.*

There were no messages, of course, no letters. He lay in bed that night, and Cynth was just a whore, a bloody bitch, leading him on like that, spinning him tales. She'd be back with the lads in no time, passed around, couldn't get enough of it – or with Geoffrey Fairhurst at work. Women were all the same, and it had begun with the snow. Now he hated the stuff, that wouldn't go away. Tears welled behind his eyes but he couldn't shed them, because only more shame awaited him, and he knew he'd fall back wilfully into it. The traitor was *him* – to himself, for if ever he reached for love, some wretched mockery pulled him down.

It was later in the week that someone had phoned. 'A girl, I think, Alan,' his mother said. She rummaged for her notepad.

He'd just got in from school. 'Yeah?' he said.

She read what she'd scribbled. 'Something about a burst pipe and her parents had only been a couple of doors away all the time. Apparently it was nothing after all, dear, she said. Nothing. They've moved back in, so there's no need for you to do anything. She was quite insistent. You needn't do anything at all. Does that make any sense? It doesn't much to me. Who was she? Come back here, Alan.' His mother called after him. 'Where do you think you're going?'

HANGING ON IN the dark while his limbs jolted, he snarled the newly naked Triumph through the one street of Potten End. The hated sidecar lay back where he'd left it, unbolted on the garage floor. His headlight stabbed between invisible fields along the edge of the Common, and when the road dropped into Warner's End, the freed beast strove and roared as though it would take off.

By the Top of the World, he slewed to a halt. His stomach heaved from the dizzying ride up past the castle, beside the steep pasture, through the icy hairpin on the crest. The inn's ugly windows were swaddled, the crossroads deserted. He flicked the bike's idle, getting his breath back, and his nerve, while the exhaust clattered off the brickwork. Down in the cleft below, the new town sprawled. But there was no moon now, and the distant lights held no romance.

He clicked up the gear lever, and the bike snatched at first gear, sweeping him off again, down towards the sodium street lamps of the council estate. Between front gardens and parked cars, forty felt like sixty. That was nothing – the hundred-and-twenty on the dial wasn't just for show. The engine thumped brutally as he levelled out behind Boxmoor.

He sat with the bike running on Blackbirds Moor. Something had made him slip his sheath knife on to his belt. He put his hand to the back of his jeans just to touch it and then swung the machine into her lane. But there were no lights in the terraced cottage, no inkling of anyone at home. The downstairs curtains were undrawn; the rooms behind the nets looked as empty as when he and Cynth had come to find her parents and younger brother.

He got off the Triumph. There was no answer to his knock. He tried again, waiting under the high eaves, stepping back to look up at the house she'd disappeared into – just as he had when she'd closed the door to get ready, just as she had that first night of all. He peered through the door's pebbled glass. There were no sounds from the hallway, no footsteps on the stairs. He left the bike and went round by the canal to the path at the rear. There was the same mass of ice springing from the burst pipe halfway up the back wall – like a malign star exploding in the darkness. Nothing had changed, no one was home. She'd been lying.

The bypass swerved to the left. Alan felt the sudden lift from the valley's foot as the road leapt blind over the mouth of the railway tunnel heading east. He skirted Leavesden Aerodrome with its glimmer from the Rolls-Royce works. He rode hard through an industrial nightscape flickering with neon, the printworks' illuminated clock, the black half-mile to where the motorway fed in at Berry Grove and the gypsy camp sucked a living off the crashes.

The Bee was like a shrine to a tough god, its windows all denim and leather. Alan drove into a car park crammed with bikes. He toured the glittering rows, dismounting next to a hot Ariel VB and heaving the big Triumph back on to its stand. He scanned about him – for that other sidecar. But there was no Nob, no obvious sign of the Stanmore gang – because he didn't believe a word Cynth had ever told him, with her *authorities*, and *theirs* and *ours*. She was a fantasist, a compulsive liar; her 'over-dramatise' wasn't in it. Still, he hesitated, nursing his limbs exactly as he'd done before. His mouth was dry. He took a couple of steps and touched the back of his belt, this time slipping his fingers round the handle of the knife. Because he no longer cared what happened, or who got hurt. Because she'd bloody betrayed him, hadn't she.

LADS MILLED IN the aisles and gangways. He could hardly see the counter for the press of bodies. A thick tobacco haze wafted darker flavours: grease, burnt oil. The buzz of voices threatened to drown out whatever vintage Elvis was grinding on the jukebox. No one turned a hair or gave him a second glance as he shoved a way through to the counter.

He bought tea, grimly steered the brimming mug between tough leather backs towards a space by the juice and milkshake machine. The boys at the tables sat with greased hair and grimed hands, clutching bottles, gesturing heatedly with cigarettes. The few girls wore their quieter leather or thin, pastel raincoats; one in the corner teased up her hair. There was no sign of Cynth. He edged his way down one of the aisles until his elbow caught someone's shoulder and his tea slopped over his fingers on to the sleeve below. 'Sorry, mate.'

'Eh?' The thin features confronting him were those of Pete from the fight.

' 'S'all right. Sorry.'

'Yeah.' Pete brushed at the spill and turned back to rejoin his conversation.

But Alan seized the chance. 'Good fight, that.'

Pete looked up at him again. 'What?'

'You and that Jimmy Chapman. Boxing Night.' There was a sudden burst of merriment from behind his back.

'Chapman.' Pete took a drag on his cigarette. 'Yeah. Fancies himself, don't he?'

'You seen them? Stanmore?'

'Seen fucking Chapman. The rest ain't showed, mate. Why? D'you know 'em?' There were tea stains in circles where Pete's hand lay across the chipped yellow Formica.

'Just curious.'

Pete clicked his tongue. He made to turn away.

'That girl . . . ,' Alan said.

'Eh?'

'That tart.'

'What fucking tart?'

'Cynthia. Or something.' He dug his nails into his palm.

'Yeah?'

'I wondered . . .'

'Fancy her, did you?'

'No.' There was a cough in his throat. 'Nothing like that.' His words trailed off again. 'It's just . . . she was the cause of it. Wasn't she?'

Pete shifted his arm from the table and squared round. 'Look, mate. Nobody's seen her.' His eyes narrowed. 'Have you?'

'No . . .'

There was a movement in the crowd. A voice shouted, 'There's dicing!'

' 'Bout fucking time.' Pete stood up with the lads around him. They crammed for the door.

Engines were running outside. Another started, and

another. Alan watched from the crowd in front of the entrance. At least five bikes emerged from the lines, then a dozen more, like cavalrymen breaking ranks. The dicers swept towards the road, jockeying. The only starting grid was the car-park gate. The leader opened up his throttle and the rest pelted after him, swinging left in pairs and threes, screaming flat out up the incline towards Edgware. Their red tail lights flicked in and out of thin, invisible trees.

Someone said, 'What's the score?'

Alan heard, 'Apex and back.'

'Eight minutes tops. Come on, I ain't freezing my bollocks off.'

Just inside the frontage, he looked at his watch.

'Oi! What time d'you make it?

'Ten to nine.'

'Give us the shout, mate, will you?'

He was surrounded by a knot of lads who smoked and jostled while he checked off the minutes. Others hunched outside, slapping their arms, stamping, shifting from foot to foot. Girls whispered. The song on the jukebox was 'Return to Sender'. Up by the Spider's Web, past the bus works, over the top roundabout, then down along the ice-cold strip to Mill Hill. Three and a half minutes . . . four. A new record started playing.

He pictured his own first ride. Round Apex Corner and then crashing up through the gears, five minutes, climbing, six, brakes, drop two cogs into the big roundabout. Into the long final straight – not forgetting the Elstree – and try for the ton. Alan sucked air through his teeth and

looked down at his watch. He gave the nod. The crowd
around him shoved and surged out. Sure enough, bikes
could be heard in the main straight. As the note grew,
figures rushed across grit and gravel to line the fence at
the road's edge.

There were headlamps among the trees. There was a car,
too, and a lorry's tail lights. The exhausts rose to a scream
and the first bikes were home, sprinting full bore one after
the other past the Bee, and the next wave, and the next,
trailing off again into the distance, slewing up to the
motorway junction to turn and coast back.

They were brief heroes. Doug sat astride his Norton in
the car park. Big Mick unzipped his jacket, lifting the
goggles from his eyes. More tailed in behind them. They
waited, idling, revving.

'Who's missing?' A voice came over the noise.

'How many went out?'

'Only fucking Marney.' Doug reached a packet of cigarettes out of a pocket. 'Lost the tail at the top roundabout.
We seen him on the way back. He waved.'

There was laughter.

A lamp showed at the gate as if on cue. Two or three
of the racers swung their machines round. In the spot-
lights, a limping figure got off and pushed his bike uncer-
tainly across the yard towards the café. Ironic cheers went
up, and catcalls of 'Marney! Marney!'

Marney reached the glare from the windows. Then he
was stuck, his face white and drained. Before he fainted,
Alan saw the bloody leg of his jeans and the chewed-up
skin. The heavy BSA was collapsing. Hands reached to

pull it off him. He was lifted up and taken inside, but there were bells in the road, and two cop cars were suddenly heading fast towards them over the gravel. Alan rushed for his bike with the others.

HE WAS WITH a shoal of riders in a stream of red tail lights. Their patterns stretched ahead as far as he could see, flowing past lorries, swirling around cars. Machines were either side of him; he could almost touch a painted fairing, polish a sleek tank. Behind him was a roar of headlights that winked and stared like some crazy phosphorescence.

Or at Apex they were locusts, bunching up in a plague. Nothing else dared move, and the traffic backed up until they were through. They were retracing his journey, Mill Hill, Hendon, Golder's Green. Then they crossed the River Brent and swung right on to the North Circular, in and out of the astonished motorists, jumping traffic lights, dodging islands, rocketing zebra crossings. He had no time to think: North London unreeled like strips of film, its parades, factories, unlit warehouses, dingy runs of ribbon development. He braked, accelerated, slipped up and down through the gears, living on his wits, missing by inches the snow that clung dangerously to kerbs, or was heaped black beside bollards.

Some gravity wave hit, pulling everyone up at last, and he was edging his way, creeping forward like the others, taking his turn into a crowded car park, just off the road to the right. He guessed where he was even before he looked up: at the squat clock tower and the sign and the lightbulbs above the blazing run of windows.

The Ace was tight, smaller than the Bee, and the inside was packed. The Watford crowd were on high octane from the ride. It was all Marney and the race and losing the cops. Immediately, there were London lads going out, sparked up to race in their own right, and the huge sound of their bikes surged from the forecourt, then strung as swiftly into the distance, leaving just the tune on the jukebox and the words on people's lips.

There were girls in their pale lipstick and make-up, their eyes lined, their hair lacquered up and cut in points against their cheeks like Cynth's. He was speaking to one, two, in a corner by the tables at the back. Had they seen her? Pete at the Bee reckoned no one had. Or had the Stanmore lads got her and brought her here? But the next minute the boys were back, and a new contingent rushed to replace them. Alan found himself with three others running to the door, all caught up with it, crossing the front of the café like night pilots scrambled across an airfield.

He hardly felt the kick-start, hardly knew anything but the burst of his own nervous system before he was opening up behind the rest, exploding into the night across a couple of cars, heading due south with his whole intent glued only on the tail light of the bike in front. Someone drew along-side. He shaded the throttle, staying just ahead of a big new Matchless with a megaphone exhaust, the lad flat down over the clip-ons and a girl pinched up behind. They held level under a strange, fat bridge. He just caught the sign 'British Waterways' – the same canal he and Cynth lived by, slung overhead in a cradle. There were weird meanings, and somehow she was with him, connected to him. Now he was knee to knee with the boy on the Matchless, now losing ground. They were joining Hanger Lane. A terrifying slice between cars at the Western Avenue intersection shook off his rival and took him clear out ahead. Two bikes were in front. There'd be more, Nortons, Tritons, as race-fit as his own was untried; big six-and-a-halfs, five hundreds. Even tuned two-fifties could pack a punch.

Uphill in second, breathless into third, he felt the Bonnie pull harder than he'd ever known. He let her have her head, and the revs screamed for top before he could think. He flicked his right foot on the lever. Still she pulled: like riding a bullet. Seventy-two between the eerie, street-lit trees and the dignified Ealing village set back on either hand, over the narrow crest, a double-decker pulling out on the downward slope, a van approaching . . . His exhaust shattered off the bus's panels, the van's black sides less than a memory.

He was up on the next bike. A railway bridge – the brake light showed, and Alan braked too, as hard as he could. A big crossroads, traffic, the squat dark trees of Ealing Common. He opened the throttle again, and all along the soft Gunnersbury curve he was pure spirit. Crystals of ice shone in his headlamp as he swooped out and round the emblazoned tail of a tanker. He glanced back from the wrong side of the road, and saw bikes behind him; looked up and saw others hurtling towards him – the leaders on their home-ward leg. A sign saying 'Chiswick, Westminster, A4': now there were high street lamps, far shopfronts, a confusion of road markings, and he was braking late as he dared. Green traffic lights went amber, the bike in front was through. He watched how it swung to the right, sparks coming from the footrest before amber turned red, and vehicles from the trunk road were surging across and shutting his view. He braked for all he was worth, regardless of ice.

The Triumph pitched. He forced his shoe under the gear change. The machine merely checked, howling in second. He snaked across a black cab, between a Renault Dauphine and a council gritter, past the central bollards, heading for shop windows. He couldn't lean, he couldn't stop. Then the front brake snatched and the back wheel locked and spun out on some loose gravel, and all he had to do was put his foot down on the tar. Suddenly, he was round in one piece, neither dead nor maimed, jinking his way past the other side of the bollards and back once more on to the Gunnersbury Avenue. He raised his fist. He could imagine himself arriving back first at the Ace, to the shouts of onlookers. And there would be Cynth. He pictured himself with her, as at the end of a movie, while the relentless six-fifty under him seemed to sniff and champ again, and the North Circular stretched clear as far as he could see, back towards the hill. A gasp of bitter air took him through the gears and the speedo needle climbed. It stood quivering at eighty, eighty-five beside the park, ninety until he could no longer trust himself. The bike shook, the wind ripped at his face. He even heard her voice, crying out.

It brought him back. He let the throttle slacken and the revs drop. He saw houses, shops and side roads, the dimly lit railway bridge, the little common. Burning a quieter way through, he saw the tame patches of London snow under the trees and thought of the other common he'd come over that night above his own town – high, wild, drifted deep with the Christmas falls. He thought of the scene at the monument, the bike cooling and clicking, and the sidecar full of her clothes.

He was neither first nor last back at the Ace. He sat astride his machine on the forecourt, flicking the idle with the others, feeling his heart thump, hearing the roar of engines. For a minute, he scanned the forecourt and looked over towards the doorway. Then he sneered at himself, for of course she was nowhere to be seen.

There were no casualties. Inside, they quizzed him about the Chiswick intersection. Two people had actually seen him lose the back wheel under the taxi.

'No, come on, mate. How did you do that? How did you get out of it?'

It was all a blur and he laughed it off. His body rushed alive under the bright lights as though he were still in the race, and he forgot the sound of her cry. He got talking instead to a girl who was coming on to him. She had lined eyes and pale lips and a cross on a chain around her neck.

HER NAME WAS Jen. Her eyes were heavy-lidded, her face thick with foundation. Outside, in the parking lot, there were other couples propped. Jen tasted of her lipstick and the fizzy orange she held in one hand. She sucked on the straw when she broke off from his kiss, and their breaths wreathed up together in the light from the windows. Because it was just a transport café in a freak freeze-up. To tell the truth, there was no snow left but for the oily heaps at the low front wall and the stained crusts on the sills behind them.

He caught her to him again and unzipped her jacket. She didn't resist. He pushed the leather lapels aside and laid the cotton open, unbuttoning her blouse. He put his hand inside: not a bra but a strapless thing to the waist, like they wore in the smutty Sundays. It thrust her small breasts up hard and tight, and he squeezed through the scratchy embroidery, breathing hard. Jen lifted her face. He pressed himself against her. The stiffened, lacquered fibres of her dark hair grazed his cheek, and the jukebox leaked Duane Eddy from the open café window behind them.

A bike started nearby. A headlamp flashed for a moment, catching Jen's little silver cross. It caught too the pallor of plumped flesh, cast a tease of shadow where his free hand dragged at the wired cup, forcing it down. He stared, trapped the nipple roughly between his fingers. She twisted in his arm. 'Give over.'

'Give over what?'

She watched him sullenly, then looked away. 'Just give over, that's all.'

'Sorry.' He was unrepentant. He spoke her name and began again.

She pulled her jacket over his hand. 'Girlfriend washing her hair?'

He looked straight back. 'Come on a bike, did you?'

'Course.'

'Well?' he said.

She shook her head petulantly. 'Well, what?'

He sucked at her mouth to shut her up. He took her tongue as permission, straying his hand down, working the buttons free. He could just feel her ribs, the small, yielding bones behind the synthetic lace. Then he pressed his fingers under her waistband and into the front of her jeans. He felt his lips curl back next to hers. Only the sound of a bike pulling up stopped him. Its engine throbbed and fell until he listened in spite of himself, yanking his mouth away to look up. Right next to him was a sidecar rig, the chair like a space pod that shuddered visibly to the noise. Sitting up behind its miniature screen, the puny structure seeming hardly to contain him, was the figure and face he remembered.

Nob lifted his goggles. The scars on his cheeks caught the glare from the windows. Strands of his black hair straggled as before over the frayed black collar. 'I know you, don't I?' From the chair, he eyed the telltale suede of Alan's coat and turned to his driver. Then he swung back. 'Come here, mate. I said, come here and tell me your name. That's right, darling, put your tits away.' Alan stood still.

Nob levered himself out, the grubby, fleeced boots touching down on the black grit, the black jacket loose on the slight hunch of his shoulders. His dirty jeans assembled as they straightened; his grimed hands hung down from the frayed cuffs at his sides. Then the bike's engine died and the driver dismounted. Bullet-helmeted, goggles up on the brim, he sauntered round to stand beside Nob.

Alan glanced this way, now that. Behind him were the rows of machines and the walls of the Ace. Before he knew it, his hand had gone to his belt. The next second, the button was unclipped and the knife out of its sheath. He stared witlessly at the handle in his palm, the blade pointing forward. It shone in the light. He heard himself blurting, stupid, 'Come on, then, if you're so hard.' His voice was hoarse. He stood crouched, backing off with his weapon, feinting blindly now to cover Nob, now the driver, now Jen. 'Come on!' He saw the driver reach into his pocket, heard the click, saw the gleam.

'All right, Ken,' Nob nodded to his companion. Ken's flick-knife lowered an inch. Nob stepped forward. 'Listen, son.'

Part of a bike was digging in Alan's back. A tyre pressed against his legs.

Nob moved nearer still. 'A word in your ear.'

In an instant, Alan's knife hand was gripped and he was being held against Nob's waist. He stifled a gasp of pain. He could feel the cold leather on his wrist. The cut face was in front of him, the eyes fixed on his.

'What's your name, kid?'

'Alan.'

'Alan what?'

'Alan Rae.'

'If I come after Alan Rae, there'll be nothing left of him. You hear me? Eh?'

Alan's head nodded as the lock on his wrist tightened.

'And I'll be coming after you, Alan Rae, if ever I find you've done anything to harm her. All right, you spineless little cunt? And I don't mean you.' He turned to the girl, still shivering beside the café wall where Alan had left her. 'Go on! Get back inside.' Jen scuttled away. Nob took hold of Alan by the coat front, still gripping the arm. 'You know who I'm talking about. Don't you?'

'I thought you lot . . .' He stammered the words out.

'What about us lot?'

'At her house.'

'What at her house? I tried. Chapman tried. She ain't at her fucking house. Is she?'

Alan shook his head.

'Where, then?' Nob said.

'I don't know.'

'You don't know. But you've seen her?'

'Yes . . . No. Not recently.'

'Not recently. How long?'

'About a week ago. She got ill. Then she didn't want to . . . be with me any more. I took her home.'

'You took her home. And?'

'And now there's no one there. Is there? So I came looking, didn't I?'

'Up some bit of skirt?' Nob smacked him hard across the side of the face and let him go. Alan fell back into the bikes. His knife clattered. Nob picked him up instantly and held him hard by the coat again. But he was changed, almost kindly, his kindness the more frightening. 'Look, son. If you're a bloke you get what you can, don't you. Everyone likes a bit of slip now and then.' Alan could smell his breath. 'You and I, we know how it is. Don't we, mate. I saw you leave the Bee with her, didn't I. And

I saw you up by Bovingdon with her just last week in your fucking sidecar.' He grinned suddenly, and the scars rebuilt themselves. 'Didn't I?'

Alan grinned, too, in a reflex, but he managed to shake his head. 'No. I haven't seen her. I haven't been anywhere near Bovingdon.'

'What?'

'It can't have been me. That's all I'm saying. We never went . . .'

'I'm warning you.'

'Honest. I don't . . . It must have been someone else.'

'Who?'

'I don't know.'

'You don't fucking know.'

'I swear it.'

'Swear?' Nob stared into Alan's eyes. 'Swear, do you?' Then he let go a little. 'Well, then. I might even believe you. Alan. Just Cynthia's special, ain't she? We both know that. She's special and we don't want nothing happening to her.'

'No.' Alan's tongue stuck in his stricken smile.

Nob's voice crooned on. 'And you wouldn't lie to me, Alan, would you? So if you do hear anything, let your old mate Nob know. 'Cause I care about her. I really do. Where did you say you lived? Out Hemel way, wasn't it?'

'Yeah. That way.'

Nob threw him abruptly backwards, almost into the bikes again. 'So fucking get looking, why don't you.' He turned on his heel and strode off towards the café door.

To get back home was easy enough. Alan took the route

past Northolt, where his dad was supposed to have gone, then through Northwood and Rickmansworth, and then across country by the Chiltern foothills. Only as his emotions ebbed did the fractured scenes of the night begin to add up. She wasn't at her house. She wasn't with the lads. Nob was as in the dark about her as he was. She hadn't lied: it hadn't been the Stanmore gang after all, that night at her house. And she'd been seen at Bovingdon, the Yankee air base. He thought again of the torn scrap of paper on her hall floor.

Bovingdon village wasn't even far away, as though the white lanes had been guiding him there all along. It was just up over the back of Ley Hill. All through Church End, Sarratt, Chipperfield, there were signposts pointing along the lanes like dim white fingers.

The airfield itself was tucked off the dark hilltop, unadvertised, but there was no hiding anything on that scale. Soon, he was driving slowly past the entrance. He made out the greatcoated guards where the barrier rested on oil drums, the Nissen huts and hangars, the square control tower sticking up from its murky snowfield. He stopped by a farm gate and stared in through the perimeter fence, as though he might see Cynth, too, far off beside the floodlit runway – as though he might somehow put two and two together. All too clearly, he remembered the sidecar and the old Standard Vanguard with the faded Confederate flag. He remembered exactly the look on her face at the mention of his father.

Somehow, it connected: not only her parents but now she, too, had been taken, and the hunch he'd backed from the beginning had locked shut on her ... He studied again the unblinking runway lights. All this time she'd been genuinely at risk while he'd wallowed in shame and rage. She'd broken off with him *because* he was Lionel's son – to spare him ... His body knew it. His body knew her; it always had. But there was nothing he could do.

IT WAS DAYS later, the twenty-third, a Wednesday evening at nine. Alan looked up from his probability equations and caught exactly the TV news he'd half-dreaded, half-prayed for. An Englishman had disappeared from a room in Turkey, and the pundits were all up in arms. So sure was he, so psychically primed, that even when a photo flashed up on the screen, he could hardly believe Kim Philby's wasn't the face of his dad.

His mother's eyes were shut, her head against the wing of her chair. She was dozing over some knitting, as sometimes she did when the dinner was in the oven because her husband was working late, and she was simply waiting for him to come home. Soon, his car would pull up the concrete slope of the drive, as usual.

When Alan was small – long before Lionel's career in weapons – there was a grey metal box, smaller than a toaster, with a lead going in near the base and a red light when Lionel pressed the switch. His father had called it a lidlock; he'd invented it. Alan remembered this now with a sinking stomach. Every object in the room was in its place. The Rayburn in the hearth gave warmth; just as

Lionel's flawed heating system did not. Every detail of his and his mother's seamless lives was accounted for. She was an icon of respectability, of snoozing, triumphant normality. He put down the maths file from his lap, got up, and hurried out to the front of the house.

Crusted, half-cleared snow gave back the starlight as he dragged at the iced-up garage door. Now, he even remembered helping Lionel solder the little device. Probably, it had marked the start of his apprenticeship. Bespectacled Lionel had spoken to his mother: 'Look how good his eyes are with that iron.' Alan looked up at the impassive stars, the black shreds of cloud, and put his hands up to his head. He'd made it all up. Nothing was real, or true, and he was going crazy. Bad wiring, his father would say. There was no one he could tell, about Cynth, about anything, because there was nothing to tell; and no one would believe him because there was nothing to believe. The Triumph stood in the garage, behind the family car, as large as life.

All Thursday morning the putative third man dominated the news and it was nothing in the least to do with Lionel. The tranny in the kitchen crackled with claims that linked Philby to Burgess and Maclean. In the High Street with Paul on the way to school, the sheets outside the newsagent near the top of Ravens Lane had 'PHILBY DEFECTS'.

An anticyclone sat over the North Sea. Nothing could warm until it shifted. Nothing would make it shift because it defended itself and its borders so relentlessly, looped over the Continental shelf like a coil of razor wire. Its air spiralled slowly down through the polar troposphere. It lingered over the glaciers in Scandinavia and the snow-fields of the Baltic Iron Curtain – Estonia, Latvia, Poland, Prussia. Only then did it drift round on the solid brine flats of the Zuider Zee and cross back into southern England. There was no cloud and the nights grew steadily colder. Any heat captured by day fled the supremely reflective glaze that covered every field and hillside, every glebe and garden, and returned by night to vacuous space. The sun served only for glare, a brilliance that grew wearisome upon thousands shivering in waterless, powerless homes.

Fogs sublimed off hard dawns through which Alan and his friend made their way to school. Everyone now walked boldly over the canal. Up at the Cow Roast, locals had got a car on the cut's thick surface. They'd driven back and forth, past the trapped barges, the houseboats, the British Waterways dredger tipped sideways by huge planar expansion.

These evenings, Alan and his mother sat together beside the fireplace, hardly speaking. There was still no news of Lionel. Alan did his homework, she added up her Tupperware sales and watched television, the large, walnut-sided set Lionel had bought second-hand. There was a hole for some other failed invention cut in the side. Wires still hung out, like a prolapse. But the news bulletins still came: of racehorses exercised along frozen beaches, of curling, skating, winter sports and avalanches, of trains cancelled, and yet more blackouts. There were bergs at St Katharine's Dock under Tower Bridge. Up at Windsor, and at Marlow, the Thames was frozen hard for the first time in the century. On the Colne at Colchester, they were using dynamite to get anthracite barges through to the power stations.

There was a party one night at Aldbury, in the house of a girl in the arts sixth. Alan stood with the boys in the kitchen, holding his glass, and they spoke of spies and spooks, Polaris submarines and what the Russians could do. There was even a Philby joke, though no one could make much sense of it. Another young woman had been attacked, up in the fringes of the town, but the police were no nearer finding the man. Alan drank to forget himself. Couples danced to the Beatles, the same forty-fives stacked to play over and over again on the portable Dansette: 'Please, Please Me'; 'Love Me Do'.

Someone's dad gave him a lift back through Northchurch, and he had to wind down his window to stop his head spinning. Past the Crooked Billet, past the Stag, the cold stung his eyes and the car slowed to drop him next to the post office. He opened the door. There was a scream; a man was struggling with a girl in the shadows. She was gone before Alan could get out, the man running down Park Street after her: 'Don't be so bloody daft! Do you hear? Bitch!' Alan followed down towards the watercress beds. His limbs were so rubbery he hardly hurt himself when he slipped. He saw high cloud, no moon. The girl might be Cynth. She might. She was so on his mind. Over there was the driveway to the Catholic church, over there the road's end, the path to the footbridge. He got up and found the start of it. His shoe skidded on the narrow wood. He gripped the handrail and edged his way along the plank.

A figure was at the far end, striding towards him. He stood still, unsure whether to challenge or call out. A man's shape formed in the dark before the canal bank. He heard the footfalls on the flimsy bridge and raised a hand as the other approached to make sure he'd been seen. 'Watch out!' There were cries. He stepped up. They were grappling face to face, the two of them, arms intertwined. Then he was staggering in soft mud through the ice of the watercress beds, his shoes filled with water, his fists thrashing.

'What the bloody hell?'

It was Geoffrey Fairhurst. He recognised the voice right beside him, peered at the features. 'Where is she?' he shouted. 'You fucking sod, what have you done with her?' He hit out. Geoffrey went down full length in the frozen stream. Alan took another step up to his knee in ice-cold ooze, but Geoffrey was escaping, blundering and crashing through the dark towards the grounds of the Sacred Heart. Alan found gravel. His other foot was mired and Geoffrey was a shape scrambling up the bank a good ten yards away. As soon as he'd climbed back on the plank bridge, Alan was sick over the rail, the cheesy snacks of the party cascading on to the undamaged ice at the other side. Of the girl there was no sign, no sign at all.

He searched the tow-path, the canal bank, the bushes in the hedge. His stomach hurt. He was Cynth's lover, but he could neither find nor save her. Where was his dad? Where was she?

It was another three weeks before he found the body in the lock.

IV

SWITCHING

SHE WAS READING the *Daily Mirror*. Geoffrey leaned over while they waited at the lights. As a press feast, the Vassall Inquiry had everything – short of a cabinet minister in an orgy at a stately home. Its lurid entrapment scandal was knocking Philby off the front pages again: two more journalists risked jail for refusing to disclose their sources. The red changed to green.

'A penny for them,' he said. They were passing the cinema.

'Oh, nothing,' she said.

'Poor devil, though.'

'Who?'

'Vassall. Can't help the way he is, can he? Then the Russians blackmail him into spying for them and he gets eighteen years.'

'Yes.'

Her thighs were crossed under her blue raincoat, the sheer stocking just below her knee, the high-heeled boot with its toe angled past the base of the long gear lever. 'You all right?' he asked.

'Yes.'

'Sure?'

'Yes, Geoff. Course I am.' She lifted her hand and put it to his cheek.

He flinched and the car veered slightly. 'Sorry,' Cynthia said. 'I was forgetting your bruise.'

An oncoming Rover hooted. It was Astraea, but he had no time to wave. He let his breath out, the pain slight now, the mark of Alan's fist more decorative than troublesome. Astraea's car was in his mirror, a retreating black shape next to the grubby line of remaining snow.

It had been like a gift, Cynth turning up that night, and all the long gamble with himself brought down to a moment. He stole another glance at her legs while the lines of the pop song reran inanely in his head, that he should keep his mind on his driving and his snoopy eyes on the road ahead.

His mind harked back to the previous year, first noticing her beside the daffodils on the edge of Verulam Park. The ache in his heart then – it *had* been like a pop song, an industrial *fin amour*, into which he'd allowed himself to fall. But he'd left it at that, a fiction. And so insubstantial a detail had brought down his marriage. Only the previous week there'd been an attempt at reconciliation in Astraea's kitchen, in front of the range. Louisa recited how things had been wrong for weeks, so wrong that the mention of *that girl* was simply the last straw. She'd known from the start they should never have married; she'd always said as much, hadn't she? As for lovemaking, didn't he realise Louisa had never once . . . Was he really *that* insensitive?

Louisa had left Astraea's and gone off to her mother's; Geoffrey had begun to struggle at the lab. He'd missed Louie terribly, but the pressure at Lidlock was increasing out of all proportion. A new spurt of progress in the clean rooms absorbed all Raj's time, and left Geoffrey trying to keep up. Sleeping badly as a result, he'd continued to stretch out a hand whenever he woke, expecting to touch Louisa's reassuring body. He always found instead that icy lack, and then remembered: she'd left him, their marriage had been a sham, and all their plans were over. He'd toss and turn for an hour, then get up and pace the house, stand shivering in his dressing gown while the kettle boiled, stare out of the kitchen window into the glistening, inexplicable dark. Back in a bedroom full of memories and crushed hopes, exhaustion would take hold of him – until he'd have to lurch out of roiling dreams to the clanging of the alarm clock.

When Cynthia Somers had reappeared at Lidlock, he'd forced himself not to think of her. He'd made sure, by timing or strategic choice of route, not to run the risk of picking her up in his car. She was the precipitant of all this distress. Occasionally, he'd recall the moment when he really could have sworn it was Cynthia clinging to Lionel's son on the back of that motorbike, but he knew the mind could play tricks, that it produced its own subtle pharmacy.

Then Cynthia had turned up at his house. It was when he'd been dutifully across to ask Judith Rae about Lionel's absence from work, and all the thanks he'd got, returning across the canal, was to have been pasted on the chin by her drunken son. Finding Cynthia on his doorstep, he'd been completely taken aback, and had let her tend to him straight away without really asking why or where. He'd been attacked, he'd said, down by the canal. All *she*'d said was that her family had been frozen out. She'd taken him in, soothed him, seen to his cheek and the side of his jaw. She'd bathed all the cuts the rock-hard sheet ice over the watercress beds had made in his shins. Feeling the tenderness beneath his hair, she'd found the place where he'd hit the back of his skull when he fell.

Only when she'd finished and was plying him with hot, strong tea did she enquire into the details. Had he seen who'd done it, down there in the dark? But something had confused him, warned him, some echo in his head of the worrying office memo he'd returned to after Christmas: Philby, Vassall, missing people. It made him oddly protective of Alan, and he told Cynthia he'd been set on by a drunk. She'd seemed perfectly satisfied with that.

Her story was of her parents staying with relatives, herself left coping at home for the sake of her job. She told of burst pipes, her whole street hit by a power cut, everyone else she could think of in the same boat. No coal, her bus broken down . . . In the emergency and with the temperature still dropping, she'd simply had no idea where to turn, unless to him.

He'd been too flattered to enquire more deeply. But it was the kiss, sudden and unexpected – almost fleeting, as they passed one another in the kitchen, taking the cups back – that had set the seal. 'All right, Geoff,' she'd said later that night, smiling, 'it wasn't all strictly true.' Yes, they *had* been frozen out, but she'd come to him because *she* knew and *he* knew there was something between them, and it had gone on long enough, and when he'd told her his wife had left him . . . Well, she'd decided that if *he* hadn't been going to do anything about it, *she* would.

Flattered was too mild a word for it. He flattered himself he was not unattractive to women, but here was a pretty girl, *the* pretty girl, positively throwing herself at him. Whether he'd ever told her about Louie leaving – and when he thought about it he was pretty sure he hadn't – it should have been the jackpot. A bang on the head or not, it should have been all his Christmases coming at once.

WHITE CLUSTERS BEGAN splatting the windscreen. He flicked the switch beside the speedo and watched the wiper blades scoop them away. Another thaw had been forecast; an approaching front would bring rain, possibly floods when all the snow melted. As usual, the sky had other ideas, and Geoffrey craned his head to see the livid edge of cloud that reached over Hemel. The air was patterned with flakes until a blast across the tarmac drove them swirling between him and the car in front.

'There,' he said.

'I know,' she said.

That first night, standing dazed, still bruised, he'd simply held her in his arms. They'd slept in separate beds – for him, gallantly, the settee downstairs. In the morning, she'd made him stay home; she'd seen riders concussed. She went down to get the Green Line that would link with her bus at Two Waters. She'd returned after work. Then, on the Saturday morning, she'd taken herself off – she said to get clothes from the house, to see her family camped out with relatives. She'd tell her parents she was staying with a friend, she said.

He'd been in torment while the weekend ticked away, waiting for her return. On Sunday night he'd nearly given up and gone to bed, convinced she'd thought better of the whole idea. His head still hurt. He'd sat anxiously by the flickering fire, full of imaginings, suspended, as it were, on tenterhooks.

Only as the TV announced the latest freaks – a pregnant deer in solid ice, a woman attacked by the pigeons she was attempting to feed, a fountain turned into an iceberg – had Cynthia appeared with her things, and with her own slight bruise from having slipped against a lamp-post somewhere. Fervently, he'd kissed away the hurt, felt the night's chill on her.

She'd missed him, too. As for the settee, she told him not to be so chivalrous, and so silly. They had feelings for each other, didn't they? Were they supposed to go on play-acting? It was the sixties, Geoff, not the fifties. He'd been amazed, and thrilled, as they'd stood there in the sitting room, embracing, laughing into one another's eyes.

But now, as he drove, the memory of her nakedness was stinging. Her fine white skin burned him almost physically through her clothes, because he'd been unable to respond to it. To be precise, he'd believed she winced away from him at the crucial point. He made himself revisit the scene. Seeing that fleeting look on her face, it had been as though his spirit had been turned off, the sexual charge in the room drained out through its midnight walls. He'd been mortified and immediately taken the cause on himself. She'd been understanding: 'It doesn't matter, Geoff, does it? Don't worry about it. We can just cuddle up, can't we? There's plenty of time. After all, it's us that matters in the long run, isn't it.'

He snatched another glance and saw her looking out across the carpeted meadows to the canal, in the direction of her house. Her pale cheek had that fine blonde talon to it, the rest of her hair backcombed in a fashionable casque, warrior-style, following the curve of her ear, straying down over the collar of the blue coat. The seam at the insertion of the sleeve was torn, a little grubby. How quick the eye was to pick up the slightest detail.

The road sped under him, through the new town, up on to the chalk ridges. The wipers smudged dribs of snow to either side. Her boots and her thighs and her skirted lap persisted there in the corner of his vision, along with some tabloid taste of espionage and the forbidden. That morning they'd left the house separately, by stealth. She'd gone down to the High Street; he'd brought the car on a little later, and contrived to pick her up.

They halted at last outside the Lidlock car park. She hurried off discreetly to her office, to make it look as though he'd just given her a lift in from the bus-stop. He stared out of the car's side window: her figure through the factory railings making that tantalising movement inside her coat, the tops of her calves just visible above her boots. His pulse was agitated; he could almost hear his heart against his ribs.

Lance was loading his pipe with tobacco. 'Late, Geoff, for a star performer.'

'Am I?' Geoffrey shrugged out of his coat and hung it by the door. He went to his place.

'Missus wouldn't take no for an answer, I suppose,' Lance continued. 'What I wouldn't give for the aura of genius.' He tamped abstractedly with his penknife and sucked. 'Wait till the patter of tiny feet, matey. You won't feel like it then. Or get it. Burst joy's grape while you can, Geoff. Saves on coal. Whoever Joy was. Still no sign of dear Lionel, I take it.' Eventually, he looked up. 'Christ, what have you done to your face?'

'I got attacked. Down by the canal. Actually, it was . . .' Again, he checked himself. 'Just some drunk. That's why I didn't come in Friday.'

'Thought the place seemed different.'

'Sod you, Lance!'

Royston Gaines, the bearded crystallographer, looked up wearily. He had a nervous wife and an ulcer.

'Bloody snow,' Lance said. 'I used to be the one with the bruises. All matches cancelled these days, of course.'

Geoffrey told his carefully edited story of what had happened. 'Concussion.' He showed the marks on his shins, too.

'Could have broken them. Someone like you should have them insured. Like Stanley Matthews . . . or Margot Fonteyn. Judith cast any light on Lionel, did she? Getting beyond a joke, isn't it.'

'She just said "government work". Reckoned he used to go all over the world. She looked almost pleased, Lance.

Reflected glory, or what? And made me feel a bit silly for asking. Maybe I was. Actually, it all seems quite a long time ago. What with . . .'

'Yes?'

'Concussion . . . And everything.'

'Quite. As we were then? No one here seems to want to take up the strange case of the vanishing rocket scientist.' Lance looked pointedly round. Dr Gaines was studying his slide-rule. Millicent Throssel had her back to them both. 'Nice weekend, Lance? Not too bad thanks, Geoff. Not too bloody bad, all things considered. The remarkably inclement weather . . . and so on.'

'My wife has left me.'

'Oh, dear.'

EVEN IN HIS clean-room suit, his imagination was back with Cynthia in the marital bedroom. He sucked at his lip behind his Plexi-visor, twenty-three, caught out by the times: *the sixties, Geoff, not the fifties.* The vacuum tube of the microscope rose up before him.

And the *Gazette* had front-paged the man in the woods for the last three weeks. An identikit male portrait also stared out from the glazed doors of Woolworths, as though generated by and somehow rising from the gloomy mahogany trestles and slatted floors inside. No man and Everyman, it could have been any trilby-hatted husband out shopping with his wife. It could have been him, Geoffrey told himself. He tried to stop his mind wandering.

The working day passed almost before he noticed. He could hardly remember what he'd achieved before new snow crumped under the Mini's front wheels where she waited at the bus-stop on Bluehouse Hill, next to the Roman park. Her touch almost smarted when she put her hand on his. He tried to make light, as though all were well.

'It's all right, Geoff,' she said. 'It'll be all right.'

'It's never happened before,' he said. He saw her smiling at him.

Later still, they sat on either side of the fire like an old married couple. The coke he'd laid hurriedly, distractedly as soon as they'd got in was beginning to redden in a bank and take the chill off the room.

She asked, brightly, 'How was your day?'

'Lance and his bloody talk.'

'About you and me?'

'No!' He shook his head. 'He doesn't know. No one knows, do they? Because it doesn't quite have a name yet. Does it?'

She sidestepped the question. 'Everybody's still pleased with you, though. Aren't they, Geoff? Your Dr Raj Gill?'

He tried again. 'I suppose I should ... meet your parents. At least.'

'Yes.' She gave a tight little smile. 'But what with them camping out just now in someone else's house ...'

'We could go over. Take them out. Where did you say they were staying?'

'In towards London.' She looked down at her finger-nails. 'They might feel embarrassed. Do you know, I think they would. Let's wait till the snow clears away.' She lifted her eyelids and flashed her winning smile again. 'It can't go on much longer, can it. Don't worry, Geoff. I don't mind. Honestly, I don't. Maybe you're overworking. With the . . . what do you call them? The chips!' She laughed, came over and kissed him lightly on the cheek.

Then he poured out the frustrations of his day, the tests he'd tried to carry out on the latest batch of Raj's 'buried layer' samples without knowing quite what he was looking for. 'Look. I just couldn't focus. And I don't mean the machine, I mean *me*!'

'Just being close to you is good enough for me.' She put on some records as if to defuse the moment. She'd bought them at the weekend, she said. He gazed at the features that had so long enchanted him. She was all he could have dreamed of, setting the needle on – she wore one of his jumpers over her own, her throat and collarbone visible, still in her work skirt and boots. The film on the coals flickered and the table lamp by the bookcase cast its long shadows.

He switched on the television and they watched in silence, holding hands on the settee, drinking cocoa. The weather had 'a continued thaw', the nine o'clock news reported the Vassall Tribunal. There were blackouts in Luton, a coal lift to power stations, yachts stoven in by the ice floes in Portsmouth harbour. There were occupants driven from their homes by fractured pipes and detonating boilers – the familiar catalogue. *Panorama* had the presumed treachery and continuing absence of Kim Philby. She switched it off; but in bed her body was a reproach.

He could hardly kiss her, hardly touch her, his lips unused to her name.

'Cynthia . . . ?'

'Yes?

'Nothing.'

He lay awake. There'd been no question he'd get married as soon as he could after university. Merriam already had children, by a printer with a steady job at Hazell Watson's. He'd never imagined, when he took Louisa down the aisle, that they wouldn't spend the rest of their lives together. Her father, the clerk of the assizes, church organist, her mother a former schoolmistress, their home in Surrey, Abinger Hammer, in a cleft of the Downs – he remembered her grandparents, the old brick house with the orchard, her brothers and sister and a summer's day with the buzz of insects and the planes over Newlands Corner. Now it was Cynthia lying next to him. A sexual tide *was* coming in, at the core of it his own impotence. He felt a growing sense of dread. That night was the coldest in England for three decades. Parts of the Chilterns suffered twenty degrees of frost.

FEBRUARY MOCKED RUMOURS of thaw with yet more of the same. Geoffrey and Cynthia remained ghost lovers. Swirled in snow and strange events, they flitted by car between Cowper Road and the factory under the Abbey. When a tramp steamer ran aground on the sands of Winterton, in Norfolk, villagers braved frozen flats and icy scour to pillage its coal. One vicar in Peterborough and another in Yeovil reported wild yelps and lanterns in the dead of night. It seemed that wreckers in rags and devil riders might revive in the land.

Other moods marked other pockets of Geoffrey's time. Rae had completely disappeared from the shared lab. It was Lance who misbehaved as though in commemoration, together with Millicent Throssel, the metallurgist. Her unflattering spectacles and hair drawn back spinsterishly in a bun only proposed an ice-nixie waiting to be set free. 'Bit of a looker on the quiet, isn't she,' Lance said to Geoffrey. 'What did I tell you? Prim girls, bluestockings. Science chicks aren't just a legend.'

Coffee from the kiln gave them twenty minutes each morning away from the fussy, resistant silicon wafers. Lance smoked a thick new tobacco in his pipe. What *couldn't* they do, all three of them, with their brains and the government-funded resources at their disposal? What couldn't they get up to, down amongst the molecules? Far beyond invisible inks, exploding cigars, bugged fur hats, they conjured neutron bibles, sprayed whole tea shops with mescalin, created symptomless genetic plagues. The world was their sideline. Millie, posing as a gorgeous sales rep, would penetrate MI5. Spectacles removed, her hand at her cheek, she shook with suppressed laughter, and flashed her eyes at Lance. 'Why not?' he said, and she laughed all the more.

The micro-miniaturisation of computers would be achieved. A clutch of research notes had just been circulated – exactly where they came from and how they'd been obtained Geoffrey didn't care to ask. They revealed how quickly production-size records were being broken: smaller and smaller chips would host multiple beehives of semiconductors. Clean rooms in America, far better equipped than his own, were already stamping out logic gates less than a hundredth of an inch across, all tuned to the same goal of building intelligent war machines. Between horror and glassy elation, Geoffrey foresaw missiles that really could think for themselves, pilotless bombers, cannons which couldn't miss, and armies of robots.

But that wasn't the end of it. Here, after all, were the very building blocks of nature. Each day he and Cynthia struggled through sub-zero temperatures to work. He explained to her one morning how it was only the universe's cooling that had first created molecular and electrical forces. These were what turned energy or gas into shapes. Without cooling, nature wouldn't exist; nor would he, or she . . . He'd looked down at his own hands on the steering wheel, feeling her eyes expectantly on his. If that was the case, then so what? So what if he toyed with his probe almost at the quantum threshold, under the ice of appearance, as it were? What did the shapes *he* was making at Lidlock matter – since the whole frozen universe was just a jumble of shapes, like the letters in an alphabet? For a second, Cynthia had touched his arm.

'This whole place . . . !' Lance expostulated one lunch-time. 'People just get on with their work and go home. Everyone's so bloody staid and conformist.' He pointed to Roy Gaines returning from the Gents. 'Regular as bloody All-Bran,' he said. Dr Gaines opened his tin lunch-box at the far corner of the lab as he did every day precisely at one. But today he closed it again, then opened it, repeated the process, stood up, sat down, and appeared to stare out of the window.

Even Geoffrey laughed when it turned out Lance had stolen one of his sandwiches. It was a miniature relief, a schoolboy *naughtiness* – harmless enough, surely. Lance was emboldened, seeing his prank's effect on Millicent. 'We should use that MAC,' he said. 'You know, that thing they call Judith.'

Screwed to a wall in the waiting room next to Butterfield's office was a prototype Mechanical Analogue Computer. The three trooped out to look at it. It was weirdly beautiful, with various weights and pulleys held in an upright wooden bedstead. And there *was* something gynoid about it: two central cogs made asymmetric breasts, the lower input a cleft, and the pathway of steel ribbon a sketched, limbless torso. Only Rae, with whom it had arrived as a kind of baggage trophy – and after whose wife it had secretly been named – knew how it worked.

Lance wanted to get the typing girls up one at a time and pretend it was a lie-detector. Geoffrey demurred, uncomfortably. 'Don't be daft,' he said. 'No one would fall for that.'

'I don't know,' Lance gave a masculine wink. 'You'd be surprised at some of those girls.'

Two technicians appeared, puffing heavily up the stairway and carrying between them a large steel cabinet.

They placed it down beside the MAC and then stood up to draw breath.

'What's that when it's at home?' Lance enquired.

'Telephonic,' said one of the men, turning round abruptly.

'Eh?'

'Paper-tape reader? I dunno,' said the other. 'GPO coming to wire it in. Don't suppose they'll turn up. Do you?'

They all laughed. Then, later, Millicent remembered the sputter-coater, a device for wrapping non-conductive specimens in a layer of heavy metal, infinitesimally thin. Like so many of the new fitments, it had hardly been used. That same afternoon, they plucked and gold-plated one of her eyelashes, and afterwards, brash and young, they searched for what else to embellish. Their maturer colleagues were tolerant, or pretended not to notice. Only Terry, the head technician, voiced his disapproval. 'I suppose you gentlemen realise how much that will have cost the department. And lady.'

Lance, his face piously straight, held up the crane-fly he'd found in the men's washroom, its legs, body and wings now delicately gilded, against the gossamer wires of a spider's web. 'Sorry, Terry. Won't happen again.'

Cynthia said she should visit her family again at the weekend. Geoffrey offered to take her. She forbade him, but returned on the Sunday as before. Now with skies open, the world itself was sputter-coated, first in silver, then, from the constant low sunlight, in purest gold. Brief days were jewels against a Virgin's lapis cloak; the country at large became prankish, sainted. Two nights after full moon the incoming tide washed over the shallows of Pegwell Bay in Kent and never retreated, its briny wavelets recorded in ice. An outdoor poet was found at Windsor, stiff and enshrined in one solid block, even as a Staffordshire duck sprang alive and flapping from another. Huge icicles like the stalactites of centuries hung from the most unlikely corners, pipes on the sides of countless houses split nebular gashes, and diesel froze in the tanks of lorries, as reportedly it had during the German advance on Moscow. More power strikes were threatened. Eminent scientists in the papers predicted global cooling and a new glaciation.

Lance saw his chance when Lidlock's heating failed soon after everyone arrived. 'Frozen sea!' he cried. 'Round England! A once-in-a-lifetime attraction! Who's coming? Too cold to hang about. Or go home either. I know for a fact Rose won't want me under her feet with the nippers. For God's sake, why can't the English ever just live a bit!'

Why not, indeed? It was too tempting, too impromptu to miss. He went to spread the word: anyone game for the jaunt was to meet in the car park. Minutes later, Geoffrey stood beside one of the builders' vans with his supervisor, Dr Gill, immaculate in grey overcoat and polished black shoes. Raj had a shrewd, delicate face behind his thick-rimmed spectacles. Geoffrey noticed the hints of grey in his shiny black hair.

Some circuit designers were assembling not far off, and a knot of clerks from the office. Contingents appeared from the clean rooms, from the drawing office, from the shop floor. The event had snowballed – the whole factory, so used to hothousing, was in holiday mood. Then Lance returned with four of the typing girls, Cynthia among them. 'Right,' he called to the assembled company. 'How many cars do we need?' He shepherded Millie and two others into his Hillman Hunter. Geoffrey opened his car door but found himself giving a lift only to Raj and a bookkeeper called Dave. He saw Cynthia get into someone's green Morris Oxford. Moments later, the hastily assembled convoy nosed off towards the coast.

IT WAS A CRAZY scheme, childish and impetuous – and so they were all excited. The sea was too far away for English roads. Lance still hadn't told them where they were going. Second in the long line, Geoffrey followed his friend as they sped off towards Hertford on salt-spangled tarmac. With few lorries about, they made good time. Past Bishop's Stortford, they found themselves heading due east under the clear morning sun.

'It's quite a mystery tour,' Raj said. 'I thought we might be going to Brighton. Which way does this lead?'

Without deviation, the route struck straight across country. 'Must be a Roman road,' said Geoffrey.

'Stane Street,' said Dave, the bookkeeper from the back seat, who knew.

'Ah, yes,' Raj mused. 'Part of an empire.'

'Oh, lighten up, Raj,' said Geoffrey.

'Now part of the American empire.'

'No, we're not.' He spoke freely to his boss, only a little shocked at himself. 'Now you're being ridiculous.'

But Raj joined in the spirit of things. 'Better dead than Red. Isn't that what we're all working for?'

A while later, they slowed to a crawl. Some lumbering tanker was causing a queue, and Geoffrey fixed his eyes on Lance's chrome bumper in front of him. His foot began to ache on the accelerator; there was a cold pool around the pedals which the air from the heater never reached. He thought of the Roman military engineers, doggedly imposing their will upon mile after mile of a wooded, tribal scene, and took heart. Rae would have approved. Rae lived and breathed control, as long – Geoffrey heard that roguish laugh – as he was in it!

Past Great Dunmow, snowscapes spread out to either side, and the chalk hills gave way to East Anglian clay, with its gradually flattening roll, wide skies, and concentration of Yankee air bases. They'd come fifty miles without a break, and it was suddenly so good to get away. Geoffrey hadn't realised. At last he felt buoyed and could see things less claustrophobically, less mechanically. His luck only wanted fresh fields. Cynthia was right, they needed time – perhaps just a day to get clear of Louisa's presence *in absentia*. How could he possibly relax with the memory of her disapproval all around him? 'So where does this end up, Dave? This Stane Street?' he said.

'Colchester,' said Dave. 'Camulodunum, the old capital. Tribal centre of the British,' he mumbled, tonelessly.

Sure enough, after the traffic of Braintree and another long straight drive, when Geoffrey's legs were stiff and

his arms weary from gluing the whining little Mini to
Lance's wake, the signs of a more substantial town
appeared on the horizon. He was getting tired and caught
himself day-dreaming, but the romanticised image of an
iced and fortified hilltop grew in his mind and made him
glad, as though his spot of bother really were only temporary. He sensed he was coming to an end, as one who
trudges through unremitting winter terrain and at last
sees walls and towers – like a piece he'd once heard
Astraea play, with shimmering chords and repeated
arpeggios. In fact the prospect was so beautiful to his
imagination, almost a white pavilion, that he found
himself pinning his hopes to it, the sacred city, even the
mystical Camelot its name implied. They *would* be
married; it would all work out, because in many ways
they were the perfect couple.

'Geoff?' It was Raj.

He jinked the wheel. 'Sorry.'

Lance signalled on a crossing and pulled into a big lorry
stop by a garage. 'Thought we could all do with a break!'
he shouted from his open car door.

'You can say that again.'

Cynthia caught Geoffrey's eye in the queue at the
counter. When he sat down, she came and stood beside
him for a moment.

'All right?' he whispered.

'Yeah,' she said.

'You're a bit pale.'

'Am I? The drive, I expect.' A sign of strain had appeared
in her eyes.

He met them and touched her hand. 'Me too. Drifting off.'

She smiled and glanced about her. 'Could be a bike caff, Geoff,' she said out loud. 'What do you think?'

'I wouldn't know,' he laughed.

She went on, 'Such a good straight. And where do you think we're going?'

'Don't know,' he said. He stood up beside her and felt his body suddenly stir at her closeness.

'Clacton, of course.' Lance was passing, cup of tea in hand. 'Fun for all the family.' Geoffrey almost kissed both of them there and then. Cynthia was beaming at him.

They drove on again in traffic, through busy unremarkable streets with modern shops and traffic lights. They dropped down a steeply undistinguished hill and passed into the plain below. But when Geoffrey turned his head to snatch a glance behind, Colchester was indeed the perfect town on its hill of ice, appearing as if to order; and now the last twenty miles of the journey passed quicker than thought, filled only with the prospect of their new life together.

On Clacton front, the long tail of cars arrived in a rush. Doors slammed. Geoffrey climbed from his Mini into the biting air and they were all a crowd, hurrying across the wide boulevards and salty lawns to a municipal grandeur faded and winter-tinged. A municipal sea lay at the foot of the promenade. But it was quite true, the brine had started to freeze. He shared the amazement at the long straight beach, where stalled waves left great broken slabs, then heaped up more behind. It was nigh on a

miracle. A flat calm lapped some Arctic intention further
out. Sociable Lance, pipe alight, linked arms on the pier
with Millie, and someone called Babs, and someone called
Pat.

Cynthia and a gang of girls from accounts were already
following, and Geoffrey took a step or two after them.
Two skaters were passing and re-passing on the roller-rink,
flooded and frozen; the deserted fairground beyond was
surreal, its gaudy yellows just white-clad against the crisp,
maritime horizon. Somehow, it all bespoke her strange
allure. But before he could catch her up, he found Raj
beside him.

'Fortuitous, Geoff.'

'I'm sorry?'

'A chance to get out. Usually tripping over plasterers,
aren't we, minding electricians, rubbing shoulders with
other departments. All trying to bustle along. So much
rush to get everything up and running, isn't it. And then,
at the work itself . . . Well, I wanted to apologise. I confess
I've left you to it. The pressure of things, you understand.'
He spread his neatly gloved hands. 'People expect so much.
But now, Geoff, a chance to talk – away from it all, so to
speak.'

'Yes.'

'And you've not been looking quite yourself, lately. If
I may say so.'

'Haven't I?'

'Nothing the matter, is there? If there's anything I
can . . . ?'

'No.' Geoffrey breathed out through his nose and the

grey vapour rose up. 'Nothing at all. Things are fine. Couldn't be better.' He smiled.

RAJ PAUSED AT the side rail. He looked out over the immobilised sea. 'A chance to talk,' he said. 'Yes. Strange to have to travel a hundred miles to get it. Far enough, I hope. Far from prying eyes and ears. Only, it *is* a matter of some urgency. I mean what we're engaged upon, Geoff. And I welcome the chance to make sure you understand, away from all that. Do you? Understand, I mean?'

'About the work? Well, yes, I suppose . . .'

'About the work. Exactly. About the Americans, Geoff. There are one or two things you need to know. Or that I need to know you know.' Raj laughed, pleased with himself. 'Of course we're hand in glove all the way. But . . . How should I say this? Our friends aren't always inclined to share with us all that we share with them. Can you imagine that sort of relationship? Yes?'

Before Geoffrey could answer, Raj pre-empted him again, 'It's not always easy for me to speak to you like . . . a *boss*.' He was smiling under the horn rims of his glasses. 'I'm sure you understand that. You're bright. And you're . . . English.'

'Oh, come on Raj, there's nothing like that about it. You surely don't think . . .'

'You boys!' Raj was suddenly dismissive. 'Can you imagine a world in which Britain doesn't come up trumps? Plucky little Britain. This sceptred isle.'

Geoffrey hesitated, unnerved at having certain of his thoughts read, sensing he'd somehow offended.

'No.' His companion softened slightly. 'I'm not cross with you. But this business of the chips. It gives them an edge. Such an edge.' He whistled abruptly through his teeth. 'Have you really considered what all this might lead to? Exactly?'

'Well, yes, I . . .'

'Have you actually grasped what's at stake?' Raj caught his arm.

'I'm sorry,' Geoffrey said.

'For what?'

'I thought . . . I don't know . . .' He edged away. All he wanted to think about was Cynthia, while his boss kept pecking at his mind in that singsong prattle of his accent – like an insistent bird.

'While all else collapses,' Raj was saying. 'The nuclear thing, the aircraft thing, the shipbuilding thing.' He made gestures. 'And you know, of course, who already make the petrol engines of the future?' He demonstrated again.

It took Geoffrey seconds to unravel the question. 'What? Those little mopeds?'

'Exactly. The Japanese. Do you understand, Geoff? At all? And now these chips – we'll lose that race as well, before we ever knew we were in it. The British have designed and built the first computers in the world. Now you sit back and admire them. You . . . *we* squander every advantage with our pomposity and complacency.' He smiled again at last. 'And sporting decency and boyish amateurism, of course. But it is a race, Geoff. For survival, I think.'

'With the Russians, surely.'

Raj snorted. 'Hardly.'

'What?'

'Well, yes and no. But these damn things they've made . . .'

'The Russians? You mean the space shots.'

'The Americans, Geoffrey. The chips! My dear chap, get *with it* – if I may say! The chips!'

'Sorry. I'm sorry, Raj. I'm . . . I suppose I might have taken my eye off the ball a bit lately.'

'Not at all. You're young. You're relatively new. How could you be expected to see everything at once?' Now Raj chuckled and strode ahead. Geoffrey could have wished he weren't so touchy, quite so . . . foreign. He scanned for Cynthia while he kept up. He and his chief walked together, beside the skaters. A pair of herring gulls swooped past the edge of the pier, crying and skimming low along the deadlocked breakers.

'We've kept an eye on you, Geoffrey.'

'Oh?'

'Don't worry. You've done well. *We*'ve done well, you and I. There's even a chance . . . ,' his companion looked modestly down, 'that a very limited and temporary advantage may accrue directly. In the race.' He faced back squarely to Geoffrey. 'Temporary. And very limited. You must understand that. *If* the politicians don't manage to blow the whole damn world up in the next few months. A big if, that one, of course! And as this particular project began as an all-American baby, you can bet your boots they'll pour every damned thing into it except milk. Of course they will.' The chuckle played around his precise lips again. 'Nevertheless, we may soon open what the military call a window of opportunity. As soon as tomorrow, even, if they get the damned heating mended.'

Raj looked about him, a little melodramatically Geoffrey thought. There was no one near them on the broad planking of the pier. 'With our latest batch, let's say I'm very encouraged, Geoff. Imagine it! The vertical dimension as well as the horizontal, all in the one chip. Buried layers, like a cake. Successive deposition with connections and isolations! Are we the first? If we are, Geoff, *if* we can pat ourselves on the back, there may still be an opportunity to secure a British foothold in the new industrial order. Sooner rather than later. We shall see tomorrow. You and I.' He was excited, like a child.

'That's excellent news, Raj. Congratulations. But you said "a foothold"? It's not as though . . .' Geoffrey felt his eyes widen. The cold off the frozen sea was intense.

'I know. You imagine I'm over-egging. That's the phrase, isn't it? Wog nonsense. No, Geoffrey, it's all right.' He laid a hand on his arm again. 'But America, West Germany are thinking twenty years ahead. The Japs think thirty. Only you . . . us,' he smiled again. 'Only *we* rest on our laurels, our native wit, our gentlemanly genius. I'm telling you, my friend, if we let this chance go, too, then in thirty years' time British industry and whatever's left of that British pre-eminence we both still desperately want to believe in will be . . . ,' Raj held his nose and made the gesture of pulling a chain, 'down the pan, old chap.

Gone, all that . . . damned pomp and circumstance. Quite
gone.'

GEOFFREY REGARDED HIS boss, normally so self-effacing.
He doubted he'd ever really had so long a conversation
with him. They walked on to the tip of the pier. An oily
calm below them heaved with slight undulations.

'Yes, Geoff, we've had an eye on you. Now you keep
all that under your hat. Understand? And another matter.
Very hush-hush. Very, very significant.' Again, he looked
to either side of the bare world. 'These things, if they can
be made small enough . . .'

'The chips? Or the computers?'

Raj clapped his gloved hands. 'The one follows from
the other. And cheap enough? What are they? Silica. Grains
of sand. Numberless as souls.' Raj pointed under the
decking they stood on. 'Cheap as . . . dirt. At the NPL at
Bushy Park. Computers linked up,' suddenly speaking
very quickly, too fast to follow, 'communicating with one
another, Lidlock, Turing, so that the existence, the being
if you like, isn't vulnerable, central, Northwood,
Whitehall, but distributed, in the event of an attack.
Nuclear. Capable of reassembly. The Post Office know all
about it – telephones and all that. Inconsequential little
places like ours scattered here and there, but connected by
a . . . a network. There. Did you understand any of that?'

Geoffrey felt himself blush.

'Of course you didn't. That's the point, my dear chap.'

Raj cackled, delighted at his stratagem. In fact he could hardly stop laughing for a while. Then he began again, speaking lucidly this time, but almost as quickly. 'The message is broken up, Geoff. Click! Message switching. Packet switching, if you will – split into little packets. As opposed to circuit switching.'

'Are you meaning some sort of new machine code? I don't . . .'

'Forget the code. Assume Algol, Cobol, whatever language you like. I'm talking beyond all that. It's a technique, a British technique. The Lidlock factory was first converted to try to cash in on the American advance. Small pioneering companies securing patents – that's how *they* do it. As I told you, we're just about keeping pace. But this other, it is perhaps our only continuing, momentary, lead – set aside what you and I are doing – by which computing machines in a distributed network could soak up the slack in talking to each other. Can you imagine? No, you can't, yet. It offers – possibly – an industrial future, possibly *the* industrial future, to the first country to develop such a technology.'

'It's like the pictures. Mind control, little green men, worlds to come.'

'What it is, I suggest . . . ,' Raj paused for dramatic effect, 'is make or break, Geoffrey. And until the one or the other, until we establish some leverage in this, or squander it as we've squandered every other advantage since the war, then both it and the attempt that's already in place will *and must* remain very secret. Do you understand? The more progress we make the more it becomes incumbent . . .'

'Of course. Of course, Raj. Of course,' Geoffrey stammered.

'Because once the leverage is obtained – by whomever – then it becomes normal scientific property, published and shared in the normal way of course. But until then . . . ,' Raj tapped his head, 'keep it under your hat and work like . . . a black.' He held Geoffrey's eye.

'I'm still not sure I really understand just what it is I'm supposed to keep under it.'

'Good. Very hush-hush. Turing was the man. Now there are people at Bushy Park. My own little project . . . ,' once again Raj looked modestly down, 'tomorrow, even, and we might just steal our little march on them, you and I.' Raj grinned and nudged him. 'The Yanks. Of course, they too are working on . . . networks.' He breathed the word. 'A distributed system. Military at the moment; but can you imagine the commercial, the *political* possibilities? Can you *imagine* that, Geoffrey? You've seen the new paper-reader next to Dr Butterfield's office? Our own code-name: Schrödinger, would you believe? We're getting a KDF9 delivered in April. You know what a KDF9 is?'

At that moment Geoffrey saw Cynthia. She was coming towards them. 'Hello, Geoff,' she said.

Geoffrey turned to Raj. 'Miss Somers, from typing.'

'Pleased to meet you,' she said.

'Enchanted,' said Raj.

'My . . . boss, Dr Gill.'

'I know.' There were calls from the promenade. 'Oh,' she said. 'There's Babs, and Pat. We're going to get some chips.'

There was a moment's silence. Then they all laughed. Geoffrey looked over at the other typists, arm in arm, headscarves framing their smiling faces, the one called Babs wobbling slightly on her high heels.

'Coming?' said Cynthia.

'Maybe later, I think.'

'OK. See you, then.' She walked off to join her friends.

They couldn't stay long, the whole trip such a mischievous gesture, and he had no opportunity at Clacton to speak to her again. He drove with his passengers back along the Roman road, talking of the trip and the stunned grey sea. The sun took an age to set.

'People call her Boadicea,' Dave was explaining from the back seat in his peculiarly flat tone, 'but her actual name was Boudicca. She gave them Romans something to think about. They raped her daughters, see,' Dave said. 'Right in front of her. Over the body of her husband. If it happened today, we'd all have to decide what side we were on.' He laughed. 'Bosses or workers. The locals came right along here to St Albans, then did all kinds to the women they found there. Bit like the Indian Mutiny, really.' Dave went quiet, Geoffrey hoped with embarrassment.

He drove on in silence. Raj had mentioned Turing. It nagged him, at the wheel – the one name he hadn't recognised on Lionel's papers. No slouch, he'd guessed 'M switching' immediately: message switching. That gave 'C.S.' as circuit switching, didn't it? *C.S. amenable to voltage.* But wouldn't any design depend on the voltage across it? And there was something else Raj had said that he'd forgotten. It was starting to bother him, but he couldn't quite get his head around it, what with Cynth, and the sun constantly in his eyes over the blinding fields. Something was the matter. Something was very much the matter.

The car park at Lidlock seemed an unfamiliar corral beside the empty factory. Lance was already there, standing in the dark with Millie. The others arrived; their day out unravelled. Dave wandered off, Raj offered petrol money. When Geoffrey started the car again, he saw through the windscreen Cynthia with Babs, was it, or Pat. Then Cynthia's blue coat, washed colourless by sodium light, was leaving the other girls at the factory gate and turning right in the direction of the bus-stop.

He waited until all the day-trippers had dispersed, and the drivers of the convoy had gone. He watched Raj Gill wave as he wobbled his bicycle off towards the station. Only then did he allow himself to edge forward through the gates and pull out into the street.

He stopped beside the kerb. Now *he* was being melo-dramatic, on the very edge of his new life. It was out there in the future, that glistening construction, that romantic pavilion, elaborately white and final. It could hold him and Cynthia together. He could see her, far down the pave-ment, an anonymous figure under an anonymous lamp.

He engaged the gear again and began to creep forward. She stopped, turned to look back. She must have seen the car, coasting beside the pavement just outside the Lidlock car park, but she made no sign. Instead, she continued on her way. His feet seemed paralysed, too heavy to work the pedals, and the car drifted to a halt. He watched her to the end of the street, watched her until the ugly yellow darkness swallowed her. Beyond and to the left, the silhouette of the abbey tower was visible. Louisa had played once in a concert there. He thought of the martyr and the great Norman edifice rising over the blood and the stones ripped up, ever higher, more massive. He wondered how it would have felt here in Raj's other empire, centuries before that, waiting for an army of Daves to arrive from Colchester?

How cold he was, his legs cramped from the drive, and every quarter of his being invaded by a wilful frostiness. But he didn't wish for a thaw. He was at home with the cold at last, with chips of ice and rock; he wanted the snow to continue. It was shimmers of ice she brought to him, that he saw about her, that he brought to her. He had no family to welcome her into, no stories, only his cold self.

And that disappearing figure, picked out by his chemical imagination and still ahead of him somewhere, was *offering*, for heaven's sake, what Louisa had always grudged. Because she loved him, she said. Why, then, did his body refuse? Now the darkness was tentacled, icy, lapping around the streets and at the walls of the abbey like some malignity of perpetual winter. He had his own peculiarly morbid idea: that it was his death he was wrapping her in.

He let in the clutch. The car nosed forward and gathered pace. The road curved along beside the old houses, skirting the old town, and he came to the Verulam Road as he'd done that first time in the snow.

The bus was just turning down in front of him into Bluehouse Lane. He waited. He waited a fraction longer for it to stop. A car he hadn't seen in his mirror hooted, and he got going just in time to pick her up. But when they reached home and he'd set the fire going, he immediately made excuses to go out again.

IT WAS A MUNDANE ecstasy, a contrary elation, driving without her under a clear night sky; he could almost hear the temperature falling. In Astraea's house the lights were on – visible through the trees as he wound his way steeply down, plunging between the dark hedges on the other side of the ridge. Once or twice, his wheels skidded on the packed snow in the narrow, twisting lane. Her driveway was no more than a tunnel through the high boughs. He parked. There was no sign of Ben's Rover. He got out and stood for a moment under the stars, complete, brilliant, maintaining their arrangements out of the cloudless black.

Astraea answered the door in her old-fashioned jodhpurs and another jumble-sale jumper. Her long straight hair, sharp in the light behind her, was parted like curtains. It showed her eyes and her smile. 'Geoff?'

'I was passing,' he said. 'Just wondered if there was any news of Louie.'

'Nothing special, I'm afraid. Come in.'

'Only, our phone . . . We're still waiting. *I'm* still waiting.' He hesitated at the doorstep. 'Though I should count my blessings . . .'

'Please *do* come on in, Geoff.' She scolded him and led the way inside. Because these things happened, didn't they. There was no sense being juvenile about it, for heaven's sake – and she could be friends with both him *and* Louisa, couldn't she? And Ben, of course.

They sat together a little stiffly by the fire in her sitting room. Geoffrey thought of the last he'd seen of Ben, that day he'd brought the cello and got drunk; and of the spark that had passed between him and Astraea when he was leaving. He told her about the Clacton visit, the frozen sea.

It felt good with her, like a pressure lifted off. He wanted to talk. He liked describing the stubby pier to her, with its ridiculous funfair, the extraordinary grey icicles the waves had spattered on to the rusted stanchions. It *had* been extraordinary, yet slightly tawdry, like all seaside things – he laughed, for he'd never really been much of a talker, certainly not to women. He told Astraea about Millie and Lance's antics with the sputter-coater, and that made her laugh in turn.

She offered him a hot drink. When she returned with the cups, he spoke of childhood summers on the estate at Waddesdon; how he'd keep pace behind his father through the thickets and coveys, with always one eye on the leather of his gaiters or the barrel of his gun poking down, a dull steel from the crook of the man's arm. He told her how he'd used to run to the pig shed to stand next to the pig man and see the sows farrow down, and the piglets coming out, each in its own transparent sac – individually wrapped. That made her laugh again. It was nice to have company. Ben was abroad, as usual. In Berlin, actually, though she wasn't sure she was supposed to say so.

Geoffrey let himself chatter on: how his dad would go to get sacks from the grain store and the dog would chew the sparrows stealing corn one by one as they fluttered against the bottom window. One crunch, and they were goners. That made her cover her ears. He could describe the manor house, but of the cottage where they lived, he could remember little. Except, he said, waking up and seeing the snow one morning, covering everything. How strange it was that just a few weeks ago, on looking out of Cowper Road the first morning after the blizzard, and before Louie left, he'd recalled that scene again. It had been just a memory, he said, loaded neither with pleasure nor with pain. And he wanted to tell her everything and cry in her arms, but he couldn't. He was cold to the marrow, with no recollection of what warmth might be. For Louisa, or for his parents, he felt not a jot, nor ever really had. He knew it. They were right about him: it was his own fault and the world was deadlocked on a four-minute warning, had always been and would always remain so – because all his mind had tried to do was latch on to a girl who disappeared in darkness.

'It's all right, Geoff.' She laid a hand on his shoulder. 'She'll come right, I expect. Louie. Give her time. She probably just needed to get away for a while. She'll come back.'

He looked up. 'Yeah,' he said.

The bedroom was eerily gold that night in Geoffrey's dream, and there were sputter-coated wings and he was driving Alan's motorbike along Stane Street with Cynth up behind him. He knew it was Alan's bike. He knew he shared something intangible with the boy. He could feel Cynth's arms around him, and her body pulled close, hear her crying out. She was in pain; something electrical was hurting her, terribly. Up ahead of him he saw Colchester rising out of the plain, a white horror he'd never understand, never, until the Cold War ended.

He woke, shivering, and aroused, and now it was Astraea's body his imagination lingered over, like an island of gratification. He could hear Cynthia breathing beside him; such an irony that while she slept he had the capacity. But it would be the act of a beast simply to wake her for sex. He risked switching on the lamp. She stirred and turned over. Now even fickle desire ebbed, and with it every shred of the day's lightheadedness, as though he were there alone; and he remembered the feeling of panic that had gripped him when he'd first seen the names on Rae's notes and the phone numbers beside them.

They were still there in the pocket of his sports jacket. It was the coat he pulled on for work every morning and otherwise left unheeded as his own skin. In the lamp's glow, he swung himself carefully out of bed, unfolded the papers and looked at them once again. He really liked Rae. He missed him at the lab. Surely the notes were just the random jottings of his trade. Message switching, circuit switching – Lionel was a top-level designer, after all.

It was then he remembered the missing detail Raj had

told him on the pier: *Schrödinger*. It was the rather fanciful code-name of their own projected terminal, the reason for the new punched-tape reader being installed. Lionel's list of great theoreticians suddenly made sense. What could *Planck*, *Bohr*, *Einstein* and *Turing* be but the *other* nodes: Northwood, Whitehall and so on. His breath was tight in his chest. Underneath the names must be the GPO exchange numbers the computers would dial to. Which meant Lionel had been in on the whole secret since before Christmas – a secret Raj Gill had only conveyed to Geoffrey with extreme hesitancy, in that weird and roundabout way. He felt real dread again. It was a surprise, at the very least, to find Lionel quite so . . . well-briefed. For all his status as a former weapons engineer, a definite whiff of espionage hung, and Geoffrey's duty was clear, surely. But it was almost as though espionage were code itself – for something worse; as though he were already implicated, as though the touch of the papers might suck him into a spun darkness from which it would be impossible ever to escape. He forced the thoughts down. He needn't do anything. Not yet. Not just now. He couldn't.

He went to the window and drew the curtains back a fraction. The glass was completely opaque with condensation – from the paraffin stove he lit every evening to make the room bearable, and from his own breath. He touched one drop; it ran down. A lower one stayed still, frozen already to the inside of the pane. He turned the lamp off and then came back to stare, rubbing the glass clear. There was just the street outside with the eternal white of the roofs and the glimmer of moonlight on the enduring snow.

THE COLDEST WINTER since 1740, they said, though two months below freezing over southern England hardly spelled the end of the world. But Geoffrey spent the rest of that night beside Cynthia in anxieties and inexplicable nightmares, and he turned up at the lab in the morning badly rattled, to find the boilers at Lidlock fixed, with the womb-like ambience of the laboratory reassembled. Lance was making notes at his corner of the bench, Millie was in conversation with Dr Gaines about some photographic plates. And the designers – Bill Hollingworth and the others, some in white coats, most just in tweed jackets – were busy with their routine tasks.

Geoffrey went straight down to the clean room to put on his spacesuit for the day of Raj's tests. With an increasing sense of foreboding, he passed through the airlocks. In the presence of the probe, he felt the breath being sucked from his belly, and almost gagged at the waxy electrical smell from the filters meant to sanitise it.

He'd achieved his heart's desire, and he was at the culmination of his work with Raj. His star should have been at its zenith. Instead, everything normal and familiar kept slipping away, accelerating into a void. He thought of the furthest galaxies and of the micro-matter he studied, both hurrying towards some absolute zero of the soul. The costly new instrument reared up in the cramped cabin; its dark notes buzzed in his helmet, unusually insistent, unexpectedly hostile.

Sudden light cast his little workstation in an odd relief. He looked up. A sci-fi figure was at the soft door of the oxidation room. Raj hovered where there was no room to move. He carried a tray. It contained his mounted, sterile wafers ready to go into the specimen chamber. 'A good day yesterday, Geoff.' His voice was muffled by his visor. The door flapped shut behind him. 'We should do it more often.' There was a pause. 'Geoff? Are you all right? Are you ready to start?'

'Sure.' Geoffrey's own voice came out at last, echoing in the helmet. 'Fine. Didn't sleep too well. That's all.'

'All that driving, I don't doubt. For which, much thanks, by the way. Not coming down with something, are you? Sure you're OK to carry on?'

Geoffrey nodded his headpiece.

'Only, it's as I told you.' Raj's visor was angled so that Geoffrey couldn't see into it. 'I was in with Butterfield first thing. Damned man thinks folds and buried layers are too unreliable at this level. A step too far. A shade too clever, more likely. Just because he doesn't understand the process, he doesn't believe in it. So either this shot does the trick or we're back to . . . square one.' Raj spread his unearthly, latex-clad hands. 'And then who can say what will happen?' The remarks hung in the clean air. 'In our court, eh, Geoff? Let's get going, then,' he cleared his throat, 'as our friends across the water say.'

Geoffrey stared. Raj's soft visor reflected red glows and illuminated dials from the probe. For a second, he didn't know where he was. But then this *was* science fiction, nigh on, and he should be used to odd effects. Crystalline layers, formed in their alien world by the alien machines next door – gas-dopers, photo-electric micro-engravers – were undergoing treatments invisible to the eye, undetectable by any human sense. These were the treatments on which so much now seemed to depend.

Impurity was the key. He tried to concentrate. p- and n-type taints, laid down at infinitesimal remoteness and then trenched through: they might just hold enough structure in the substrate – and hence enough logic – to give the behaviour of electrons shape. It was an alleged behaviour, of course. Everything was, down at this level. He imagined them, electrons, streaming in the ether, golden probabilities. They might not even exist. Assuming they did, they could behave in irrational ways, both in semiconductor circuits and in the microscope itself – in which the whole point of using them was that they were already finer and smaller, whatever that meant, than the identities of light, whatever they were. There was even an effect known as tunnelling by which the electrons appeared to 'get under the skin' of what was being observed. Perhaps.

He steadied himself. It was simply his business to secure Raj a yes or a no. But he was so tired. And before the probe could operate at all, an extreme vacuum was needed. Hence the fortified tube at the heart of all these humming units, the power supplies, the magnetic lens casings, the extraction vents – like some deep organ pipe snatched from the age of faith, de-sanctified and equipped for blast-off. The coercion of angels . . . He jerked his attention back once again. His hands were shaking. He took a deep breath.

'Geoff?'

His throat was dry. 'Never better.' Gloved, sanctioned, the pure scientist, he stood up to position Raj's first sample in the vacuum lock at the focus of the inner beam. But his fingers took an age, his head ached, the blood pounded in his ears, the buzzing hum of the machine . . . He could feel Raj's disquiet. It was Raj next to him but he thought he heard Lionel's voice, ironic, insistent. Surely it was Lionel. He hadn't noticed him come in. 'All previous systems, all pointless theological speculations . . .' Was he glad or shocked at Rae's return? 'It's only this gets results, Geoff. Gets measurable results. We need this, Geoff. A result.' He swung round abruptly in his chair. 'Steady on, Geoff.' The soft words were Raj's. A white-gloved hand touched his arm. 'Easy does it.' He wasn't thinking straight.

He managed to seal the chamber. Straight away, the diffusion pumps began removing whatever air had been admitted, and he sat down in his swivel chair to wait. There was brief light again as he turned to speak to Raj, sudden fear when he saw the retreating figure. 'Back in a minute, Geoff.'

He began his notes. The special pen skidded in his gloves. He found his thoughts wrenched from every known fact, every safe and functional outline, with that same sickening pull – like a weird gravity. It was for his ability to identify with the machine that he'd been hired. The imaginative facility he'd demonstrated as a student had got him noticed over researchers with higher qualifications and more experience. But now he, like the microscope, was being pumped out, as though he'd already left the earth and was looking down, seemingly possessed by that same imagination; while something spinning, like flying saucers, something banished from the reasonable world of his homely planet, was contriving to leak in.

He leaned forward. He touched the steel tube. Once, the previous summer, they'd been driving home, and Rae had been at the wheel. Unprompted, Lionel himself had owned up to a weakness for space stories – not the lurid popular market, of course, but the theoretical stuff. It was his only vice, he confessed: found only in one American magazine. He called it his 'drug', the steely projection of pure scientific ideas. And actually, Geoff, he'd an idea for a tale of his own; one day he'd get around to writing it, and sending it off.

Geoffrey would have laughed politely, but Rae had grown serious. Unprompted, he'd launched there and then upon the plot: some sealed object found floating in the cold of space, a lonely asteroid bearing unmistakable signs of intelligence at work. The hero's fate was to penetrate it, said Lionel, then decode it. What would be found there? 'That's just it, Geoff – what *is* it?' Rae had laughed suddenly, bitterly. 'Now I've given it away,' he'd said. 'Now you'd better keep quiet about it or someone will steal my big idea.'

It was nothing, nonsense, the harvest of exhaustion. One bad night . . . He squinted up at the vacuum gauges. The needles were reaching the critical level. Geoffrey's pen hovered.

Raj ballooned back in, his encumbered figure infinitely strange. 'How're we doing?'

Geoffrey looked at his gauges. 'Low enough. Let's make a start.' He just needed to get back on his feet, get the situation sorted out, get back to normal. He switched the high tension on and began attending to the current in the lenses.

'HERE WE GO, Raj. Prepare for lift-off. Isn't that what you have to say?' He controlled his voice.

'Oh, yes. Stand by. Fasten safety belts.' Raj paused. 'You're actually not well, are you?'

'It's nothing.'

'If you're sure.'

'Quite sure. Thanks.'

Raj took the copilot's chair, and switched on the monitors that imaged the scan. Geoffrey held his breath, and tried his damnedest to judge what would be going on inside the tube. But he could hardly move his limbs. He felt squeezed from above and below, secretly gasping for air. The beam was tightened in by the condenser coils. Stronger windings were in place to concentrate it on the surface of the specimen. Electromagnetic deflectors created the scanning effect, flicking the focus back and forth faster than thought, driving it neatly down a page far smaller than microdots, gospels on postage stamps, or any fanciful miniaturisation. The initial routines made him calmer at last. He just had to keep everything on course, in order to interrogate a stream of high-energy electrons in mid-flow. Built into the vacuum tube were offset detector plates. The reflected scatter would be picked up, amplified and sent back to the monitor. Tamer electrons in an ordinary cathode-ray tube could be made to display it – a reflection of a reflection of a reflection.

An image of sorts began to appear on the screen. It was hazy and indistinct, a pale monochrome fizz with one or two darker patches. He altered voltages sequentially, tuning the energy to a point. It was what he'd been schooled for, and soon there was an identity in a lower corner. He homed in on it, checking this lens, justifying that.

'There!' Raj said, pointing.

Geoffrey edged the scanned area across the surface of the specimen. It was clearly the prototype circuit: there showed the angles of deliberate engineering, and there was the trench cut through.

'Like the damn canals on Mars,' said Raj, his voice more jubilant and emotional than Geoffrey had ever known it. 'Ha! Didn't I tell you? What level are we looking at?'

Geoffrey worked his slide-rule for a moment, then jotted a calculation. He spaced his fingers against the screen. 'Say five microns.'

Raj whispered excitedly, 'That's good. That's very good. That's smaller than anything the Americans have achieved.'

'How do we know that?'

Raj turned his headpiece towards him. 'Just take it from me.'

'If the pathways are clean . . . ,' Geoffrey said.

'If the pathways are clean, we're ahead of the field. We need to go in closer.'

Geoffrey took them down further still. Difficult minutes passed while he readjusted the control values. Raj was on edge, fidgeting in his chair, but at greater magnification the etched layers showed ominous marks and scuffs. Another few seconds and dark recurrent landslips loooked unmistakable in the terracing, along what should have been distinct boundaries. There were little crystal rods like fallen trees.

'Damn and dammit!' Raj breathed out through his teeth. 'I can't . . . I won't believe it.'

Geoffrey chewed his lip. The more laboriously they trawled, swooping low over the silicon micro-surface, the more final the conclusion seemed to be. The one clear thing was the breakdown of a print technology seemingly stretched beyond itself. Butterfield, it appeared, had been right.

'I'm sorry, Raj,' Geoffrey said.

'Yes,' said Raj. 'Well, well. I'm bloody sorry too. Never mind. Let's try another.'

They went through the whole process again with another sliver, and another, and one more. Geoffrey tried to tell himself it was the familiar drudgery of research. He said to Raj a hit first time would have been against all the odds, and that they were pretty much out on a limb in any case. They broke for lunch and then began once more. But as the day wore on and the failures mounted up, Geoffrey knew almost beyond a doubt that something fundamental hadn't worked, and most likely the silicon simply would never accept such an artificial geology. He could feel Raj flagging beside him, his boss's massive disappointment virtually palpable.

Paradoxically, he himself felt a growing relief. Bizarrely, he found he was almost gladdened by the failure, almost amused. In fact, by the end of the afternoon, it was Raj who seemed the nervy, unstable one. 'The truth is we're playing at it,' he said, wretchedly. 'We just haven't got the resources, as usual. The government want rabbits pulled out of hats without being prepared to make the investment. So, back to the bloody drawing board. Except I'm beginning to doubt there's much else we can do. Oh, bloody hell!' He stamped his foot. 'Well then, Geoff, prepare for a world the shape of Texas. That's it. That's what I'm afraid of.' He left abruptly, before Geoffrey could speak to him man to man or order him to pull himself together.

Suddenly buoyed up on this strange elation, weirdly deluded that he'd got away with something, and that his good-natured, entirely rational character was intact, Geoffrey set up a last fling. Now it was his turn to break restraints and go it alone – almost alone. There were a couple of samples left, and with just him and Lionel there in the tirelessly persistent buzz of the machine, he could cope at last. He looked to his right, just to make sure. Inside the helmet, he smiled knowingly and settled once again to the microscope. It amused him that he was hallucinating. He set one of the samples in place.

Afterwards, he couldn't quite remember how he did it. It hadn't been anything particularly inspired or creative, simply a moment when he grasped what was needed. Actually, he'd just persisted, in a kind of abandon, with an angle slightly askew from common sense. That was the best way he could explain it to himself. And it had worked. Features of the specimen had started to show up far better. Yes, on a second glance, whole sections of the circuit weren't blemished at all – as they'd appeared throughout the day. In fact they were very good, and the result was a stunning success: so much so, that he redirected the beam and made plate after plate of the winning chip before he went out though the oxidation-room door, out through the airlock, still in his spacesuit, joyously out past the grinning Lionel into the main building to find Raj.

SHE CAME IN when he was back in the lab, completing his notes. It was late, almost time to leave. She walked straight towards him and stood next to the bench where his shiny photographic prints lay scattered.

'I hear you're something of a hero, Geoff,' she said. 'Everyone's talking about you and Dr Gill making a breakthrough.'

He felt, for an instant, that he was still wearing the clean suit. He let his gaze slip away. 'Everyone?'

'It's all over the factory. You must be terribly proud of yourself. Aren't you?'

The fear he'd thought safely past flickered up in his chest. 'I wouldn't exactly call it a breakthrough,' he said, cautiously. 'I didn't know people knew. They're not really supposed to.'

'Oh, come on, Geoff, don't be so modest.' She picked up one of the plates and started to look at it. 'Is this the

scene of the crime? It doesn't make much sense to me.'
Gazing up at him, she was smiling artlessly, and his heart
was sinking, he didn't know why.

'It's a temporary advantage, what I found. What we've
found. It's a way to get the crystal surface to accept ...
Cynthia, you know I shouldn't really be telling you, or
anybody, about it. It's Raj's result, actually.'

'Ten four, lieutenant!' She smiled again, but turned away,
holding the exposed plate in the light from the window.
He got up hurriedly to stand beside her.

'So what does it all mean?'

'Really, Cynthia, I shouldn't ... And here at work.'
Close beside her shoulder, he could smell her scent.

'So this is Raj's famous layered chip?'

'How did you ... ?' His laugh was ghostly; his arm
touched hers. 'Yes, it's the multiple surface of the silicon.'

'It doesn't look like anything very much,' she said.
'Look, here's a man. And there's a face. To me, it's just
like reading the tea leaves. You'll have to explain it to me,
Geoff.'

Just below the banter, he felt some desperate battle of
wills and craved a way out. They gazed together at the
print. Swirls and random shapes beyond the channels did
suggest a perversely aroused male figure. It even reminded
him of Lionel, with that characteristic, rather grotesque
stance. And the face she'd indicated could almost be his
son, Alan – or was Rae so intolerably present today that
he couldn't get the wretched family out of his mind?

But there were other details and the scene was absorbing,
engrossing him. Raj was right after all, he wasn't well. All

kinds of pictures were starting. He saw a great fanged gape, like some medieval contraption, and now his head was aching. A steel strap was tightening inexorably around his skull, and suddenly the pain was hideous, intolerable. He just had time to wonder how migraine felt before the image on the paper started moving, shimmering. The electrons that had made it were writhing up in their photographic glue, and a sound came from his lips. Truly, he wasn't himself, standing there with Cynthia. He was right back in a vacuum, and the pain wasn't in his head but in that stream of them falling headlong through a huge voltage drop, winged, their vibration searingly bright, their song an amber scream drawn out.

'Geoff,' she was saying. 'Geoff, where are you going? Are you all right?'

He hung on to the toilet bowl in the washroom while his stomach convulsed. All the disturbance of the day gave birth through his mouth, all the tension and exhaustion of weeks came back at him, discharging. But the agonising parade in his head still kept on, an unholy hijacked carnival, cackling, sneering, still embracing the planet he occupied, his secure home, his quiet valley. And they were wheeling something on, some piece of stage machinery, some sealed rock, far out in space. He saw deep inside it, glimpsed spitted forms over fires, human shapes hanging from poles, souls in torment, their trussed commerce flaunted, weird sexual lights of paint and gloss and sheen. He saw a vast dark figure holding a probe, and his own practice was the torture of all nature, her womb, the electricity streaming through it, the currents of pain tunnelling, tunnelling under Cynth's lovely skin, the intolerable pressure to answer, clearly, objectively, to get the next result and the next and the next in the race, the cold inquisition of appalling detachment.

He was staggering past the sinks to the washroom window. He fought to get it open and inhaled great gulps of freezing air, one after another; until the pain that had come on so savagely started to ebb, and he was staring at the snow outside. And all he could think of was the bedroom in Charles Street, with Cynthia handed to him, last night and every night, on a plate, as if in some pact. And at last he realised what it was his body had known from the beginning. Finally, he saw what he'd been refusing to see, blinded all this time by his own self-conceit: Cynthia Somers amenable to voltage.

His head cleared. He stood, panting. At least there was something he could do about it all. Turning, he took a step towards the door. It was only a question of whether he had the nerve. Lance had told him to work it out, *for God's sake*. Well, now he had worked it out, because everything made bloody horrible, monstrous sense. But it was nothing Lance could ever have imagined.

He got out of the washroom. He told Cynthia he was going off to get something for his stomach and that she was to meet him at the bus-stop as usual. Then he made his way straight down to Raj's office. He was in luck. Dr Gill was off somewhere in one of the clean rooms, his secretary said. 'Is it urgent?' she asked. 'Shall I ring down for him, Mr Fairhurst?'

'No,' he said. 'Nothing urgent. Just give me a few

minutes, will you. It's only some papers. I'm sure I can find what I need.'

SHE LAY IN his arms. The bedroom was dark, and his hand saw for him. His fingers strayed the length of her back, caught the stretched hems of her underclothes. He felt the stitching of her bra, the fastenings, the edge of her suspender belt. She'd said nothing as they went upstairs, only offered herself again, automatically. The air in the room was so cold it stung his nostrils.

Far off down the valley there was a goods train. He could hear its steam pulse fade, now strengthen, as the engine laboured the other side of Bourne End, maybe, three miles away. He stroked her back, toyed with the shoulder straps. A late car droned up Charles Street; a couple of motorbikes burned along the High Street, their note swelling to a roar then tailing into the distance. He made up his mind. He could see no other way to set her free.

He got out of bed, went round and stood beside her. How beautiful her shoulders were: he could just make out the white of the lace straps. The night plucked at his own bare skin, but he knew he was right: an act to ransom shame. He stretched out to touch, to caress her one last time. He was aware of her eyes.

She was watching him intently. 'What's the matter, Geoff? Geoffrey? Not feeling ill again, are you?'

'No.'

'Why've you got up, then? What are you doing?'

His voice was unsteady. 'I'm finishing what I should never have started.' The quiet was palpable. 'We can't go on with it. Can we, Cynthia.'

She was tightening the covers over her. 'Go on with what, Geoff? Go on with what?'

'You're a very good actress. I'll give you that.'

She said nothing, and he could hear her breath, shallow, in her throat.

He stroked her forehead. 'It's all right,' he said quietly. 'It's the least I can do. Really, it is.'

'Geoff?'

Her lips remained parted; he could just make out their shape. He pulled himself away abruptly. The pain of vision flashed momentarily in his head. He waited a second longer. Then he moved decisively across the rug and bare floorboards to the door, went out on to the landing and crept downstairs in the dark.

He'd left his briefcase against the bookshelves in the front room where it was easy enough to find. It was a little heavier than usual, the handle just pressing into his palm. How strange it felt carrying it back up again.

He still didn't turn on the light when he got back. He simply laid out Raj's documents on the bed and told her everything she needed to know. In a calm, measured voice, he outlined the production methods and details of the layered chip. He even gave her the photographic prints they'd both been looking at earlier in the lab. Standing shivering in his pyjamas, he repeated everything his boss had told him about the packet switching, the locations of the terminals in the telephone network: Bushy Park, Northwood Central Command, Marconi at Elstree, and their own modest test node soon to come on stream at Lidlock. He explained the precise relation of all these to what he now understood, so clearly, to be that potential holy grail of technology: computers speaking to one another in a nuclear-proof, distributed network.

'You understand what you're doing, Geoff?' she said softly when he'd finished.

'Yes, I do,' he said. 'I understand exactly. In the morning, I'll just have to find some way to put all this stuff back.'

Downstairs, he stood and listened while she phoned. He even wondered whether it was Lionel Rae's broken voice he could hear echoing through the black Bakelite earpiece that hadn't worked for weeks. She looked up apologetically as soon as she'd put the receiver down. 'They're sending a jeep to pick me up,' she said. 'Right away, it seems. I . . . We'd better get dressed.' She began hunting around distractedly for her things.

'A jeep,' he said. 'It is the Yanks, then?'

'Spot on, Geoff. Ten four, lieutenant.' She smiled at him wearily, but there were tears at the corners of her eyes. 'And a man with a camera. They'll want to photograph all the documents.'

'Cynthia, I'm so sorry.' The embers in the fireplace gave off a feeble heat, while the table lamp spread a yellow cast on the Picasso print, the copper bowl, the finch in the glass dome still in its Santa hat.

'I was just a pawn, wasn't I,' she said. 'In a game of

high stakes, apparently. My looks, my parents' citizenship. They made me . . . amenable.'

He winced at the word, then controlled himself. 'Your parents?'

'DPs. Czech. They've got them at the air base. And my brother.'

'They?'

'They're holding them. It's not far away. That's where I've been going at weekends.'

'If there's anything else I can do. Anything.'

'Not your fault, is it.' She sat in the armchair and put her head in her hands. 'The worst thing is the effort of having to keep it up,' she said.

'I'm just so glad I couldn't . . .'

'I said, it's not your fault, Geoff.' She spoke sharply, but then she was beside him with her arms around him – comforting him, of all things.

'Who picked Lionel up?' he said.

'Ours. I know it was ours.'

'But . . .'

'I gathered the Russians had things on him.' She broke off and stood limply. 'He'd been feeding them titbits, I think, from when he was on the rockets.'

'And British Intelligence caught up with him?'

'They were running him. Isn't that the phrase? They picked him up because the Yanks put pressure on. And handed him straight over. He's been through the mill. What they did to me was nothing.'

She seemed so bitterly grown-up, experienced far beyond her years. 'You must hate me.'

'I could never do that.'

'No?'

'No, Cynth.'

'I hate myself. Geoff, I didn't really understand anything, you know. Please believe me. I just did what I was told. I don't even *get* why they were suddenly so keen to snoop in at Lidlock. Why bother? Isn't there supposed to be a . . . what d'you call it, a special relationship? Has Lidlock been compromised or something? Did they think Lionel . . . ?'

Now he was on surer ground. 'It's nothing political. It can only be commercial.'

'Commercial?'

'Britain and America neck and neck, the Yanks with all the cash. We've got our wartime advantage and what we smugly think of as our intellectual pedigree. We invented the computer; they invented the chip. They've got . . . I think I've heard Raj say "Arpanet"; we've got this thing at the NPL.' He spread his hands. 'The wretched chip changes everything. It makes everything possible, and anything. Can you imagine? No. No one can. What can be invented will be, but it's the timing. Who gets an inch ahead now, wins.'

'If you say so.'

'I got it from Raj. At the moment, probably by some fluke, he's actually an inch ahead.'

They stood looking at each other.

'Out here in the sticks with their bikes,' she said, 'all dressed up like rebels, like lads. They're supposed to be our friends, looking after us. Bloody swine!' She said it suddenly and with such anguish. He'd never heard her swear. 'Far-fetched, isn't it,' she went on, 'the lengths people go to. You couldn't make it up. I almost didn't believe it, till they threatened me. Right on my own doorstep. I said no, and they went away. But they came back the same evening – a fake bike gang of them – and that was when they took Mum and Dad, and Denny.' She was on the verge of tears again. He touched her shoulder; she looked up at him. 'I was born here.' Her voice was breaking. 'I'm British, Geoff. How dare our people hand bloody Lionel over, if it's *them* and *us*, and not the Russians at all.'

He could only guess. 'I suppose they were just asked to do a Cold War buddy a favour. After all, they're on the lookout for Reds, not Yanks – certainly not expecting our best pals to use a bunch of their military to take out the industrial competition, friend or foe. By the time someone at the top gets to realise what's happened it'll be too late; and no one's going to risk a diplomatic incident. Not with our allies, of all people.' He was stroking her hand. 'And poor Lionel.'

She hissed suddenly. 'There's nothing poor about Lionel. It was him found out about my parents. Before all this.'

'When he still thought he was working for the Russians?'

'They probably told *him*.'

'So nasty a circuit.' He sighed. 'And such a complex one.'

'Using Lionel to get to me. To get to you. Poor Geoff.'

'I'd no idea I could be that important,' he said. 'No idea.'

She made a weak smile, and resumed looking for her belongings. The light clicked on in the dining room. Then he heard her soft footsteps through the ceiling from upstairs. She returned with her bags, holding her boots in her hand.

'Will they let your family go?' he said, quietly.

'They've got what they wanted, haven't they.'

'And let you go with them?'

She bit her lip and nodded. 'Geoff, I'm sorry, too. I really am. And grateful.'

He embraced her one last time. They heard the sound of an engine outside, and then suddenly, briefly, his house was alive with impossible shadowy figures. There were flashes and sharp accented whispers. Afterwards, as he sat alone in the dark of his room, his mind was clear. At last, he could breathe. He lifted the phone: the line was dead again, as he'd known it would be. But now that she'd gone, he felt so free, so wonderfully free.

V

GRACE

SUN BETWEEN THE rail and paddle racks had melted the top layer of snow. One patch under the lip of the lock gate had lost its opacity and was almost clear, like a window pane. A trapped shape, foetal, pink-tinged, caught Alan's eye. He guessed some pike-chewed rudd or dead, deep-frozen water vole.

A whim had brought him, just a chance inclination. No one used the gates any more, with the canal so solid. He peered more closely at the ice. The curious shape most of all resembled a human ear. Instantly, he remembered that girl running down Park Street, back in January, her attacker, the drunken fight with Geoffrey. One summer, there'd been a dead dog floating. Paul and he had thrown stones at it, upside-down and bloated in the mucky reach by Alsford's, its legs splayed stiff like some push-along toy. He'd heard nothing from Cynthia, seen nothing.

He jumped straight down into the lock, his soles thudding on the surface, but once he'd cleared the fringes of the patch it was obvious the grizzled cheek and hairline were a man's. Baffled, he crouched at the grisly find, until a terrible and overwhelming familiarity came breaking upon him, and he brushed desperately again at the edge of snow. Now he stood, rubbing the hidden profile hard as he might with the sole of his shoe – to no avail. He stared all around him.

There were thick slabs of ice at the lock's edge. He seized one, knelt again and polished it fiercely back and forth across his patch, pressing for a melt, conjuring the image. Once, he and Lionel had planned to grind a mirror – using just such an action. Cans of Monsanto reagent to cast it from were still under the bench in the workshop: silvered over, it would have given them the stars. He swallowed. Cautiously, he lifted the block, and the mush he'd made began minutely to resolve. The pane swam once, then froze tantalisingly from below.

He emptied his duffel bag. The schoolbooks flopped on to the snow: his plimsolls and sports kit, Lionel's battered black case of drawing instruments, Lionel's steel rule. He took that, tamped with it and screeded, then smeared it like a palette knife over the blur. The ice glistened, until all at once a depth opened, green-black, a glassy interior containing a face. There was the nose, and the suggestion of a mouth. A huge emotion welled up in Alan's throat. No matter how blurred or crystalline, he knew the truth: it was his dad, of course.

He rocked back on his heels. Then he saw the hole, neat behind the ear, quite large. He shielded his eyes. It was red. His father's frozen wound was the shape of a heavy-calibre bullet.

When he stood up, his right knee wobbled uncontrollably. The stained black bricks of the lock walls, the snow-laden hedges, the white railway embankment all veered, and he clutched at the timber of the lock gate, peering over the baulk down at the canal below. A woman was carrying her shopping bags, and the sun streamed and glinted on the willows beside the paddock. He turned back, and away again, but he still kept seeing his father's pinkish-grey, stubbled, murdered skin. He took hold of himself. Eyes averted, he made himself strew the ice pane with a little crusted snow, scuffing the edges, camouflaging the object he'd just struggled so hard to bring up. Then he picked his way to the far end of the lock and swung himself up and out.

At home, still in his coat, he washed his hands in the sink, over and over again. He stared at his reflection, stooping at the mirror, and caught Lionel's face staring back. A whirring and clattering began from the floorboards beneath him, and he almost bit through his tongue before he realised it was the twin tub in the kitchen.

HIS MOTHER HAD her back to him, her hip thrust against the machine's white cabinet, her gloved hands wrestling it back at the sink. She twisted round awkwardly, sensing his presence while the drier raced and span.

Her face was made up as it always was, even for housework, her hair done in its perm. She wore her gingham apron over her blouse and crimplene skirt, the neat bow tied at her waistband. Her stocking seams ran straight down to the backs of her heeled court shoes.

'Haven't you got homework?' She had to shout.

He caught the humdrum words, but ignored them. He asked her, crazily, above the noise, 'Any letters?'

'No, Alan.'

'Phone calls?' It was madness, his heart nearly bursting while his voice made conversation. She *must* know. She must know *something*. The washing machine was inching across the floor at her while he held her attention. Spikes of grey water leapt up around the washtub's metal lid; a splash went over her sleeve.

'No!' She turned back and shoved at the bodywork. 'Now look what you've made me do!'

'I've just been at the lock. He's frozen in.' He spoke it weirdly, flatly, to hear how the words might sound.

'What was that?'

'I'd better go again. I need to go and make sure. That he's . . .'

'What!' She was pushing the machine, arms outstretched.

He snatched the picture of Lionel from on top of the fridge and held it in front of her. She angled her head away. 'Stop that. What are you playing at?'

'Aren't you worried? Don't you care?'

'How dare you!'

'Well?'

'Of course I care, Alan!' she yelled angrily over the drier.

'But have you done anything? Spoken to anyone? Rung anyone?'

'It's not my place to, is it? Or yours, for that matter.' The machine splashed at her again.

Should he laugh, or cry? Should he tell her, or kill her? She was ridiculous. 'About this Philby thing,' he said.

'What about it?'

He indicated the picture. 'Look! Beside his plane! *See* him? Working for the enemy.'

She dashed the photograph away. It fell to the kitchen lino tiles so that the glass smashed. But she ignored it, and him, while the spin drier finished and slowed, leaving only the heavy thrum of the main wash still going, and a voice on the transistor radio, suddenly audible, announcing a quiz show. 'How dare you speak about your father like that!'

'The family hate us. He's an ... *embarrassment*, Mother.'

'The family think very highly of him. I know that.' She was quivering, holding her face averted, stiff with rage.

'You here keeping up appearances! I can tell you he's never coming back. I know *that*. What did Daddy do in the war? Eh? Mother! Do we know? Has he told you who he's working for? Mum!'

She let the machine go at last and turned to face him coldly, her rubber gloves dripping in front of her. 'I don't want you speaking like this. Do you hear me! You're not yourself.'

'Not myself,' he said bitterly. 'Since when have I been that? With a father who thinks he's a Martian.'

'It's his way.' She spoke icily, picking up the lid of the machine.

He thought she was going to hit him with it. The dirty water surged and rolled, the extremities of garments showing over and over like the grey tips of emotion. He remembered the cane across his legs when he was just a kid and she said he was lying. The aluminium lid shook in her hand, the word Hoover embossed across the serrations.

'Your father is a good man, Alan.'

'They don't have good on Mars. They don't have good, or evil, just control circuits, servo-mechanisms. That's what he's always going on about, isn't it? Isn't it? They're all just bloody mad robots keeping on, and on, and on, and round again, bloody doing it . . .' He didn't know what he was saying, and the look on her face made him slink abruptly out of the house.

But there was no mistake. Sure enough, under the snow he'd so recently scattered back in place, the ice window was still there, clear now, glazed again by the cold. And though the sun was falling, edging behind a mercuric streak of cloud, he could still just make out the features he knew so well, the slaughtered, unbearable cheek he'd once pressed against his own, the lips he'd childishly kissed. Below him was an oblong arena into which all the happenings of the past two months had been congealed, and the black wooden gates were thrust tight against their frozen spill.

ALAN LOOKED UP from the pale oak stalls. The E-major chord, construction of hope, hung in the organ notes and in the voices around him. He could almost see it rise, lingering and lapping at the chapel vault, touching the arches. In their round sandstone, they echoed the great abbey at St Albans, where temperamental Mr Flower had once taken him to hear the Mozart Requiem.

E major soothed and embalmed the sawtooth wave of grief that still came from the lock. He'd simply turned and gone the old way that afternoon, along the tow-path and up the slope to the lock, maybe to put off going home. He'd climbed up the bank from the watercress beds and got on to the stile. He'd stepped up on the foot-plate all unaware, grasped the rail and pulled himself up on to the black wooden arm of the gate before just glancing down. Now he stroked the oak of the choir-stalls. The chord still sounded – against a paternal figure bursting up from the ice, who held the tool of his trade over a child's limp body.

Sun shafts in the apse stained the stone floor. Colly Flower turned round from the organ console and peered over his spectacles at them all. He picked up the new music they'd been attempting and struck it with the back of his hand. He said it would be hard for a school choir, but worth it. It would take all their efforts at accuracy and concentration. 'Unaccompanied in performance,' he said. 'But I think we might pull it off.' There were nods and movement, and some groans. The strange piece had been taxing, for all the transparency of its ending.

The words to it were stranger still, like an old painting. Alan's eye rested once more on the poetry stretched out under the stave to match the notes. *In a garden shady this holy lady . . . Blessed Cecilia . . . Translated daughter . . . I cannot err; There is no creature Whom I belong to . . .* He flicked the pages . . . *against the still Long winter of our intellectual will . . .*

*O trumpets that unguarded children blow About the fortress of
their inner foe.*

Colly went to the piano. He, too, was moved and seemed
to collect himself. He played the fugue of the second section
in order to explain how the troubled soul was split among
the voices, soprano, alto, tenor and bass. He showed subse-
quent excursions into C, and then A, for the invocation
and prayer. Alan had never heard Colly speak like this, had
never imagined a deliberate interior structure in music, or
in any art. It seemed to mollify the hurt, as though the
piece were written only for him, and now.

Then the practice was over, and the choir dismissed; but
all down the narrow lane into the town, with the weeks-
old snow still lying under the stark, overarching trees, Alan
kept the image: of the girl martyr, *like a black swan as death
came on,* who *constructed an organ to enlarge her prayer,*

> *And notes tremendous from her great engine*
> *Thundered out on the Roman air.*

He hummed to himself, trying to hold the printed notes
and their sounds, while grids or diagrams stretched out
across the tints of evening. The days were lengthening.
Herringbone cloud glittered over the dormitory houses of
the boys' school.

The High Street by the Swan looked over at
Woolworths, the poster still in its door frame and the
women going in and out. Alan retraced the Roman road,
the snow-tucked route where drovers had walked cattle for
centuries to market, where boys had trod for generations,
speaking grammar-school Latin. A couple of tuned-up

bikes were parked over at the new milk bar. He could see the leather jackets of the lads inside. Cars queued at the Kings Road traffic lights.

He went on past Cowper Road and the almshouses, then crossed at the post office into Park Street. He passed as he did every day the smashed ice beside the plank bridge where he'd fought Geoffrey Fairhurst. Now there was green in the silted gravel: exposed watercress just stirred in the trickle that passed its roots. To the other side, his own splash of vomit showed beyond the wooden handrail. The tomato, bread, and pineapple bore recent signs of plunder, and the sudden breeze was soft. He crossed the canal by its faintly melting ice.

> *O cry created as the bow of sin*
> *Is drawn across our trembling violin*

If ever Lionel might have sung those words, or drawn penitent breath ... He propped his music on the piano at home and picked out the chords, fumbling for the keys. He looked out. Where the front lawn sloped down, an edge of grass was just visible, the green stalk of a single snowdrop gilded by the late light. The air was warmer by a degree. He remembered when he was ten, making thermometers. They'd all lived in a flat somewhere, and Lionel had pumped the brass blowlamp on the kitchen table, while the capillary tube, newly bought from the chemist's over the road, glowed orange. Alan would blow into the molten glass and watch the bulb appear, cool and harden. Over the flame again they'd draw in meths and seal up the end. He remembered when they'd made the little radio Lionel

designed, when transistors were tiny new miracles. It was
the one he still listened to in bed. He remembered his
father's hypocritical embrace against 'bad dreams', against
all thermodynamic visitations of the night – Lionel,
condemned to his heat death in the ice.

> At sounds so entrancing the angels dancing
> Came out of their trance into time again,
> And around the wicked in Hell's abysses
> The huge flame flickered and eased their pain...
> O weep, child, weep, O weep away the stain.

SHE LAY IN his arms. A misty light stole in from the
chamber windows. He lifted his head and saw branches
on a salmon-flecked sky. Then he watched her wake, one
hesitant eyelid lifting before the other. Her lips widened
as he leaned closer to kiss them. He rearranged strands of
her hair, ran his hand over her shoulder, smoothed her side
down to her hip. She pulled him to her and they made
love for the second time.

There was the smell of dry, matted towels in the kitchen,
coke dust from the range, coffee as she poured hot water
over the grounds in a blue china jug. Rooks wheeled above
a copse at the edge of the wood, and one swung suddenly
cawing past the old glass panes. Astraea jumped in her
chair, and they both laughed.

She looked over her cup at him.

'There's a word that can't be avoided,' Geoffrey said.

'Joy?' she said.

'That as well.' He smiled.

She angled her head engagingly. The hair fell across her plate. 'Bother.' She licked butter from the ends. 'What is it, then, this magic word?'

'Louisa, of course.'

'Oh, that,' she said.

'Your friend.'

'Your wife.'

'And Benjamin?'

She looked away, musing through the window at the winter scene. 'Ben's a man of the world, Geoff. It's almost the title of his job. Ben does what suits Ben. I know for a fact he hasn't been faithful.'

Geoffrey raised his eyebrows. 'You and Louie were friends.'

'Were we?' She pondered. 'Close musically. Were we even that? Did I like her? Absence can be a guided weapon, Geoff, don't you think? Or the threat of it. She's got you feeling guilty, even now. Did you do anything wrong?'

He looked down.

'Did you? Who was it walked out?' She stretched her hand over the pine table. He took it and held it, smoothing the knuckles with his fingers. He liked the feel of her skin. She looked quite beautiful opposite him, without any make-up, in one of her outlandish jumpers.

'Something amusing?' she said.

'You,' he said. It was so unexpected to feel at peace with her, the unknown girl whom already he felt he knew far better than Louisa . . . or Cynthia . . . or Merriam.

'You're not a womaniser, Geoff. I've lived with one. Dearest, we were married to the wrong people.'

In the yard, he was about to get into his car when he noticed there were buds in the hawthorn, tight, perseverant nodes with a coating of moisture. Moisture, that new phenomenon, clung to shrivelled berries and the grey-brown stalks at the hedge's foot. A bird darted on beating wings. He thought of that distant, unfulfilled anger inside him when he'd first come to negotiate with Louisa, diligently carrying her cello on his back, and smiled. Astraea stood waving in the doorway, so oddly dressed and wreathed in the just-audible notes of Roy Orbison on her radiogram. He waved back. It amazed him that not all women were the same.

There was a crowd out shopping in the High Street. Shouts rose from the market traders as he picked his way between the canopied stalls on the one hand and the Gothic façade of the Town Hall on the other. Fish gleamed under the arches, whiting in boxes, cod and bright-eyed haddock on slabs, their long-lost smell reaching out once again across the pavement. He passed them by, picked up his potatoes and greens, and some meat from Waitrose, the butchers. Then he went into the cobbled alley by the timbered Church House. Snow only lay in the gutters, almost visibly receding. Wet fell on his neck and he looked up at the huge icicle hanging like a stalactite from the eaves above him. It was tipped with another drop. All along a carved cornice there was a glisten.

It was the oldest part of the town. He took further passageways, clutching the brown paper bags of his purchases, past the boys' school, across the open ground that stretched down towards the canal. Tweed-jacketed youngsters hurried between Saturday classes. Before the bridge, he turned back, coming up Castle Street beside the cottages and the cramped eighteenth-century house fronts that overlooked the churchyard. There was busy traffic again at the lane's head, slogging through the High Street narrows. A woman was cycling by, her basket full of bulbs in flowerpots. She nodded to him, and smiled. Wheels swished on a wet film; all along the kerb was a black, dissolving slush. He thought of Cynthia and himself, her body, in his mind, fenced around as though with glass. Melting ice on the pavement crunched under his shoes.

THE PALACE ROSE up beside the grey river, a brick catalogue of chimneys that twisted, jutted, aspired with lazy smoke into a still-wreathing mist. Yet high overhead there was blue, with strokes of sunlight on cirrus. A party of skaters, a father and his daughters, cut cautious figures before the bridge on the towing-path side, because the ice looked ready to break up at any minute.

'It's not like your canal,' Astraea said. 'It's all so wide, and so fragile. Look how they daren't go near the arch, nor out near those poor ducks.'

Half a dozen mallards made a group at the centre of the stream, seeming to wade in a dent just under the bridge's span. Water covered their webs with the forecast of a pond. An incongruous seagull stood with them.

DEREK BEAVEN

'What do you mean, *my* canal?' Geoffrey said. 'Because you live just over a hill?'

'Of course. Over the rise, we're the true country folk.'

'We?'

'We milkmaids and farm girls,' she laughed, putting on an accent. 'Us out in Hockeridge Bottom. Us don't have no truck with no canals. Why, did you think I meant me and Ben? Were you getting jealous?'

'Of course,' he said in turn.

'Well, you needn't be. You needn't be.'

He put his arm round her, and they walked on beside the river and up on to the Hampton Court Bridge. Far-off sounds of the fair on the Green came in snatches, the old-fashioned pipe organ, the clashing rock and roll of the dodgems. A poster tacked to a board billed it the 'Last Chance Frost Fair'. And there did seem an honest, if optimistic, attempt at one of the great Thames festivals the newspapers had referred to so nostalgically all during the freeze; though the river at London had remained too quick, too salty, and probably too filthy to harden right across. Yet East India Docks had gone up solid, and at Chatham the Navy had used ice-breakers to get its warships out.

So the Hampton Fair had a point, Geoffrey thought, and an off-season eye to the main chance. There were people in antique costume selling toffee apples or offering to read fortunes, and booths were set up around the base of the Ferris wheel. A Tudor strongman bent iron bars in a little crenellated pavilion beside the car park. The youth in charge of the rifle range wore a feathered cap and a leather jerkin, on to which the ash fell from his cigarette. Geoffrey had a go, and won a box of Allsorts. 'I can see who's put a glint in *his* eye,' said a woman spinning candyfloss in the machine. She'd tucked some sort of bolster around her hips; her coat swelled out like a farthingale.

Side by side on the carousel, Astraea and he sat giggling like newly-weds, licking the fleecy sugar while the carved horses swept up and down, and a furious Victorian tune bellowsed out over the whirl of Bushy Park, the grey road, the old stables, the palace, the moist and misted silhouettes of trees.

No whole ox, no blazing oak logs, but four rotisserie chickens finishing off over charcoal – Geoffrey and Astraea stood looking at the Park, clutching the smoky pieces in their fingers between slices of bread. Stragglers of the deer herd were huddled under the trees. Where the snow still lay, small heaps of fodder had been left out, and the marks of innumerable hoofs radiated. But pools of unfamiliar grass lay here and there like green oases, and Geoffrey let his eye stray over them, and into the distance. Half a mile beyond the tranquil scene, screened from view by the majestic oaks and chestnuts, would be the Upper Lodge and the NPL research complex. There the great, archetypal ACE would even now be humming and chattering to itself. And its capstans of memory tape would be spooling abruptly back and forth, mechanically dreaming of nodes and networks.

Astraea led him away between the helter-skelter and the dodgems. A sign pointed to the river. He glanced sideways at her, lovely in her grey coat and filmy headscarf, and was amazed at how one circumstance could so flip into another. Then she turned and kissed him quickly, before the cars came hooting as they crossed the road. A gate gave access to the bank. A wooden footbridge led over to the islands above the lock. Down on the ice of the river, the printing press was in an extra booth rigged from tarpaulin and pitched daringly upon the shallows.

The operator had knotted a cloth round his head. His hands were inky from the work. 'We keep having to move ground,' he said, tightening the impression. He pointed to wet holes where the legs of the stand had previously been set. 'The weight melts the ice and the damn thing starts to lurch. We just shift a few feet along and carry on. But it's an honourable tradition.' He laughed and called out to the nextcomers. 'Roll up! Get your souvenirs! Last chance before the thaw!'

Coming away with their verse snippet, *Along the shoare of silver streaming Themmes*, they passed a party of young people. Of all the people Geoffrey might have expected to see, Alan Rae was the last. He stopped in his tracks, while Astraea, intent on the still-wet page of commemoration, continued on.

The boy seemed as surprised. He stared, first at Geoffrey, and then, following the direction of his hasty glance, at the back of Astraea. There was a moment of embarrassed silence. Then Geoffrey called, 'Strey! Sweetheart!'

She turned and came back.

'Yes?'

'This is Alan. Alan Rae. His father works . . .'

'At the same place? Lidlock? Hello, Alan. What a coincidence!'

The sounds of the fair seemed magnified, the raucous public address from the dodgems competing once again with the jubilant, barrelling carousel. The lad was there with a teacher and his wife. A couple of pupils from a school trip had stayed over after the theatre – because the teacher's parents had a house on an island downstream, and how wonderful to look out that morning on the tideway just below Teddington with the broken ice sheets floating past. Geoffrey and Astraea made polite conversation: of the fair, the thaw. They spoke of the other great houses beside the Thames – Strawberry Hill, Ham, Marble Hill. Not forgetting the Hawker Siddeley factory, the teacher added wrily. The baby cooed and wriggled in his wife's arms.

HE'D THOUGHT IT had been her – that girl with Geoffrey Fairhurst at the fair. He'd really thought it had been Cynth. Then she'd turned, and the face framed in the headscarf was some other woman, and he'd been strangely glad, almost elated, because Geoffrey hadn't got her, and if she was alive at all . . .

He drove up next to some iron railings in the pavement. It was dark in the middle of Old Hemel, but the odd star was overhead and melt was dripping on him from the high-timbered gables. He yanked the Triumph back over its stand, and went down the stone steps under the Spinning Wheel to elbow a way inside through the beery press of listeners. A man with a beard was knocking out 'Madam, Shall I Tie Your Garter' on the tiny wooden stage beside the bar, and 'Oh, no John, no John, no John, no!' rang in his ear as he ordered his drink. He located his schoolmates and took his pint over, sipping at the foam: Mickey and Brian, and Barry Evans from his maths group. Now someone had brought on an ancient bowed instrument, and to its delicate scraping they could hear themselves speak.

'Jonesy and Slim are getting the bus,' Brian told him. 'Jonesy broke his mum's car. Fifteen quid for a new front wing. He's had to get that job on Sainsbury's bacon counter. Saturdays: "Will that be all, Mrs Smith?" "Yes, thanks, young man." Pzing! Those things on wires. Heard they've caught that bloke, then?' he added.

Alan started involuntarily. 'What bloke?'

'The bloke in the woods, man. At least, they haven't so much caught him as everyone knows who he is.' Brian was lean, dark-eyed. He made a wry grin. 'All right, to be strictly accurate, Jackie Barton reckons she and her little buddies know.'

Alan was laughing. 'How's that?'

'They were round at Loopy Lou's – in the fifth form, that dark-haired one Harpo went out with. Lives in one of those posh houses somewhere up Gravel Path. Her dad was there.'

'Jackie's?'

'Loopy's, you dick. And someone said, joking, of

course, "Hey, Mr Mitching, that poster in Woolworths looks exactly like you." And Jackie says the old bugger went completely white, and sort of had to leave the room. And then there was just this very awkward silence before normal service was resumed – to coin a phrase.'

'Is that it?'

'Well, there've been no more attacks, have there.'

'I don't know.'

'And they reckon he's a bloody rummy sod. Ex-army. Very ex. So perhaps it is. Keep it in the family, eh?'

'Yeah,' Alan said, though he kept scanning the crowd, as he scanned every situation, thinking he might see her. She wasn't there, of course. She never was. Every so often he got haunted by ideas of her death, her eyes open and lifeless on a slab; because Death was everywhere, since the lock, almost visible, almost with bloody skulls and a scythe. Sometimes, he couldn't help thinking of her laid out at the air base, suspended somehow. But, to his astonishment, his mood always lightened again.

Brian was asking him, 'Hey, man. Anyone at home? What have you been up to, then?'

Alan brought himself back. A bald chap was singing with his eyes shut about the lark in the morning. 'Nothing much. Went to the theatre up in London. The Mermaid. Marcus and Sylvia took us.'

'Yeah?'

'Two Greek tragedies. Bernard Miles stabbing his eyes out.'

'Laugh a minute, then. Like that bloody thing ITV did. Christ! *Elektra*, wasn't it. In the original, to prove they weren't just lowbrow piss-peddlers. What a bloody flap that caused.'

Barry Evans broke in. 'Bernard Miles does those country stories on the radio, doesn't he? The funny bloke from up Ivinghoe.'

'It was good, though,' Alan said. 'We stayed over at Marcus's mum and dad's. Went to the fair. Sylvia brought the baby along. Good time had.'

It was Barry who asked directly, 'Your old man turned up, then?'

'No,' Alan said. 'He hasn't. Not yet.'

The bald chap had finished. People all around them were talking, and the air was thick with smoke.

'Oh, well. I expect you'll hear soon enough.'

'Plays,' Alan said. 'I never really thought. Stuff right there on stage – so close you can almost get hold of it. Almost.' He swigged at his drink to hide emotion. 'Marcus says it's all happening these days. There's never been anything like it. He wants to do *Serjeant Musgrave's Dance*, or maybe *A Man for All Seasons*.'

'Sergeant bloody who?'

'If it wasn't for Marcus ... They've been fantastic. Just one character walks in from the wings and there's a completely different story.' Now there were girls with guitars, and a protest song was starting up. 'I opened the box,' Alan said, quietly, 'and the cat was a goner.'

'What?'

'Schrödinger. I opened the fucking box!'

'You should have taken the money.'

They all laughed.

'Now you've really lost me, mate,' Brian said. 'Bike going all right?'

'Yeah.'

THE ROAD TWISTED now with the railway, now with the canal. Alan threaded under the one at the Old Red Lion, accelerated over the other by the Gade stream, past Nash Mills and Apsley paperworks. He gripped the Triumph's handlebar: there was the brake, the clutch, the throttle, the advance-and-retard. At home on the bench in the workshop there were still radar parts, and salvaged components in wartime sweet tins. There were rectifiers, HT units cannibalised from this or that chassis. There was the oscilloscope, the Avo-meter, the cardboard box full of valves, the corpse of a projection television cradling its miniature, graphite-grey cathode-ray tube. There were Boolean test beds, flip-flops, the transistorised mock-ups of AND, OR, NOT. All these things were present, hard facts, large as life. But Lionel was dead, Lionel who'd first guided his understanding, who'd read him to sleep and told him all the workings of devices, made the cardboard clock by which he'd learned the time, and shown him first metals, then numbers, turned newsprint to papier mâché, resolved milk into plastics, built the kite from bamboo and brown paper to fly on Ivinghoe Beacon, had hustled him from this childhood location to that. It was because of Lionel that he knew the Hornchurch stooks, the creaking barn at Reigate, the brook down from Weston Turville which ran under a main road and kids could scuttle through its echoing concrete pipe to the secluded spinney on the other side . . . That first ice on it had chapped his legs because he was five. Lionel, whom he loved, was dead. Why did a great chord of celebration keep welling up?

It was only revving up the concrete to the garage at home that he got the logic of it, and the music. If the one was dead, the other must be alive – Cynth. It was only a matter of time.

BEFORE EACH LOVERS' meeting, Geoffrey Fairhurst was still a little on tenterhooks. He looked at his watch and stamped from foot to foot. It was eleven thirty-five, and Astraea and he were going to walk to the Cow Roast for a drink and a sandwich. She'd forgotten, changed her mind, spent the night with her husband. The bad man from the woods had got hold of her. He scolded himself and peered from the ridge in the direction of her house. The wind stirred the treetops, and the sun dappled strands of old snow on the coppice floor.

Then came a flicker of movement between the trunks, and she was striding up the path from Hockeridge Bottom in her old coat and woollen hat. He waited, impatient. She had new black boots.

'How do you like them?' she called, out of breath near the top.

'They're astonishing.' He went to kiss her.

'Are they sexy enough? I really fancied the high-heeled ones, but I suppose one has to be practical.'

'Very sexy,' he laughed. He wondered if he'd ever get used to footwear that could force the male imagination so theatrically upward under winter hemlines. He joined hands with her, and they walked along Shootersway to a point which looked right across the town to the Common. The Northchurch woods marked the Chiltern edge, and Geoffrey fancied he could see right through to the Bridgewater Monument, there, that faint stone stroke in the far-off woods. Astraea laughed. Down in the valley, the railway lines glinted, and the melting canal glinted next to them. The road all along Charles Street glinted through gaps in the houses, where water had flooded from three burst pipes. Crystal to liquid – he tried to remind himself of being caught so recently in a changeless state. Impossible, now, such scenes: the milkman pulling deliveries up on a sledge, the bottles themselves with the tops perched like red or silver hats on little pillars of frozen cream, the garden birds looking on, parched and ragged.

Glass was shattering. There were shouts from off down a trackway, and ribald laughter. He hurried through the trees to look, but it was only a couple of lads smashing the windows of an abandoned factory. Bricks and tiles stood in stacks. Long weeds had grown through the concrete yard and turned black. Snow still lay. Just as he was about to go back, he caught sight of a third figure with an air rifle to his shoulder. Another pane fell inwards with a crash as the young man turned a serious face towards him. Astonishingly, it was Alan again, and he felt himself start. Then he was smiling awkwardly. 'We can't seem to stop meeting,' he said.

'Wouldn't credit it, would you.' Alan dropped the gun into the crook of his arm, and the gesture reminded Geoffrey of his old man, out on the estate with the shotgun or the .22, a couple of rabbits dangling from his grip.

Geoffrey looked around. 'What is this place?'

'Old brickworks. There's clay pits down there, I think.' Alan swung his barrel to point down the slope. The two others looked on, a little sheepishly, half-bricks in their hands. There was another gun propped against a wall.

'Oh.' Geoffrey stood for a moment. He wanted to set things right. 'I think there was some misunderstanding, Alan,' he said. 'That night on the bridge. I mean the foot-bridge over the watercress beds. You know? I'd just been to see your mother. About your dad. She'd have mentioned it, I expect, as soon as you got home.'

'No, I'm afraid not. She never said.'

'Oh, well.' There were rooks above the branches. 'Have you . . . heard, I mean? Do you . . . ?'

'Geoff?' Astraea was coming down the path, calling.

'It must have been a difficult time,' Geoffrey said. 'There are things you probably need to know. Only, it's . . .' He glanced back to where Astraea had halted, diffident, at the edge of the scene.

Alan was staring at him inscrutably. Then he smiled. 'Look, I'm really sorry I clouted you, Mr Fairhurst. I'd had a couple too many – you know how it is. My mum, she's been under a bit of a strain. You can imagine. But I really shouldn't worry. Really, I shouldn't. Because Dad usually turns up. You know? I expect he'll be back once it thaws. Don't you? When the snow clears away.'

'Are you coming, Geoff?'

'Be right with you!' he shouted. 'You've heard from him, then?'

Alan made a kind of shrug. 'Sort of.'

'Ah. Must be a relief. For you both.'

The boy nodded.

'Well, no doubt I'll see you around, then. If I'm dropping him off, perhaps. When things get back to normal.'

'Yeah. See you, Mr Fairhurst.'

Geoffrey walked back to Astraea.

'What was that all about?' she asked.

'Only that kid we bumped into at Hampton. Odd, really, seeing him again. Son of a bloke at work – I told you. It's nothing, love. Nothing. Last throw of the ice.' He laughed. 'Let's get going, shall we?'

Later, it was bright and almost mild, and on the way back from Dudswell they took the longer route round by the farms, up across Grim's Ditch – a superstitious title given to every prehistoric trench in the area – and along the lane that ran straight as an arrow past Champneys. Then there was a footpath over the fields, and they heard the tractor working at last, and saw a great cloud of birds following the share. New-turned furrows ran close to where they were walking, the fissured clay shiny with the steel's polish. And there were nuggets of chalk and flint, with a few edges of broken tile here and there. Geoffrey stooped out of curiosity to pick one up: just a fragment, muddied, stained.

'You're going to tell me that's Roman, I suppose,' Astraea said.

'It probably is,' he laughed, twisting it over in his hand. He found a slightly larger piece, in which the break was a dull terracotta, very clean, perhaps newly hit by the plough that afternoon. He licked his thumb and smudged at the slight imprint of an irregularity. 'I don't see why not,' he said. 'Who'd bother lugging a handmade roof out here just to dump it? There must have been a building of some sort, don't you think.' He threw the bits back. 'Look, a few steps on and there's nothing.'

'If you say so, Geoff.' She hugged his arm.

'Just imagine,' he said. 'The whole place crawling with the buggers. Them and us.'

'Yes, Geoff.'

Back at the house, they went straight to bed. Afterwards, as they lay in one another's arms, they could hear the tractor, the sound coming through the trees, and the rooks cawing overhead.

BOOT POLISH AND elbow grease made something of his black chisel-toes. His hands were scrubbed, his hair was slicked. Wearing no other clothes than his own – his school suit and the thin knitted tie his aunt had given him for Christmas, he stepped out into the March evening.

Ice-breakers had been reported ten miles off, rocking their way up from the curve around Northwood and Cassiobury Park. In another couple of days they'd smash under King's Road, freeing trapped barges, carving James Brindley's old cut back to utility. In another couple of days, the watermen would bring their picks and spikes to bear on the winding gear on the lock. The paddles would go up at last, the stacked volume would flood out from under the crust and Lionel's block would crash twenty feet to discovery. There'd be police, and palaver – about the rocket scientist inexplicably slain and dumped at his own doorstep.

Alan climbed the stile. Starlings wheeled against the sunset over Durrants Lane, buds in the hawthorn twilight were about to burst. He crossed the plank bridge. Sparrows fussed, their sudden wings close to his shoulder like nerves tingling. Her letter was in his inside pocket. He stopped once to touch it, then took it out in the High Street to read over again. An indefinable warmth reached down from the upper air.

The Town Hall door leaked light on a propped black-board. He queued with the lads just come over from the Swan. Girls were going in, their lacquered hair glowing in the entrance, their low-heeled shoes rehearsing dance steps on the flagstones. In the wooden hall it was 'Midnight in Moscow'. On the dais, the trumpeter wooed the clarinet-tist, the bass player slapped out his line. A spectacled guitarist attempted Hank Marvin, and six couples danced under the sparkle. The rest of the boys gathered around the drinks table, eyeing the girls as they chattered or jigged at the far side. 'The Locomotion'. The hall was filling up. 'Little Town Flirt'.

There was still no Cynth among the tabard dresses and white blouses. But he knew she'd come. Two girls were next to him. They'd been in his class in the fifth year –

girls he'd hardly spoken to. The band played Chubby Checker, and he asked one to do the twist, and he was unpractised, laughing, his legs soon out of time and aching. Then he drank bottled beer with the others. The night began to jostle and swirl. Still she hadn't arrived. He didn't mind. When the lights dimmed, he was buoyant, thrilled with anticipation.

Bike boys burst in from the cold and stood menacingly under the painted beams. Word went round they were Bennett's End estate, looking for action. But Alan recognised one from the Bee and got talking: Matchless, Norton, BSA? Triumph, mate. Bell-mouth carbs and brakes like butter. Yeah. He glimpsed a scarred face nodding.

Suddenly she was there in the crowd. She was coming towards him. They were just teenagers at last, and the songs spoke for them. 'Your Cheating Heart'. 'His Latest Flame'. The ageing trad band gave way to four lads from Adeyfield with electric guitars and a drum-kit. There were flashing lights. 'Lone Rider'. 'Can't Help Falling in Love'. Their teenage embrace filled the foolish little Victorian hall.

Outside, it was as though he'd just met her. They were walking back to pick up the bike, down King's Road and under the station, stopping to linger by the castle, dawdling slowly up Bridgewater Road. Stars appeared where the cloud parted; the moon had a misty circle. He could still hear the guitars, the perfect exchange of this chord for the next.

They came up the hill to his house and didn't bother going in. The garage door was open and the bike stood ready. He sat astride it while she climbed aboard. Then they were driving up by the back roads over the Common, going the longest possible route to Boxmoor. Soon there were high lanes, where the slopes still glowed white, where the frost-lit beechwoods swept them in under arched tunnels and on through wooded folds, the sparse Chiltern fields half-visible. The night roar of the Triumph echoed across bracken stalks, rattled off the tree-trunks, past Nettleden, Piper's Hill, Gaddesden Row, Stag's End. He could feel her warmth. She dug her hands into his coat pockets, huddling herself against him.

Acknowledgements

I'm particularly indebted to Nicholas Pearson and Derek Johns for their wonderful support and help with this novel. I'm very grateful to my children, Kirstie and Jonathan Beaven, for talking initial points through – and also to Kirstie for lending me her computer to write on. I owe heartfelt thanks in a variety of ways to the following people: John and Jane Bazalgette, Adrian Blamires, Sam Boyce, Mary Chamberlain, Joan and Philip Cooley, Silvia Crompton, Eleanor and Peter Griffiths, Robin Harvie, Marjorie Marten, Ted and Jo Parton, Anjali Pratap, Christine Ruff, David Thorold at St Albans Museum, the Met Office archivists, Watford Library staff – and, as always, all the library staff at RBWM.

Some Notes on the Story
of the Silicon Chip

His Coldest Winter is a work of fiction. Its events and characters are imaginary, and all personal names, except those of people on record, were chosen arbitrarily.

History, on the other hand, deals with fact; and the fact is that throughout the fifties and early sixties, America's eventual pre-eminence in computing, based on the invention of the 'silicon-based monolithic integrated circuit', really was by no means assured. All industrial nations were engaged independently on the quest for workable military electronics, and, until about 1960, the American space and missile programme was still playing technological catch-up with the Russians.

Britain actually held many of the best cards in computing. Even the idea for an integrated circuit was first mooted by G.W.A. Dummer at the Radar Research Establishment in Malvern, six years before Kilby or Noyce came up with it. Many of the requirements for modern computing machines, including the use of binary digitisation (put forward independently by Von Neuman in the States), had been formulated in the UK by Alan Turing and others. 'Colossus', built to Turing's ideas for decoding the German 'Enigma' code during the Second World War, is now acknowledged to have pre-dated the American ENIAC as 'the world's first computer'. The first machine to have *all* the features of the modern device was the 'Mark 1', constructed at Manchester University in England, again with Turing's inspiration. By 1960, another Turing design, the huge ACE at the National Physical Laboratory in Bushy Park, made Britain again the world leader in artificial intelligence.

So, although the Americans had got the chip off the ground, so to speak, the two very different Atlantic research economies could still be seen as almost 'neck and neck' in 1963. Astonishingly, the first American integrated circuits were regarded by American electronics manufacturers as uncompetitively priced for most purposes, and the US Air Force had its own rival notion of 'molecular electronics', into which vast amounts of cash were poured to no avail. It was only Kennedy's plan to land a man on the moon that really kick-started the American mass production of ICs and thus assured US dominance.

As regards the 'net' – that Cold War solution to the prospect of nuclear hits on command structures – it was Donald Davies at the NPL who developed and oversaw the theory of packet-switching (conceived independently in the USA by Paul Baran in 1964 but not put into practice). The American ARPANET project, which evolved into the Internet, enthusiastically adopted the British packet-switching developments pioneered at NPL, and the research was officially shared at a US Association for Computing Machinery symposium at Gatlinburg, Tennessee, in 1967. It's not so far-fetched to imagine Davies and his team working privately on the idea in early 1963 – though the first documentary evidence of it is in a paper he circulated in 1965, by which time the computer race had been categorically lost, and with it any motive for mutual secrecy. Both ARPANET and the pioneer local network at the NPL were effectively the first computer 'nets', however, and packet-switching still forms the basis of Internet communication.

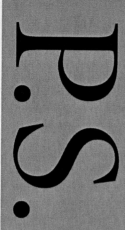

P.S.

Ideas,
interviews
& features ...

While the Ice Lasts

Derek Beaven talks to Travis Elborough

I think I'd like to begin by asking you to say a little about the germination of the novel. The effects of science on the way we make sense of our world, and our moral choices and our relationships, particularly sexual ones, are perennial themes in your work, and find expression here.

Yes, that's true enough, but the way this book actually began was the other way round: it was from the heart rather than the head. I'd just begun structuring the plot as a teenage love story when I bumped into a woman I hadn't seen since we'd both been teenagers at a school thirty miles away. I put it down to coincidence. Nevertheless, difficult events threw us strangely together, and then the development of the book echoed – to our surprise and delight – the development of the relationship.

I wondered, though, did the story grow from an interest in the development of the silicon chip? Or were you initially working with certain characters – teenagers in love, as you say – or a milieu in mind? Am I right in thinking that your own father worked in the defence industry during the period that the book is set? Although, obviously, this is fiction, that world evidently is one you were familiar with, and convey, strikingly, in the novel.

A memory popped up as I was trying to tune in to what the novel wanted to be about. I was twelve, and a friend of my dad's – yes, in the missiles game – was describing something he was working on. I overheard: 'The Yanks have already got these down to the size of a pencil point.' He must have been referring to integrated circuits, and the thought immediately made me start raking around in the history of the chip to see whether they really had been developed that early, and whether there might be any mileage there for the book. The answer in both cases was yes.

I was struck that rather like the binary silicon chip technology itself, there are a number of dual motifs pulsing through the novel: the rival bikers fighting over Cynthia mirror the American and British scrabble for the crucial breakthrough, we have fake and real biker gangs, Lionel and Geoffrey's treachery, a cold winter and a cold war and a series of couplings that culminated in Cynthia and Alan and Geoffrey and Astraea coming together. How conscious was that symmetry? It's almost like a dance, isn't it? On a vaguely related note, it's easy to take Alan and Cynthia in the opening part of the book as a pair of star-crossed lovers, more, given the period, *West Side Story* than *Romeo and Juliet* perhaps.

That's very sharp of you, and puts me on the spot. Proper artists are supposed to shrug off aesthetic questions like that with a smile or an enigmatic quip – which adds up to 'Go figure.' But awkwardness and rudeness are perhaps part of the persistent mystification of the artist, which I don't really approve of. ▶

> ❛ The whole plot is structured on *Romeo and Juliet* as the archetypal teenage love story, but I wanted to seek a way out of the looming tragedy. ❜

While the Ice Lasts *(continued)*

◄ And I do remember how excited I was when I first read Dante's *Vita Nuova* and found the great man at pains to explain every last twist and turn of his work. If a lot was good enough for Dante, then a little ought to be good enough for me! Here goes, then.

The binary structures in *His Coldest Winter* are certainly there, and certainly deliberate; but not because of binary code in computers. While the ice lasts, there's a superimposition of two possible histories – as in the famous cat experiment. Either the father innocently returns and Alan, instead of getting the girl, continues to carry alone 'the family's missing sexuality', or he gets the girl and a shot at relationship, but at the cost of everything he grew up with. Each state is equally present until he makes his moral choice, and inevitably the duality keeps figuring itself in the story – yes, in a dance. I'm actually delighted you draw attention to this. Binary symmetry is also suggested by the section title 'Parallel Courses', where I was thinking of that other famous quantum thing, the double slit experiment, which Geoffrey dreams about. The play is on the notion that what happens to one entity must affect – uncannily – the other. This gives rise to the mysterious brotherhood between Alan and Geoffrey.

As for plays themselves, you're right on target there: the story is threaded through with various 'theatres'. The whole plot is structured on *Romeo and Juliet* as the archetypal teenage love story, but I wanted to seek a way out of the looming tragedy. I was feeling better about relationships than in my earlier books, and so the narrative move was to appeal to a kinder universe than the strictly Newtonian one. The post-Newtonian world of the book, which I claim as fully theoretically legitimate, permits the couples to resolve at the end. It's like trying to find a contemporary way to reclaim the territory of Elizabethan comedy – with, in keeping, an on-stage dance at the end!

Alan is an astonishing fictional creation. His awkwardness, the teenage moods and the sexual confusion are, at times, painfully well realized. I have to confess that in comparison I found Cynthia rather too ethereal, possibly because we only glimpse what she has suffered through Geoffrey. How would you react to this criticism?

I'm really pleased you found Alan convincing. About Cynthia, though, I'm tempted to ask, too ethereal for what? Let's put the point you make even more strongly. In contrast with the two men, Cynth is never given a narrative point of view. Although the novel stays in the third person throughout, we do always sit 'on the shoulder' either of Alan or Geoffrey – there's almost no 'narrative' presence outside the two guys. That means Cynth is only ever available to the reader via Alan's or, as you say, Geoffrey's perception, or through her own words. She also has to be plausibly in two states at once until Geoffrey's moral choice is made: an ordinary girl going about a life of no more complication than work, bikes and boyfriends, and a Juliet ▶

> 6 Cynth has to be plausibly in two states at once: an ordinary girl going about a life of no more complication than work, bikes and boyfriends, and a Juliet tragically implicated in a vicious geopolitical web. 9

BORN

South London, 1947.

EDUCATED

Attended eight schools in England and in Australia – including Ashlyns, an experimental comprehensive in Hertfordshire – and read English at Oxford.

CAREER

After university, taught English at a grammar school and then trained as a dancer at the Laban Centre in London (now part of Goldsmith's College). Worked with a small opera company, becoming their ASM, before returning to teaching, tutoring English and Drama at a sixth-form college near Heathrow Airport. Now writes full time.

LIVES

Maidenhead, Berkshire.

AWARDS

A Commonwealth Writer's Prize 1994/5 for *Newton's Niece*, which was also shortlisted for the Writers' Guild Best Fiction Book of 1994. *Acts of Mutiny* was shortlisted for both the

While the Ice Lasts *(continued)*

◀ tragically implicated in a vicious geopolitical web. She has to be able, potentially, and convincingly, to turn out either way.

So my response to the criticism is, yes, you're right, Cynth may seem ethereal. But can we look more at this business of character? What makes the original Juliet, for example, such a wonderfully convincing 'character'? OK, better writer – but she's also given so much to say and do by a playwright who's obviously very much in tune with her. Romeo, by contrast, is little more than a poetic convention; though this is only a problem if we read the play rather than see it, because in performance a handsome star actor will soon make up any lost ground, and the illusion of equal presence for all the cast will be complete.

Novels, however, are a written form, and while this one draws on plays it's definitely not trying to be one. I know a lot of contemporary novels do seek to mimic that same performance effect by whizzing telepathically from the interiority of one head to the interiority of the next, and back again, and I guess I could certainly have fixed it for poor Cynth to get to the reader more. Instead, I chose not to.

We're habituated nowadays to film and TV, where the camera gives flesh and blood even to the slightest figure in the action. In fact, the camera panders to our hard-wired tendency to hang full character on any hint of a face we happen to see. And maybe it's such exposure to performance that conditions us to demand equal 'presence' of the whole cast list. But that hasn't been the written tradition, and this book simply isn't about Cynth's character. I'd like readers now and then to resist a filmic trance and think about the illusions of character and perception being presented. Which you've just done, of course. I should be pleased!

By the way, I have used the female point of view a great deal in previous books, and did even start this one using Geoffrey's wife Louisa as a third point of view. But she started running away with me and had so many buddies and such trenchant views on the men in her life – views I reckoned I'd given enough space to elsewhere – that I had to drag her off the keyboard; even if that left two painfully tongue-tied chaps to deal with icy events all on their own.

Your writing, it seems to me, is often concerned with the notion of Englishness. In *His Coldest Winter* you consider the nation's recent past in an unflinchingly unsentimental way – you make the austerity of the era and the unease that Geoffrey, for instance, feels about moving beyond the class of his birth extraordinarily palpable. And yet there is deep love of the landscape, and an overwhelming sense of loss pervades the novel. Would you be prepared to describe yourself as an English romantic?
God, I hope not! It's just that I've nowhere else to write about. That sounds flip, but you do have to work with what you're given. I write about the England I grew up in because I haven't yet sorted out a way to get past my teenage years. I do try to be objective about ▶

LIFE AT A GLANCE *(continued)*

Guardian Fiction Prize and the Encore Award in 1999. *If the Invader Comes* was 'longlisted' for the Booker Prize in 2001.

While the Ice Lasts (*continued*)

◄ this country and I'd hate to be identified with nostalgia. And at least I have some claims to internationalism: I've done stuff about Australia and Malaya – and my children are half Indian. But I know what you mean, and it would be disingenuous to deny it: England does preoccupy me. In my view it might be good if we managed to resist bringing back judicial torture and covering the whole place in concrete and GM crops – or is that romanticism?

The novel is set in 1963, but there's a moment on the beach when Raj says, 'Well then, Geoff, prepare for a world the shape of Texas,' a line that has a double resonance for the reader given the current occupant of the White House. Did you see the novel, however obliquely, as making a comment on Britain and America's current special working relationship?
Not so obliquely as all that, I hope!
(Incidentally, the logo of Texas Instruments, for whom Jack Kilby invented the chip, is precisely the shape of Texas. All their components used to come with the Lone Star State stamped on them – they may still do.)

You came to novel writing slightly later in life than some. Would you agree with Joanna Trollope, who has claimed that while you can't be too old to be a writer, you can be too young?
I don't think I would. I'd love to have had a full career in writing, and am angry that I didn't. I set out at seventeen with the

ambition, inspired by one of my teachers, of writing plays. But the task always felt like pushing a melon through a keyhole – toilsome and of pitiful output. It took a lot of grief to account eventually for the shape of the melon and the existence of the keyhole; and another thing I had to wait for was the invention of the word-processor, which lets me use both hands and not care about mistakes. I'm naturally right-handed, but my left hand has all the ideas. Using the computer feels like the luxury of muddying about in some clay: fists prodding, fingers sliding, knuckles carving away until something begins to take shape.

Who were the writers who really first inspired you then?

All the big names. I was bowled over by Shakespeare at school. All the classical and Renaissance poets and playwrights. As far as the novel is concerned, Tolstoy, Thomas Mann, Herman Melville, Dostoevsky, Günter Grass, Conrad, George Eliot, Jane Austen, Joyce, Hardy, Golding, etc, etc. But the writer who quite unexpectedly made me think a novel might be possible was Evelyn Waugh. I read his advice that goes something like, Write only what the characters do, and what they say, and I thought that might help. ■

TOP TEN FAVOURITE NOVELS

These are the ten works of fiction that are really sticking in my mind at the moment. Thomas Mann's *Dr Faustus* is the most astonishing novel I've ever read. *Moby Dick* is endlessly wonderful. Orhan Pamuk's *My Name is Red* does everything the odd way round but brilliantly. *The Spire* by William Golding fascinates. I can't leave out *Love in the Time of Cholera* by Gabriel García Márquez. Hilary Mantel's *Beyond Black* is written with a razor and takes the novel to new places it needs to go. *The Tin Drum* by Günter Grass and *Midnight's Children* by Salman Rushdie go together and both knocked me out when I first read them. I'm going to claim two collections of short stories by the American writer David Means as one item: *Assorted Fire Events* and *The Secret Goldfish*. And I was delighted by Ahdaf Soueif's *The Map of Love*.

Between Gods and Groundlings: Intuition and the Art of Fiction

by Derek Beaven

BAFFLED PILATE SAID 'What is truth?'
Lovers, lawyers and literary critics have stayed
baffled. Absolute truth eludes philosophy.
Science, on the other hand, has always been
bidding for the territory. We should be
worried.

At least truth isn't fiction – by definition.
Interestingly, the novel appears in England
exactly side by side with organized science
around the turn of the eighteenth century. So
fiction – making stories up – slotted naturally
into a hierarchy of two; and it took on that time-
honoured and available female role of being *the
cause of the problem*. In fact, every complaint
ever made against fiction – that it's trivial,
inconsequential, depraved, prissy, romantic,
gossipy, pornographic, subversive, irrelevant,
cheap, expensive, wordy, fantastical, morbid,
corrupting, ill-educated, illiterate, facile, fickle,
meretricious, difficult, time-wasting, lacking in
rigour or for entertainment only – has also been
applied to women. The hierarchy of enlightenment culture seems to have mirrored neatly the
hierarchy of marriage!

When *His Coldest Winter* was first published,
I included notes on the history of the silicon
chip at the end, in case people thought I'd been
… making things up. Maybe the notes turned
out a bit of a red herring, because I was actually
looking to celebrate *intuition* in the story rather
than the triumphs and disasters of technology.
The tale emerges from subliminal signals: Alan

and Geoffrey both pick up startling intelligence – correctly, as it turns out – as if from a hidden world, and both act directly upon it. Some readers have skidded on this issue, and lost the plot a little. Perhaps it seems too indeterminate, like black ice. We're at home with the detective whose eye reads those super-subtle clues the more plodding coppers miss. But pure intuition . . .? Maybe that traditionally feminine ability 'to see round corners' now feels unacceptable in a narrative about men, science, spies and motorbikes.

Once upon a time, though, intuition was a regular plot driver. I'm thinking of Greek theatre with all its sibyls and soothsayers. The career of Oedipus, say, is first shaped by oracular knowledge and then destroyed by an intuitive bombshell. Characters in the English or Spanish playhouses, too, steered a course between gods and groundlings, borrowing from that same classical tradition. Snippets of information sent from 'beyond' were so often crucial to the action, and in the heyday of the Globe a whole 'unseen' world was at work: harmonious music came down from heaven, apparitions rose up from the footings, and Hamlet's father's ghost presented his ambiguous tidings now from up here, now from down there.

By common consent, these were special moments in the history of storytelling – sublime writers making transcendent works of art. In fact, great literature is called great ▶

‘We're at home with the detective whose eye reads those super-subtle clues the more plodding coppers miss. But pure intuition . . .?’

Between Gods and Groundlings:
Intuition and the Art of Fiction *(continued)*

◄ because it strikes us somehow as enduringly 'true'. Yet the truth represented is nothing science would recognize. Sophocles, Shakespeare, Calderón, etc., are indeed consummate writers, but might it be that great stories also demand a world-view capable of delivering them? What of the idea that the stage machinery of the pre-scientific age held – heresy of heresies – a more accurate mirror up to nature than our own? It's a difficult one. Like it or not, Newtonian science is our orthodoxy. The more truth it claims, however, the more story it seems to cripple.

I'm no advocate of 'woo-woo', or mumbo-jumbo. I'm as glad of 'the appliance of science' as the next person. Who wants to live in the dark ages, subsistence farming for some warlord? But I know intuition exists, though it can never be verified, and the problem is that it exceeds science, because it isn't repeatable – it can't be tested by experiment. So the difficulty for the artist is how to include such things in a contemporary representation of the world. Sure, they exist in the ghettos of fantasy and modern fairy tale. What I'd like to see is the job done through legitimate fiction.

It takes a descent into the flesh. We hear tell of gut feelings or 'the pricking of my thumbs' – though the body's intimations are notoriously fleeting. So the water diviner tensions a stick to amplify the miniature movements in his arms; the crystal gazer uses a glass flawed like 'a cloud bank' or 'drifting fog' – according to Hilary Mantel's *Beyond Black* – to sort out the pictures crowding her mind; and just so does the wicked queen in *Snow White* gaze into her own favourite amplifier to learn … what she already knows in her heart.

I chose the electron microscope as an amplifier in the scientific sense, of course. But the significant thing for the present age is that it can take us legitimately, without benefit of sprites, spectres or the willing suspension of disbelief, down to that level under the skin of things. There, matter is just that tad more likely to be uncertain – we're not necessarily at the quantum level, indeed, but symbolically down that way. So the instrument in my story helps Geoffrey see flaws in microchips, but it can also bring home to him the information his own body has already sensed. That is his experience. And, while we're speaking of amplifiers, doesn't the thought experiment of the poor cat, which Schrödinger devised, show just how easily the quantum world can, with all its moral dilemmas of participation, reach into our own?

Orthodoxy won't usually allow us this move. Science gets defensive. But science has recently been wooing the arts hard, and the arts should resist. The arts should reflect that something Bluebeard-ish is still in play, an implicit violence against nature that screens itself behind arcane symbols and impenetrable maths. Science needs to come clean before anyone gets into bed. Fiction holds a key. Only fiction has a chance of unmaking the hierarchy science still insists on. Fiction ought not to be complicit in it any more, nor shrink from the intellectual hard stuff, nor withdraw any longer from the table when the serious talk starts. ∎

> ❝ I know intuition exists, though it can never be verified – it can't be tested by experiment. So the difficulty for the artist is how to include such things in a contemporary representation of the world. ❞

Have You Read?
Other books by Derek Beaven

Newton's Niece (1994)
From the disturbing goings-on in a modern
South London mental hospital, Beaven's
extraordinary début hurtles back through the
past to the eighteenth century and Catherine
Barton, Isaac Newton's niece. What unfolds is
a lavish and richly detailed portrait of
London and a story full of music, science,
politics and intrigue.

'Magnificent set pieces, a richness of thought,
a prodigal and original talent' *Time Out*

Acts of Mutiny (1998)
Now a middle-aged man, Ralph reflects on a
fateful voyage he, his mother Erica and her
smooth-talking American lover, Mr
Chaunteyman, made on an ocean liner to
Australia in 1959. Then the young Ralph
witnessed the beginning of a love affair
between two passengers – Penny Kendrick, a
woman sailing to join her husband in
Adelaide, and Robert Kettle, a scientist on
his way to work at a satellite tracking station
– and discovered a deadly cargo stowed in
the ship's hold. A devastatingly acute
examination of lost innocence, sexual
betrayal and English class and
manners, *Acts of Mutiny* is a quite
unforgettable novel.

'The psychological accuracy with which
Beaven describes character, and the
truthfulness of his observation of childhood,
is matched by the enjoyable precision with

which he evokes time and place ... a
beautifully written book' *The Times*

If the Invader Comes (2001)
This novel portrays a wartime Britain where
emotional relationships are threatened as
much from within the family as from hostile
enemies beyond these shores. The
protagonists of *If the Invader Comes* are two
troubled lovers, beset by circumstance.
Clarice Pike is a feisty, elegant doctor's
daughter; Vic Warren is an unemployed East
End shipwright. Following their seemingly
impossible affair, Clarice journeyed to
Malaysia with her father; Vic married
Clarice's cold, faithless cousin, Phyllis. Their
eventual reunion in an England now at war
forces Vic to consider the relentlessness of
male brutality. Beaven's third novel is a bold,
ambitious but immensely satisfying work of
fiction.

'Offers reminders of Graham Greene's *The
End of the Affair* ... [A] powerful, sharply
conceived novel' *The Times*

If You Loved This,
You Might Like . . .

Youth by *J.M. Coetzee*

Anthem by *Tim Binding*

The Sweet Shop Owner by *Graham Swift*

A Quiet Life by *Beryl Bainbridge*

Spies by *Michael Frayn*

The Gate of Angels by *Penelope Fitzgerald*

Printed by RR Donnelley at Glasgow, UK